THE DRAGON MAIDEN

KENDALL LESPERANCE

Cover design by: ebooklaunch
Map Illustrator: Manuel Figueirido
Editor: Jessica McKelden
Book Description Editor: Gina Denny
Chapter Motif by Freepik

Paperback ISBN:979-8-218-40928-9
Ebook ISBN: 979-8-9905684-9-5

Printed in the United States of America

CONTENTS

Chapter One 1
Chapter Two 5
Chapter Three 10
Chapter Four 17
Chapter Five 22
Chapter Six 27
Chapter Seven 33
Chapter Eight...40
Chapter Nine..46
Chapter Ten..53
Chapter Eleven...59
Chapter Twelve...67
Chapter Thirteen 73
Chapter Fourteen..75
Chapter Fifteen...86
Chapter Sixteen 92
Chapter Seventeen 104
Chapter Eighteen 108
Chapter Nineteen...111
Chapter Twenty..117
Chapter Twenty-One 124
Chapter Twenty-Two..130
Chapter Twenty-Three 137
Chapter Twenty-Four..141
Chapter Twenty-Five..148
Chapter Twenty-Six 151
Chapter Twenty-Seven 162
Chapter Twenty-Eight..168
Chapter Twenty-Nine 184
Chapter Thirty 190
Chapter Thirty-One..194
Chapter Thirty-Two 198

Chapter Thirty-Three 201
Chapter Thirty-Four 203
Chapter Thirty-Five 208
Chapter Thirty-Six 212
Chapter Thirty-Seven 227
Chapter Thirty-Eight 230
Epilogue 235
Acknowledgements 239
About the Author 241

CHAPTER ONE

VALORA

My feet hurt, my belly was empty, and best of all, my mood was foul. For almost a year, I had traversed thousands of miles searching for my brother, Ronan, always just seeming to miss him as I traveled from town to town. I desperately missed home. If I closed my eyes, I could almost recall the scent of my mother's freshly baked bread wafting through the air, the perfect start to a morning. My stomach growled at the memory, protesting at the fact that I had nothing edible left in my pack. Yesterday, I'd run out of food and needed to find a place to purchase more. Hopefully there would be bread.

The Shadowvale Mountains, named for the clan that inhabited them, had been in view for a few days now. I knew if I followed their silhouettes, I would eventually come across a town. Mountains meant dragons and dragons meant villages. All dragons took up residence in the mountain ranges. There were five distinct ranges strewn across the continent, each governed by a different clan of dragons. Their kind had worked out a treaty ages ago that in return for their help and protection, humans would provide labor and goods for them.

Further out from the mountains, there were a few settlements, too far from the dragons' watchful eyes. Due to the remoteness of those towns, they had more freedom on how to use their resources, only needing to provide goods or taxes. My village provided lumber for the Shadowvale clan. What they used it for, I had no idea. They lived in the mountains, so surely there was no need for buildings.

As expected, around midday, I came across a village. The houses were small and close together, arranged in a circle around the town square, where I assumed a market would be. As I approached, I could see stalls set up, but all were vacant. In the center of the town square was a platformed stage, but that too was empty. The hairs on the back of my neck prickled. Something was wrong, but I did need food. Otherwise, I would have to wait until I came across the next town.

To my surprise, only a handful of people were outside. On a lovely spring day like this, I would have expected children running around. The weather was cool with a nice breeze, a wonderful day to be out in the fresh air. In a village of this size, usually more people would be bustling about.

I could feel eyes on me as I walked through the nearly empty square, both from the people hiding inside, staring through their windows, and the few that were out with me.

Taking another look at the empty stalls, I approached the nearest person. He was a bearded old man, his hair peppered with a few black hairs. His leathery face was well-wrinkled, and his worn clothes had seen better days. As I walked over to him, he watched me with a dark expression.

"Excuse me, but is there anywhere I can buy food or supplies?" I tried to sound as polite as possible. He did not seem like the type who had much patience by the way he glared at me.

He looked past me before brushing by, hurrying into a nearby house and slamming the door behind him. I was shocked by his behavior, and when I turned to look at the other people in the square, hoping one of them would be of help, my jaw dropped as I realized they had all disappeared as well.

The feeling that something was off grew as my stomach turned from hungry gurgles to nervous roiling. Trying to remain calm, I began to walk out of town, resigning myself to another hungry day. The sooner I got out of there, the better. Hopefully, the next town would be more welcoming.

With my head down, I walked to the other end of the square, doing my best to ignore the prickling stares through the windows. People were not trying to hide their attention, children pressed their faces against the glass. My pack shifted, and something inside poked my back uncomfortably, most likely my father's book of stories. I shrugged off my pack and knelt to rearrange the contents. My heart skipped a beat at seeing the charred book, one of the only things I had left from the fire. The other was my mother's brooch, pinned to the inside of my pack so it would not get lost. I moved the book to the bottom of the pack, wrapping it in a blanket and shuffling a few other items around.

Suddenly, a large shadow passed over me and a gust of wind came from behind, blowing my raven hair into my face. I clawed desperately with one hand to try to see, my other hand gripped on my pack. Before I could look, I was swept off the ground. Immediately, my stomach dropped as I watched the ground quickly disappear from below and looked at the two green claws wrapped firmly around my midsection. I scrambled to close my pack, a few unimportant items already falling, plummeting through the air below me.

As I looked up, a scream erupted from my throat, disappearing into the wind. Above me was a scaly belly with two gigantic wings quickly pumping the air.

A dragon had kidnapped me, one that was in a hurry.

We were flying so quickly that my eyes watered, the wind instantly chilling me as it whipped through my clothes. The roiling in my stomach had gotten worse and I struggled to see straight. I guess for once being hungry did have its benefits. If I had eaten today, I was sure my stomach's contents would have been expelled by now.

The scenery below sped by, the forest I had spent weeks traversing through passing in mere minutes. My eyes were glued downwards until all views of the ground disappeared entirely as the dragon took us through the clouds.

What use am I to this dragon? I thought. *What does it want with me? Am I going to be punished for entering that village?* A shiver went down my spine at my next thought and my stomach lurched. *Is it planning to eat me?*

CHAPTER TWO

VALORA

As soon as I had the pleasant thought of being eaten, the dragon entered a steep dive. Another scream of terror escaped me before I could stop it. I could feel my stomach moving to my throat, my mouth flooding with moisture. My hands gripped my pack in whitened fists as I struggled to hold back my vomit.

We came back through the clouds and I could see the ground once more. The dragon dove straight for the clifftops, towards an entrance high up on the rock face. It was a lone entrance as far as I could see, accessible only by flight. Based on how steeply we dove, that was where he was taking me, and as we approached, I closed my eyes, bracing myself for impact.

My heart quickened as I felt the claws release me. I tumbled to the ground, nearly face-planting on the hard, rocky floor. My knees and arms ached from the impact and my bag flew from my hands as I attempted to catch myself. Several moments passed as I caught my breath, trying to figure out which way was up. As I righted myself, my stomach heaved violently and I spilled its contents all over the floor, a bitter aftertaste left behind. Slowly, I wiped my mouth and noticed a pair of glittering, cobalt claws in front of me. These were different than the ones that had brought me there, but were no less sharp and dangerous. They would easily be able to slice me open if their owner was so inclined.

Leaning back on my heels, I looked up into the imposing face of a dragon. Smoke poured from his nostrils, his silver eyes shining ominously. Spikes protruded from his forehead and continued down his spine, towards a pointed tail that wrapped around his legs. A pair of giant, leathery wings folded against his shoulder blades, a darker hue than his deep blue scales.

From my abdomen, I felt a tug, and I placed a hand on my stomach, trying to calm my insides. In my periphery, I could see a gathering of other dragons, but my attention was fixed on the one in front of me—the one closest who could roast me alive and eat me if he wanted. I felt my mouth open into a gape, never having seen a creature of this size so close before. His glittering blue scales shimmered in the sunlight streaming from the entrance.

"I thought I told you to bring her here unharmed," he spoke, his gaze shifting to look behind me.

I looked backwards to see a light-green dragon who looked almost ashamed, if I did not know better. The color of his scales matched the claws that had brought me there. His stature was smaller and thinner than the one standing in front of me, his spikes spaced farther apart.

"I'm sorry, my Lord, but I knew that you wanted one swiftly," the green one said, his eyes averted.

"But not damaged," the first one spoke again. "You will be punished for this, do you understand? You must be more careful in the future."

"Yes, Lord Dracul." The green dragon bowed and walked away, his claws clacking on the stone floor. His head was dropped in shame as he walked past the other dragons, all of whom eyed him with disapproval, except for a darker-green one who whispered a few words before dismissing him.

The blue dragon, Lord Dracul, made a noise, and my attention turned back to him. His gaze fixed on me. "I trust that your trip was not unpleasant?" he asked, raising an eyebrow.

I opened my mouth to answer, but no words came out.

He repeated his question, irritation creeping into his tone.

I swallowed to dissipate the dryness in my mouth, ignoring the horrible taste left behind from vomiting earlier. "What?" My voice came out as a squeak, and I winced at the sound.

"I trust your trip was not unpleasant?" Lord Dracul repeated once more, beginning to frown slightly.

A sinking feeling entered my stomach, overriding the weird pulling feeling from earlier. It appeared that I had been brought there on purpose. Lord Dracul's look was almost enough to make me vomit again. I was not sure why I had been brought there, but judging by his growing look of irritation, I was starting to doubt my chances at survival.

"I don't know what you mean," I said slowly.

"You were not injured in any way?" he asked, a look of exasperation passing over his face. He seemed dissatisfied in some way, and I could not pinpoint why, but his disappointment bothered me.

I paused, taking stock of my body. "I don't think so. My stomach just seems a little out of sorts."

"Good." He nodded, satisfied with my answer. "Now, if you'll follow me, I will show you to your quarters." He turned to leave.

"Wait, excuse me!" I said, panic entering my voice. I tried to stand to follow, but fell back to the ground, my legs still weak. My cheeks flushed in embarrassment, but I forced myself to keep my head held high despite the other dragons exchanging looks of amusement at my actions.

Lord Dracul turned back and raised a scaly eyebrow at my outburst.

"But what am I doing here?"

The dragon's eyes widened at my question, his tail swishing behind him. "You do not know? Your people should have informed you."

My heart began to sink. I did not want to believe what I thought he was going to say next. Context clues pointed to me staying there indefinitely. "Informed me of what?"

"This is your new home," Lord Dracul explained gently, probably in response to seeing my panicked expression. "You were chosen to stay here, and in return, we will continue to protect your village and not destroy it."

I felt the color drain from my face. I put a hand on the ground to steady myself, a soft whimper escaping. An icy chill enveloped me when he confirmed my worst fear. I was still searching for my brother; there was no way I could stay there. He had the answers I sought.

Quickly, I glanced behind me and made a decision. On unsteady legs, I jumped up and sprinted towards the entrance, not giving myself time to think. My pack was somewhere in this cave, but I could not stay there a moment longer.

From behind, I felt a claw snag my clothing, pulling me backwards, but not before I caught a glimpse of what was outside the cave. Everything happened so quickly that I had forgotten that there was only a steep cliff that fell away completely. The only fate that would await me that way was certain death, and would have been, if I had not been stopped.

"What was that about?" Lord Dracul hissed, leaning towards me. His claw released me once he saw my expression. I could hear the other dragons murmuring amongst themselves in the background.

Maybe I could explain to him that I did not belong there. Surely, he would let me go then. I did not belong to the village I was taken from. "I don't live in that village. I was just passing through," I explained, desperation edging into my voice. Looking at his expression, it did not seem like I would be able to leave. "I'm searching for my brother. I need to go."

Slowly, I began to edge away from him, but the dragon swished his tail around me, effectively blocking any exit. I could feel tears pricking my eyes, but rapidly blinked them away. I could not break down and cry; it would not be helpful. Not right now.

"Be that as it may, the people picked you to be a Dragon Maiden, and this is your new home," Lord Dracul said. The title sounded vaguely familiar, but I could not recall any details about the position. Living far away from the mountains had that advantage. "Now follow me to your quarters. I won't ask again."

A protest escaped from me against my will. "But—"

The large red dragon with a stocky body to the right of us leaned forward and said softly, "You best do as he says. If you don't agree to be a Dragon Maiden, there are other... alternatives for you." From the look he gave, it was not too hard to guess what those alternatives were.

Lord Dracul's tail moved, and I spotted my pack a couple feet away. I walked over and picked it up, clutching it to my chest. Right now, it was the only comfort in this sudden, unfamiliar world. Once more, I glanced behind me at the entrance, towards the sunny skies, before turning and following the cobalt dragon further into the mountain.

CHAPTER THREE

VALORA

As I followed the large dragon in front of me, I paid close attention to the twists and turns we took. Maybe later I could try to escape, once I figured out how to get down the cliff. It did not escape my notice that the tunnels were vast enough to fit a dragon, but I was mostly surprised at how smooth the walls were. Certainly, it did not look like the tunnel system had been clawed out by dragons. Maybe this was the reason they needed human labor? Every few feet were lit sconces, intricately carved vines holding the light sources in place. We moved too fast for me to take a closer look, but it did not look like it was flame that kept the sconces lit.

At last, we stopped at the opening to a large cavern. "Here we are," Lord Dracul said, gesturing to the room.

My mouth dropped open and I gasped at the enormity of it. Lavishly made beds were scattered around, each covered in a different colored set of blankets and embroidered pillows. Dark mahogany wardrobes overflowing with clothes lined the walls, filled with all sorts of finery in different sizes, and next to each was an open chest filled to the brim with different shoes. Next to each wardrobe, a mirror hung on the wall, a stool placed in front of each one. And in the middle of the cavern was a bubbling lake, the heat of which could be felt from the doorway.

My head spun as I turned to Lord Dracul for answers. "I'm not the only one that lives here, am I?" I asked, my eyes alighting on the multiple beds.

A smirk crossed his face. "No, you're not."

He roared loudly, and I covered my ears, wondering what was going on. To my surprise, five women rushed into the cavern from a doorway across from us that I had not noticed before. They stopped in front of Lord Dracul and knelt at his feet.

"How may we serve you, my Lord?" one of the women asked, her face still pointing downwards. She seemed older than the others, with graying, mousy-brown hair that was gathered into a bun at the nape of her neck.

"This is to be your newest Dragon Maiden," Lord Dracul announced, nodding towards me when all their heads shot up in unison at his words. "I expect you all to treat her well and to train her when she is not receiving specific instructions from me."

"My Lord, does this mean one of us is to be replaced?" the woman asked, her face paling. The other women gasped at her words.

"Not yet. I have not decided what to do with her yet, other than she is to become a Dragon Maiden." He gave each a look to reassure them.

"Yes, my Lord." The woman bowed once more and did not move until Lord Dracul left the cavern. I felt the knot in my stomach begin to loosen after he walked away.

As soon as he was gone, everyone swarmed me. Once more, I felt under scrutiny, not dissimilar from my visit to the village earlier that morning.

"Oh my goodness, where did he find her? She looks positively dreadful!" One woman's tone was filled with scorn as she looked me up and down, her green eyes focusing on my travel-worn clothes. Her emerald velvet gown matched her eyes and a golden necklace draped across her throat. When my eyes met hers, she smirked and twirled a lock of her short, red hair around her finger.

"Hush, Vimery," the older woman chastised. By her age and the authoritative way she spoke, I assumed she was in charge of everyone. "You don't want Lord Dracul to overhear you."

"Yes, ma'am," Vimery said, bowing her head slightly.

The older woman turned towards me. "I'm Alonsa Evertree. Now what is your name?"

"I'm Valora," I said, leaving out my last name. These women were still strangers to me and based on Vimery's reaction, I did not trust them.

"Welcome to the Dragon Maiden chamber, Valora," Alonsa said, coming forward and linking her arm through mine. Gently, she pulled me further into the chamber and out of the doorway. "Now, how were you chosen? How did your people pick you?" She led me to a set of cushions and sat down, the other women following and sitting as well, gathering to hear my story.

Slowly, I sat, still clutching my pack to me. "I wasn't chosen," I said, trying to pick my words carefully. "At least, not the way I think all of you were."

"What do you mean by that?" The youngest of the women was excited, her dark-gray eyes sparkling with her enthusiasm. Her expression was warm and kind, I could tell she meant no harm by the question.

"Shh, Bethany," Alonsa chided softly, pushing back a stray lock of blonde hair that had fallen into the younger girl's eyes. "Let our guest speak."

"Well, I did not live in the village where I was taken," I said, shifting under their stares. "I was just passing through. I was out of food so I needed to stop. There were a few other villagers about when I entered the market, but they all disappeared as soon as they saw me. And then I was taken by a green dragon."

Silence followed my words and I could see the shock in the other women's faces.

"I tried explaining to Lord Dracul that I don't belong here, but he just ignored me." Tears once more pricked at my eyes and I blinked them away.

"Regardless, you were picked for a reason. Just as we all were," Alonsa said, gently placing her hand on top of mine. It provided me a small amount of comfort. She reminded me of my mother. "Now, I should introduce everyone. We have Vimery Cottonthrall, Bethany Twisten, Gwen Unilow, and Hyacinth Unilow."

Each of the women nodded as their name was spoken. I was unsurprised that Gwen and Hyacinth were related. From the same last name and their looks, I would assume they were twins, both wearing their dark-brown hair in a tight bun and possessing the same passive hazel eyes. Out of all the women, they also wore the plainest dresses made of undecorated blue muslin.

"It's nice to meet you all," I said after a moment's pause. My pack shifted in my hands, drawing everyone's attention.

"Oh, let me show you where you can put your things," Alonsa said, standing and leading me to the bed closest to the doorway. It was covered in cobalt blankets and pillows, matching Lord Dracul's scales. Looking around, I was somewhat dismayed at the lack of privacy as I put my things next to my bed. "Today, you can settle in, and tomorrow, we'll begin your training. Unless Lord Dracul has other ideas in mind."

Fiddling with the hem of my shirt, I asked, "What exactly does a Dragon Maiden do?"

Vimery snorted at my question, and I felt my face flush.

"That's right, you aren't from the usual towns," Alonsa said, giving Vimery a look. "Each of us is assigned a Dragon Lord to attend to. There are five main Lords, and then the High Dragon Lord, Lord Dracul. Once a month, we polish our Lord's hoard and pick up their cave. Occasionally, they will have us cook for them, help with administrative duties, and look after any of their younglings. And any banquets, we help organize and prepare those as well."

"Why did Lord Dracul make it sound like they pick a Maiden from this town once a year?" I asked. "And what about the other towns? Do they go through the same thing?"

Alonsa smiled. "There's a need for six Dragon Maidens," she said. "Each of the Dragon Lords has one of us assigned to him, but Lord Dracul has been without one for a long time. Each year, he searches for a Dragon Maiden, but for the most part, they have disappointed him. Then he either sends them to the Pits or…" She trailed off, wringing her hands. The Pits already sounded awful. I could not imagine what was worse than that.

"Or he roasts them," Vimery said gleefully, her mouth turned up into a cackle.

Immediately, I felt all color drain from my face.

"Vimery!" Alonsa scolded. "You don't need to try and frighten her. Her world has already been turned upside down today." She turned to me and said, "He doesn't actually roast them."

"Then what happens?" I asked quietly.

"We don't actually know," Bethany said. "They just disappear and we never see them again."

"If being picked is such an honor, why did no one volunteer?" I asked, trying to keep disdain from entering my voice.

Alonsa pursed her lips and I could tell she was unhappy with the question. "There could be many reasons," she said at last. "Perhaps no one wanted to be taken away from their family. Not everyone is designated to become a Maiden if chosen. Some are sent to other areas in the caves to work. Taking a person from the village once a year does take a toll on the population. This year, they may have not wanted to send one of their own. Whatever the reason was, you are here now." She clapped her hands. "Let's get off such a dreary topic," she said. "Our newest member here looks like she could use a bath, so out with all of you."

I smiled, glad for the distraction, feeling my body relax as everyone left. As their attention slipped off me, it was as though a weight disappeared from my shoulders. A bath would be wonderful. I had not had a proper one since I had started traveling almost a year ago. Bathing in cold streams had been a necessity, but not a pleasant experience.

"The pool is where you'll take your bath," Alonsa said, going over to a nearby chest and grabbing an armful of towels and a comb. "Here you are. We'll return in a little bit so you can have time to yourself."

"Thank you," I said gratefully before she disappeared after the others.

Quickly, I stripped out of my dusty clothes before stepping into the steaming pool, a sigh escaping as the hot water soothed my aching muscles. I had not realized how tight I had been clenching them all day. It had been one surprise after another. I leaned back for several minutes, enjoying the swirling bubbles as they caressed my body. Eventually, I scrubbed myself clean and got out, grabbing a nightgown from a chest near my bed, assuming it was for me.

Shortly after I finished, the others entered the cavern and began readying for bed as well, chatting amongst themselves. I sat on my bed, combing my hair while watching them, trying to pick up on their bedtime routine. Even if I did not want to be there, I still did not want to stick out like a sore thumb. My eyes felt heavy and weary, but my mind still whirred. I knew it would be a while before I could fall asleep.

After everyone was in bed, Alonsa went around the cavern, dimming the sconces that lit up the vast room. I laid down and settled into bed, when the gravity of the whole situation washed over me like a tidal wave. Not for the first time that day did tears prick my eyes, but this time, I let them flow. In a single day, my entire life had turned upside down and I would probably never see my brother again. The thought made the tears flow harder. Ronan would never know what happened to me, what happened to our parents. He would just return to the charred remains of our house and all of us gone, if he ever did return. I began to cry softly and struggled to keep quiet so as not to disturb the others, but apparently, my efforts were not enough.

"Shut up," I could hear Vimery hiss from nearby. "Stop crying like a baby."

"Vimery, she just lost everything she knew. You were emotional when you first came here too." Alonsa's kind voice came from the right of me. "Show a little compassion."

I sniffed, trying to hold the sobs in so as not to disturb everyone. After a couple minutes, Alonsa came over and rubbed my back, whispering comforting words in the darkness. Eventually, I dozed off, tears still streaming down my cheeks.

Chapter Four

VALORA

Once more, the nightmare that had plagued me almost every night since I left home returned. My parents were slaughtered before me, blood pouring down their necks. Taunts of the soldiers surrounded me as they cut me with their swords, enjoying my agony. I curled into a ball to protect myself, but the pain continued. Eventually, they grew bored and left me to bleed out, though not before setting the house aflame. Their last act of cruelty was to burn me alive with the corpses of my parents staring at me. With much difficulty, I summoned up my remaining strength, grabbing what I could—my father's book and my mother's brooch—before scrambling for the exit. Smoke filled my lungs, and coughing, I barely managed to escape before the house collapsed behind me.

With a gasp, I awoke, unfurling from the ball I had subconsciously rolled into during my nightmare. Immediately, my face flamed as the other women sat up and looked at me. Their faces were more curious than anything, although Vimery's still reflected her animosity towards me.

"I'm sorry," I mumbled before lying back down.

One by one, the women went back to sleep, their even breathing filling the cavern. I stayed awake, tormented by the memories. Ronan had left shortly after I came of age and six months later, the men had come. I knew deep down that he had done something that had caused their grisly visit—something so horrible that they had punished us in order to punish him. After taking a few months to recover from my wounds and regain my strength, it was winter. I had stayed with one of our neighbors until spring. That had begun my search for him, one that, at this point, I would not be able to finish.

It was almost dawn before I was able to doze off again into a restless sleep. I awoke by hitting the ground, aggressively pushed out of bed. With a groan, I opened my eyes.

Vimery stood over me, a smirk on her face. "Time to get up," she said.

"Vimery!" Alonsa said in a shocked voice as she looked over to see what happened.

"What? I was just trying to shake her awake," Vimery said, shrugging. "She was the one that flinched so hard she fell out of bed."

Alonsa looked skeptical, but when I remained silent, she did not push the point further. I didn't know why Vimery hated me so much, but I figured it would be better not to antagonize her and make her treatment of me worse.

I stood and winced as pain lanced upwards through my right leg, having fallen on it strangely. Luckily, after a few steps, the pain lessened and it was easier to hide now that it was dulled rather than a sharp, stabbing pain. A quick glance towards Vimery, and her disappointment was palpable that I did not seem to be in more agony.

Alonsa motioned me over towards one of the wardrobes and handed me a light-gray dress. I quickly put it on. It hung off my frame, the hem heaping at my feet. Alonsa clicked her tongue in slight displeasure before going to a different wardrobe and picking out a smaller dress from the back of it. It was midnight blue, so dark it almost looked black in the right lighting. To my relief, it also had long sleeves to cover my scars. Though they were healed, they were not even close to fading, and I felt self-conscious about them.

"This is one of the smallest ones we have," Alonsa said. "Hopefully it'll fit." She reached into a chest and pulled out a pair of matching silk slippers.

I put it on and it fit perfectly, hugging my frame well. Looking around, I noticed all the other women fixing their hair at the mirrors. There was only one left available, but it was so ornate, obviously the best quality out of all the mirrors. Using it felt wrong. I did not want to presume it was mine so I braided my raven hair by touch instead of sight.

My stomach growled with a vengeance and I clutched it, realizing that in the shock of everything yesterday, I had not eaten. Now it was empty and angry, and a new wave of nausea passed over me. Before I could ask about breakfast, a girl in a well-worn gray dress rushed into the cavern carrying six bowls on a tray. She set them down on a table before rushing back out, her head bowed the entire time. The disparity between her clothing versus what the rest of us wore did not escape my notice. She was even barefoot.

"Ah, breakfast!" Bethany exclaimed, her expression brightening as she walked towards the tray and picked up a bowl.

All the others came forward and took bowls as well, scattering about the cavern to eat. I waited for them before moving to grab one. In it was what looked to be lumpy porridge, and after I swallowed a mouthful of the tasteless lumps, my stomach gurgled happily, glad to finally receive sustenance. While this might not be the tastiest breakfast, I knew it would keep me full for most of the day. I quickly began to scarf down the rest of the porridge, my first real meal in days.

My back was to the door, but I felt a presence approaching. My suspicions were confirmed when everyone went pale and dropped their empty bowls, gazes fixed on the doorway behind me. I swallowed my last mouthful before turning around.

Immediately, my stomach churned at the face staring back at me. I swiftly regretted eating breakfast so quickly, feeling it wanting to come back up. That pull, that knot from yesterday, was back once more. I heard the swish of fabric from dresses as the other Maidens knelt to the ground, but I remained frozen. After a moment, I was able to break free from the trance that Lord Dracul had on me, and knelt as well, bowing my head.

"How may we serve you, my Lord?" Alonsa asked. I was glad that she was the spokesperson, as I was not sure I would be able to work any words out. "If you came for the newcomer, we expected to have at least a few days to begin her training."

"I would rather train her myself before turning her over to your care," Lord Dracul said. "But I do appreciate your willingness to help."

From behind me, I could hear slight murmurings from the other women. Apparently, that decision was abnormal and not how things were usually done around there. That fact made the knot in my stomach tighten. What could he possibly want with me?

Lord Dracul's head turned towards me, and even from across the room, I could feel the heat from his gaze. "If you would follow me," he said.

Numbly, I stood and followed him through the stone halls. The sound of his four clawed feet scraping against the floor tortured my already frayed nerves. I kept my head high, but could feel tears spilling down my cheeks. I tried to surreptitiously brush them away, but when I looked up, Lord Dracul glanced away quickly. Great, just great. This dragon who controlled my fate had certainly seen me at some of my lowest points in the span of less than a day.

I struggled to swallow past the lump in my throat as he led me through more hallways, further inside the caves. The huge cavern he led me to seemed more secluded from the others we had passed. My mouth dropped open, as it was bigger than the giant cavern I now lived in, and was filled with golden trinkets and treasures. Everything sparkled in the light of the sconces, and my mind went blank. I could not fathom how much all the gold here would be worth.

"Here we are," he said, taking in my silence. "Today, I want you to get started on polishing everything in here." He lifted a claw and dropped a polishing cloth into my hands. Immediately, my heart sank. "I'll be checking in on your progress throughout the day." With that, he turned to leave.

Finally, unbelievably, I found my voice. "How is this supposed to *train* me?"

He turned back to me, an eyebrow arched. "I expect that the others explained what your duties are?"

Silently, I nodded.

"Polishing my hoard is one of your duties. It's best you get started on that now. You can see how much there is." A wry smile stretched across his lips, revealing his many sharp teeth. Once more, he turned to go, but before leaving, said, "I'm very sorry if you don't agree with how you were brought here, but I hope you learn to accept this place as your home."

"And if I don't?" The words came out unexpectedly and much sharper than I had intended.

His expression was sad, which surprised me. "I hope you do," he said. "I really hope you do."

As he left, I once more felt that knot loosen. I turned my attention back to the mountains upon mountains of gold. The thought occurred to me that there was no way to get this all polished in a month, let alone a week.

I gritted my teeth, gripping the polishing cloth in hand, and grabbed the nearest object to set to work.

Chapter Five

DRACUL

Around midday, I went to check on the newest Dragon Maiden, to see what she had accomplished and bring her lunch. No one was allowed around my hoard except for my Dragon Maiden, so there was no one else to bring her food. Yesterday, her arrival had certainly been a surprise. No Dragon Maiden had tried to escape before—most were ecstatic to be chosen. It meant their families were to be well compensated and taken care of for the rest of their lives. I could not imagine what the Sherok villagers had been thinking when they offered up a complete stranger to become a Maiden. Perhaps this year, no one had wanted to volunteer.

But by far the biggest surprise was that the newest Dragon Maiden was my *dragaria*—my mate, the one the stars chose to be mine. From the moment Verlak had unceremoniously dumped her on the ground, I'd felt the pull to her. Even now, I could feel a rope-like presence tugging me towards her. She would feel it, too, in time, once the shock of everything wore off. Right now, she was sad, hurting, and confused, but I could sense a resilience underneath, a hidden strength.

Never before had a Dragon Lord had a human as his *dragaria*, at least not to my knowledge. Such a fact would cause ripples throughout all the clans, and I could only imagine the rumors my enemies would come up with if this fact became known. They would say this was proof that I was not meant to be High Dragon Lord, that I was too weak to even handle a female dragon as my *dragaria*. Already, they used my age as a reason, being the youngest High Dragon Lord to ascend to the position, despite all the elders agreeing to it. I could only imagine the scorn and insults they would direct towards Valora. Even the thought of imaginary insults being thrown at my mate made steam escape my nostrils in anger.

Upon entering the cavern, I was surprised to see the amount of progress Valora had made. To the side was a small pile of items that she had already finished, shining brighter than the rest of the hoard. Though it was meager compared to what was left in the cavern, it was more than what I had seen any other Maiden accomplish in the same amount of time. Right now, she was sitting cross-legged, vigorously polishing a golden vase, oblivious to my presence. As I watched, she set down the vase in the pile and grabbed a nearby cup, attacking it with the same ferocity. I knew her arms must be aching, although she did not show it. After watching her for a couple more moments, I cleared my throat.

Immediately, she whipped her head up, a strand of hair falling out of her braid and across her forehead. Her face paled and she scrambled into a bow. "I'm sorry, my Lord. I didn't see you there."

My heart clenched. Of course she was still afraid of me. "It's quite all right," I said. "It seems like you've been busy."

She looked to the pile of polished gold as if seeing it for the first time and then at the rest of my hoard, a despondent expression falling over her face. "It's not enough," she said dejectedly. "I'll never finish this all in a week's time."

I frowned at her words. "Who says it needs to be done in a week?"

"The others said that once a month, they work on polishing their Lord's hoard for a week," she said, fidgeting with her hands and continuing to absentmindedly polish the cup. "I figured I was under the same time constraint."

A smile crossed my face. While it was true the other Lords placed that stipulation upon their Maidens, they did not have the hoard that I did—one of the perks of being High Dragon Lord. "Well, I have a much bigger hoard than any of the Dragon Lords." I held out the plate of food towards her. "I brought you lunch."

Her eyes alighted on the plate, widening in surprise as she had not noticed it before. She glanced up towards me and back down to the plate, her expression slipping into one of detachment. "I'm not that hungry," she said, turning back to the cup that she polished while we had been talking, stopping suddenly as if realizing what she had been doing. Carefully, she set it down and grabbed another golden object.

I nodded, setting the plate next to her. "I'll just leave it here then." I had made sure that the kitchen had included good food, unlike the lumpy porridge that had been sent out this morning. When I had found out what had been served, they had received an earful. No mate of mine was going to eat such tasteless mush. After my scolding, they had prepared cured meats, cheese, bread, and fruit jam for lunch, and I hoped it was to her liking.

I moved closer to her to watch what she did, questions swirling in my mind. Now that I was so close to her, I wanted to know everything about her.

Valora had turned away from me, focusing on polishing, but I could tell that she knew I had not left yet based on how stiffly she sat. Every moment that passed, I inched slightly closer, wanting to be as near to her as possible, to envelop myself in her scent. She smelled of the lavender soap all the Dragon Maidens used, but underneath was an even sweeter scent. Under my scrutiny, she polished five more objects before finally breaking down.

"What is it that you want?" she asked sharply, turning to look at me. She flinched, not having realized how close I had moved towards her during this time. Despite my size, I could be silent when I wanted to be. My face was close to hers; I could feel her breath tickling my nose.

I figured now would be as good a time as any to ask a few of my questions. "If you aren't from the nearby towns at the base of the mountain, where are you from?"

She sucked in a breath, clearly not expecting the question. After a moment's pause, she said, "If I'm to accept this place as my home now, I hardly see how that matters." Her tone was short, letting me know not to broach the topic any further.

Her ferocity surprised and amused me. I began to shake with laughter.

"What's so funny?" she demanded, placing her hands on her hips, her brilliant azure eyes boring into mine. If I was not careful, I could get lost in them and make a total fool out of myself.

"You can be quite fierce when you feel like it. It's simply amusing, is all." Having her as my *dragaria* was going to be interesting, that was for sure. Though I could admit to myself that she received more leeway than I would give any other Maiden because she was my *dragaria*. "A word of caution—with the other Lords, it is best if you do not take that attitude with them. They are not as patient or forgiving as I am."

Biting her lip, she swallowed, realizing her actions. "Thank you for the advice."

"You're welcome," I said. I wanted to push her just a little further. "But you never answered my question."

Her hands paused in her polishing and I was suddenly worried that I had pushed too far, that I had overstepped. "I… I'd rather not talk about it right now, if you don't mind." Her voice was soft as she averted her gaze.

"Very well," I said. "I won't bother you further at the moment."

Her head immediately snapped up to meet my gaze, her eyes searching mine.

"But I would eventually like to know more about you."

She nodded slowly, acquiescing to my request. Before she could speak further, I left the cavern, leaving her to her work. It was obvious she was uncomfortable around me, a feeling I hoped would disappear in time.

Chapter Six

Valora

When I returned to the cavern, it was empty. Lord Dracul stopped by once more to check on my progress and dismissed me for the day, saying that I would continue with my work tomorrow. The other Dragon Maidens had not returned yet from their daily duties. My arms ached from my work throughout the day and I collapsed onto my bed with a heavy sigh while I waited for the others to arrive. It had been a long day of polishing and I could not imagine making it through the next several days. My eyes slowly pulled closed. I surrendered myself to sleep.

I was jerked awake at the sound of someone running into a piece of furniture and cursing loudly. Looking around, I could see the other four women looking towards Vimery, whose gaze was focused on me. It was obvious the others tried to be quiet, but she had gone out of her way to be noisy. My mouth opened to say something, but knowing how Vimery was, I bit my tongue.

"Were you going to say something?" Vimery asked, a smug smirk on her face.

"Nope, I have nothing to say." I rose and went over to a basin of water, splashing it onto my face to wake myself up. The cool water felt pleasant and helped distract me from Vimery's attitude.

Bethany came up behind me. "Valora, Lord Verhorn would like to see you," she said. "I can take you to him."

I frowned, confused about the request. "Do you know why he wants to see me?"

She nodded. "He's in charge of the administrative duties around here," she explained. "He needs to formally document your arrival and go over a few details with you." Bethany turned to leave the cavern through the other entrance, and I followed her, going in the opposite direction of where Lord Dracul had led me this morning.

After a couple minutes of walking—the size of the cave system never ceased to surprise me—Bethany stopped in front of a cave entrance and entered. "My Lord, I have brought the newest Maiden," she announced, bowing her head.

"Thank you, Bethany, that will be all." A voice came from inside, and Bethany motioned for me to go in.

I walked into a cozy room. An ornate emerald rug covered the floor and a fire was lit to the right of me. At the end of the room was a hallway leading to more rooms. On the left were bookshelves lining the walls and a desk filled with papers. To my surprise, an older man worked at the table, writing on parchment. He had a long, dark-green beard with long, wavy hair tied back with a ribbon. Round spectacles hung off the end of his nose, his shrewd green eyes staring at the parchment in front of him. He did not look up until he had finished his writing, motioning for me to take a seat in a chair in front of him.

"Sit, sit," he said impatiently.

I moved to follow his orders, bowing slightly before sitting down. "I don't understand, sir. I thought I was meeting with Lord Verhorn?" Maybe the Dragon Lord had a secretary to handle these matters for him.

He laughed, a warm sound. "I *am* Lord Verhorn," he said. "We met briefly yesterday. I am the green dragon. My son was the one who brought you."

My eyes widened at his words. I had no idea that dragons could shift into human form. Once more, I bowed my head, hoping for his forgiveness, Lord Dracul's earlier warning echoing in my head. "I am so sorry, my Lord. I did not realize."

Lord Verhorn waved a hand, dismissing my apology. "It is not a well-known fact among the humans that we are able to transform like this," he said. "But it certainly helps to be in a nimbler form when completing certain tasks." He gestured to the parchment in front of him as an example.

"Do all the Dragon Lords use their human forms often?" Unbidden, the thought of what Lord Dracul would look like sprang to mind and I flushed slightly, though I did not know why.

"It depends on the Lord," he said, steepling his fingers in front of him. "Though myself, Lord Lorka, and Lord Dracul are probably the ones who are like this most often. Other dragons in our clan go about in their human forms frequently as well." He reached for a stack of parchment, rifling through it until he found the page he wanted. "Now, I have questions I'll need answered so we can formally document you and ensure your family is compensated."

"Compensated?" I asked, my brow furrowing in confusion.

He nodded. "Yes, each Dragon Maiden's family is well compensated for her service. We provide food and money for each year she is with us. I will need your full name and where you are from." He poised his quill over the parchment, awaiting my response.

"Um…I don't have a family. Not anymore," I said softly.

His eyes flicked up at me, reading me.

"I mean, I have a brother, but I don't know where he is right now."

"Hmmmmm." He tapped his quill on the parchment, thinking of what to do. "Is there anyone else you would want the money sent to?"

I shook my head. "Not really," I said.

"For now, we will put the money that we would normally send to your family aside," he said. "I will discuss with Lord Dracul about what he thinks we should do. Now, I'll need your full name and what village you come from. I need to make sure you reside within our territory."

"Valora Marchton, and I came from Horstaad Village," I said.

"That is located near the edge of our territory," he said, nodding as he wrote down my answer. "Your village provides us with lumber." He wrote additional notes on his paper before looking to me once more. "And Verlak already informed me that he gathered you from Sherok, so their tribute for the year has been met. For now, you have been assigned to Lord Dracul as his Dragon Maiden until he decides otherwise," he said. "Do you have any questions for me?"

Hearing that I was to serve Lord Dracul was a surprise to me. The other Maidens had said that he had not had a Dragon Maiden for years. I tried to ignore the knot in my stomach that seemed to jump around in excitement at the prospect of working closely with him. I still was resentful that I had been brought to this place.

"What do each of the Dragon Lords do? Bethany mentioned that you handle the administration here," I said. If I was to stay in this place, it was better that I knew more about the inner workings of this new world.

Lord Verhorn set down his quill and sat back in his chair. "She is correct. I handle the administrative affairs and ensure everything within the clan is running smoothly," he said. "Lord Noxus handles the clan's financials and ensures all taxes and tributes are gathered in a timely fashion. We work closely together. Lord Hiram is one of the eldest Dragon Lords; he provides counsel for us based on his previous years of experience. Lord Firenze oversees the army and battle tactics, and Lord Lorka is tasked with managing our farms, along with food production, collection, and storage."

Hearing everyone's tasks made me realize how much more went into keeping a dragon clan alive and well. "What about Lord Dracul?" I asked. Lord Verhorn had not mentioned anything about him.

"Lord Dracul holds the title of High Dragon Lord," Lord Verhorn said. "That means not only is he the leader of our clan, but the ruler of all the dragon clans. We help him with day-to-day tasks so he can focus on bigger issues."

"And what is my role then?" It sounded like Lord Dracul's responsibilities were different from all the other Lords, so I assumed my duties would be different than the other Dragon Maidens. "The others explained that I would be cleaning, cooking, and completing administrative tasks."

"As Lord Dracul's Dragon Maiden, your responsibilities will be different than most," he said, nodding at my question. "You will still be helping take care of him, but you'll also be playing a more active role than most. He will be providing you with more details as you go, training you privately. You may receive training from the other Maidens from time to time, but for the most part, he will be teaching you himself as to what he wants."

"If all Dragon Lords have a Dragon Maiden, why hasn't he had one before?" I knew that I was dangerously close to overstepping my bounds, especially by the way that Lord Verhorn's eyes narrowed at my question.

"That has been his decision," he snapped. "So far, the other Maidens have alternated tending to his basic needs, but now that he has chosen you, you will be taking over all the responsibilities that a High Lord's Dragon Maiden would accomplish. Up until now, he has been handling those matters himself. You are to conduct yourself with the proper respect of a High Lord's Dragon Maiden, are we clear?" His green eyes glimmered slightly ominously, almost reminding me of Vimery's.

I nodded and bowed my head. "Yes, my Lord. I'm sorry if I overstepped," I said.

"Very well," he said, pursing his lips. "That is all I require of you. You are dismissed." He waved me off, turning back to his work.

Lord Verhorn's caves were close enough to the Maidens' cavern that I was able to find my way back easily. Dinner had been delivered while I was away and the others had already grabbed their portions. I took the last remaining plate and silently ate my meal—beef and potatoes with roasted vegetables—while thinking over my conversation with Lord Verhorn. He had certainly given me a lot to think about.

Chapter Seven

VALORA

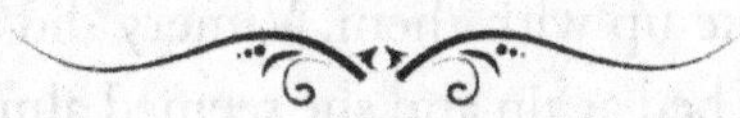

Once more, I awakened from my nightmares, unable to contain the cry that escaped. I could feel the gazes of the others piercing me like a knife and turned so my back was to them. Tears escaped again at the horrific memories. Everyone ignored me, eventually falling back asleep, but I was wide awake, knowing that I would not sleep for the rest of the night.

Soundlessly, I slipped out of bed, and before I knew it, found myself back in the cave where Lord Dracul's golden hoard was kept. I grabbed my discarded polishing cloth and got back to work. If I could not sleep, I might as well do something useful. My mind was busy as I polished, thinking about the other Maidens. Vimery was the only one that openly antagonized me, but the rest had not talked to me after I returned from seeing Lord Verhorn. They clearly did not think too highly of me either. I was sure that if the nightmares continued, they would continue to ice me out.

I had to acknowledge that I had hoped the others would help me stand up against Vimery's actions, but right now, as things were, I could expect no support. And while it was clear that Alonsa was the de facto leader of the group, it was obvious that Vimery would not follow Alonsa's instructions if they did not suit her. Based on how Vimery had acted over the past couple of days, it seemed that when it came to me, she would do what she wanted.

My hands stilled over the plate I was polishing and a tear fell. "I just want to go home," I whispered quietly, wishing not for the first time that I was back home with my parents and Ronan. I sniffed, wiping away the tear and continuing with my work, pushing down the despair as far as I could. Right now, I just had to survive.

Before the others awoke, I returned to the cavern, pretending to wake up with them. Vimery did not get a chance to push me out of bed again and she seemed almost disappointed by this. I paid her no mind and got ready with everyone else.

I was surprised that I was not exhausted as I continued to polish throughout the day. My arms were sore, but it was a kind of pain that I could deal with. I focused on it, using it as a distraction from my depressing thoughts.

Each night for the rest of the week, when the nightmares woke me, I snuck back out to the hoard to polish. I painstakingly worked piece by piece, bit by bit to finish this task that I had been assigned. Seeing the progress did give me a bit of satisfaction.

Finally, on the last night of the week, I only had a little bit left. I got to the final piece of Lord Dracul's hoard, a golden chalice, and polished it. This past week, I had gotten more done than I had thought possible, my nighttime escapades helping. I placed the chalice down and surveyed my work: a glittering, gleaming room of gold. The weight of the task lifted from my shoulders and I could feel the tension immediately draining away. I sat on the ground to rest, feeling my eyelids grow heavier and heavier. My last thought before they closed completely was that I should probably head back to the cavern.

* * *

"My Lord, she is completely out of line. She should not be here unsupervised." I could hear one voice above me, angrily growling.

Lord Dracul's voice came next. "She finished polishing my hoard in less than a week. No other Maiden has finished such a feat." Even in my bleary state, I could tell that he did not sound upset. Almost… proud?

I blinked my eyes and looked up from where I laid on the floor. Two dragons—Lord Dracul and a dark-green one matching Lord Verhorn's hair color—stood above me. The green one's nostrils were smoking while Lord Dracul looked completely unbothered.

"She has shown complete disregard for our rules," the other dragon insisted. He definitely sounded like Lord Verhorn. "She is *not* fit to be a Maiden."

At his words, steam began to escape from Lord Dracul's nostrils. "I will decide whether or not she is fit to be a Maiden," he said, his voice dangerously low. "And if she's to be *my* Maiden, what difference does it make to you? She won't be touching any of your hoard; you have nothing to fear."

"But if she is so blatant about breaking this rule, how do we know how she will treat the other, more important ones?" Lord Verhorn's voice began to rise further in volume. I had not noticed it earlier, but he had a small tufted beard sprouting from his chin. It waggled with his anger.

"I didn't know about the rule." The words quietly escaped before I could think about them.

The two did not react at first, and I thought they had not heard me until both their heads tilted in unison towards me.

"What do you mean you didn't know? How could you not know that you aren't allowed to be in the hoard after curfew? Wasn't it explained to you?" Lord Verhorn's voice dripped with scorn as he looked at me.

I shrunk away from him, backing up until I brushed up against Lord Dracul's leg. I flinched as I looked up towards my

Lord, afraid of his reaction. He was not even looking at me, his attention fixed on Lord Verhorn.

"Verhorn, just let it go," he said tiredly. "I'm sure the rule slipped the other Maidens' minds to explain. If I'm fine with this, you should be too."

"But, my Lord—" Verhorn began to protest.

"I will hear no more of this. Go eat your breakfast," Lord Dracul growled.

At his words, Lord Verhorn bowed before strutting out of the cave. After he left, I looked to Lord Dracul, trying to judge his unreadable expression.

Slowly, I shifted away from him and knelt in contrition. "I'm sorry. I really didn't know," I said softly.

"You should go back to the others to get your breakfast. Come back here afterwards." He turned to leave the cavern.

The pit that had been in my stomach when I awoke grew, and I bit my lip, afraid that he was angry. What would happen to me now? As if sensing my fear, he turned back and flashed a smile before disappearing, the knot in my stomach lessening slightly.

After a couple seconds, I raced back to the Dragon Maiden cavern, where the others were waiting. From the looks on their faces, it was obvious that they were angry.

"How stupid are you?" Vimery was the first to speak as soon as I entered, her tone scathing. I flinched at her volume and my face flushed.

"Hush," Alonsa said, holding up a hand. She took a few steps towards me. "Valora, why did you leave in the middle of the night?" Although her tone was much kinder, I could sense the steely undertone underneath it. Her brown eyes gazed at me with a coldness I had not seen from her before and a shiver ran down my spine.

My mouth ran dry and I swallowed, trying to come up with the words. "When I couldn't fall back to sleep, I decided I should get some work done. Usually, I come back before everyone wakes up, but last night, I dozed off after cleaning." I bowed my head slightly to show my remorse. "I'm sorry if I got you in trouble."

"We never *ever* leave the cavern after lights go out," Alonsa said firmly. "Now that you know, there won't be an excuse for next time. It is *forbidden* to leave at night."

I picked up a plate of strawberry-topped pancakes, my curiosity piqued. "Why?"

The expressions of the other women told me they were tired of my questions so I began to eat my breakfast.

"It's just one of the rules," Gwen said, not offering an explanation. "But if you break the rules again, you will be cast out, and those consequences aren't pleasant."

"Just be careful next time," Hyacinth added. "It's always a shame to lose a Maiden."

My stomach churned and I finished my pancakes, chewing more slowly to try forcing the food down. The others once more scattered around the cavern, eating and talking amongst themselves. Vimery looked over at me from time to time, a withering expression on her face.

After breakfast was quickly consumed, Alonsa clapped her hands. "Get dressed everyone. We have a long day ahead of us."

Today, I changed into a pale-green long-sleeved dress before hurrying back to Lord Dracul's hoard. He already waited for me, inspecting the polished gold. Seeing his back to me, I paused in the doorway, unsure of what to say. I already knew that despite what he'd said previously, I was in trouble.

"You did an excellent job polishing," he said, still facing away from me. He must have heard me coming.

"Thank you."

When he turned to face me, I bowed my head, keeping my eyes downcast. The other Maidens always did so. It seemed like a rule—if not an unspoken one—when talking to the Dragon Lords. I could not afford another mistake, not today.

"Valora, look at me." His voice was gentle.

I gulped, looking up, hoping he would not yell at me. Instead, his silver eyes shone with kindness, a small smile across his lips.

"I do not want you worrying about what Verhorn said today, am I clear? I understand the rules were not fully explained to you and probably won't be completely explained until you do something wrong again."

I felt my expression fall. Did he want me to fail before chastising me again? If I made a big enough mistake, I could easily be killed. And he was just willing to gamble my life away on that chance? I clenched my jaw, trying to contain the rage I felt building inside of me.

"I am the High Dragon Lord, the leader of all the dragon clans. Nothing will happen to you without my permission, do you understand?"

I nodded silently, not trusting myself to speak.

"I have found that you are a quick learner and work hard, so I'd like to see how quickly you learn the rules." The smile on his face grew wider.

Hot anger bubbled up inside of me and I knew I would not be able to contain myself. "What sort of game are you playing here?" All worry from earlier quickly disappeared, replaced by fury.

"Excuse me?" His expression faltered, his smile slipping.

"First, I am torn away from my life and told I have to stay here to be your *servant*." The words spat forth, releasing a cork on the pain and anger I had felt over this past week. "And now you're gambling with my life as to whether or not I can learn these stupid rules on how everything is run here. I had something important I was going to do, something that meant *everything* to me, until I was picked up by your winged follower and brought here. I didn't ask for this, so don't treat me like I was specially chosen or anything. You may be the High Dragon Lord, but that means *nothing* to me."

During my outburst, he looked taken aback, obviously not expecting my venom. After I stopped, I realized that I breathed heavily from my rant, gasping for air. He remained silent for several moments, and I broke the silence.

"Well?"

"Well, what?" He was now unreadable, his tone cool. I was unable to ascertain anything from it. My heart began to sink. This was it. I had finally pushed his patience too far.

"Aren't you going to roast me or something for talking to you like that? For being out of line?"

He was quiet once more, and I felt the need to fill the silence.

"That's not how Dragon Maidens are supposed to talk to the High Dragon Lord."

Lord Dracul's cheeks puffed out before erupting into laughter, echoing throughout the cave. "None have certainly tried before," he said.

"What's going to happen to me now?" I fidgeted as he stared at me, contemplating his answer.

"Nothing," he said. "You are certainly different from the other Maidens." His expression sobered. "But you are not to talk to me that way again, do you understand? Especially in front of the other Lords. I will be forced to punish you and that's not something I wish to do."

His answer surprised me, and I felt my body freeze. He did not want to punish me? "I understand," I said, bowing my head once more.

"Good. Now follow me. I have another task for you." He led the way out of the cave, and I followed closely behind.

CHAPTER EIGHT

VALORA

We walked through a different set of tunnels, far away from where the other Dragon Lords resided and away from Lord Dracul's hoard. I was slowly building a map in my head of the cave system, though my knowledge was still very limited with my activities from the past week. Eventually, Lord Dracul stopped in front of an opening that, to my surprise, was covered with a large navy curtain. It shielded a massive doorway, big enough to fit him in his dragon form.

"That's different," I said. So far, everything I had seen was open caverns with no form of privacy.

"I am allowed this, as I am the High Dragon Lord," Lord Dracul said. "These are my chambers." He pushed the curtain to the side with his snout and gestured for me to enter.

As I stepped into his quarters, my mouth dropped open. The entire floor was covered in thick, plush, navy carpeting. Like Lord Verhorn's study, he had bookshelves and a desk, though his collection of books was much vaster. A couple gray couches sat in front of the bookshelves near a lit fireplace, making a cozy reading area. Towards the back of the room were a few tables filled with glass vials and instruments, and a spigot leading from the cave wall into an empty basin. On the table, a few books were open, and from my vantage point, I could see that there were words circled. To the left was another small hallway leading to what looked like more rooms. Small stairs curved up the side of the cavern's walls, ending at a landing where a telescope looked out of a large window carved into the side of the mountain.

I turned to look at Lord Dracul, who I suddenly realized had been watching my reaction very carefully.

"You like to stargaze?" I asked. I had read about telescopes, but had never gotten to see one in person before. All my knowledge of the constellations, I had learned from my father. His book contained all sorts of stories about the stars.

Lord Dracul nodded, stepping into the room with me. "I do," he confirmed. "And it seems you do as well. One day, perhaps we can stargaze together."

I could not explain it, but his expression filled me with an unknown warmth. "I… I would like that very much," I said softly.

He cleared his throat, looking away from me suddenly and staring at the room. "I think I would like you to start with dusting the bookshelves first," he said. "It's been a while since someone has cleaned in here. I do what I can, but it's… been some time." He looked around as if seeing the room through fresh eyes. "I don't want you touching the back tables, though," he said, pointing towards the vials of potions and concoctions. "There are things I'm working on that I don't want disturbed." He led me to a hidden closet which housed cleaning supplies. "Everything you need should be here."

"I will get started then." I grabbed the soft cloths, my hands itching to investigate his book collection. Besides my father's book of stories, there had not been much material to read back home. Maybe if I was careful, I could sneak a peek in a few of them.

Lord Dracul let out a sigh, and steam began to emanate from him, obscuring him from view. When the steam cleared, a man stood in his place. Long, deep-sapphire hair that matched the color of his scales fell down his back, past his waist. He turned to face me, and I felt the usual knot in my stomach that appeared when he was nearby suddenly tug harder than it had before. His silver eyes were the same, but on a clean-shaven face that I was unaccustomed to. Under an open set of navy velvet robes, he was bare chested. My eyes followed the line of his muscles to the top of his light-gray flowing pants, and my gaze shot back up to his face. I flushed as he smirked at me, knowing exactly where I had been looking.

"Enjoying the view?" he teased, walking over to his desk and sitting down.

I opened my mouth, trying to say something, but the words would not come out. "I will get started right away," I stammered, walking over to the nearest bookcase, my face burning. I heard a slight chuckle coming from the desk and my face flamed further.

Slowly, I started cleaning the dust off the books, starting with the bottom row. I took each book off the shelf and gently rubbed it with the soft cloth, removing the dust before placing it back on the shelf. My eyes glanced over each cover, eager to learn what kind of books Lord Dracul had in his library. I took my time cleaning, giving myself more time to admire the craftsmanship that went into each one.

After several minutes, I heard Lord Dracul clear his throat, drawing my attention to him. He had an eyebrow raised. "Did you get distracted?" he asked, a smile crossing his face.

The knot in my stomach deepened.

His words made me realize that I had opened up one of the books and was reading it. I had stopped dusting completely. My face flushed once more and I put the book back on the shelf. "I'm sorry, my Lord," I said, bowing my head. "I didn't realize I had stopped… They're beautiful."

"Maybe when you finish your work, I'll let you take a closer look at them," he said.

A rush ran through me. "Do you really mean that?" I asked, my voice rising in excitement.

He nodded, and his smile deepened. "I do," he said. "And if you tell me what you're interested in, I can pick out a few recommendations for you."

I immediately turned back to the bookshelves and continued cleaning, this time focused on my task. I needed to show Lord Dracul I was a good worker, and he would be more inclined to let me read his books. The thought filled me with excitement and carried me through the rest of the morning.

* * *

Around midday, a young boy with cropped red hair entered the chamber with two plates. I stood on a ladder to reach the higher shelves and Lord Dracul was still busy reading the papers in front of him, occasionally scribbling something down on a different sheet of parchment. We both looked over when the boy entered, and he visibly blanched at the attention.

"H-h-here is y-your lunch, m-m-my Lord," he stuttered, setting it on a table before racing out of the room.

To my surprise, Lord Dracul almost looked amused at the boy's behavior before finishing writing his sentence and standing. "It's lunchtime," he announced, walking over to the table.

I descended from the ladder and approached as well. The two plates looked drastically different. What was obviously Lord Dracul's contained a roasted leg of lamb with potatoes and vegetables. My plate had a small piece of bread with a slice of dried meat and a hunk of cheese. There were two glasses, one filled with what looked to be wine and the other with water. I was surprised at my fare; after my first day, my meals had consisted of more food and were of higher quality. If I did not know better, it seemed like Vimery had prepared this meal for me. Resigned, I reached for my plate only to have Lord Dracul swat my hand away.

43

"No Dragon Maiden of mine is going to eat this slop," he growled. I swear I could almost see steam escaping from his ears. "This is an insult to you and therefore to me." He swiped my plate before stalking out of the chamber with his only instruction being to "Wait here."

While he was gone, I continued to clean, worry settling in my gut. I did not want the young boy from earlier getting in trouble. If Vimery had put him up to this, she was the one who should take the blame, not him. I attempted to keep my mind busy with cleaning, my ears alert for any sound of Lord Dracul's return.

It was almost half an hour before he returned, a different plate in his hands, looking remarkably similar to his meal. "Come, eat your lunch," he called to me, and once more, I came down the ladder.

He placed the steaming plate of food in front of me, the fare identical to his own.

I stopped him before he could take a bite. "You should take the new plate. Yours is cold now because of me," I said, moving to switch plates.

He blocked my hands and quickly took a bite from his plate. "It's fine," he said. "Now eat up."

"But—" I began to protest.

"Eat up," he repeated once more, taking another bite of cold food.

I did as he said, feeling terrible that I was eating something hot while his own meal was lukewarm at best.

As he ate, I noticed a ring that I had not seen earlier that morning. The large, swirling, blue stone seated on his right index finger glimmered in the light as he lifted the fork to his mouth.

After several minutes of silence, I spoke. "What happened?"

Lord Dracul paused mid-bite, as if deciding how much to tell me. "One of the other Dragon Maidens thought today would be a good day to play a trick on you since I was not bringing your lunch directly to you," he said, confirming my suspicions that it was Vimery. "I suppose she thought I would be elsewhere when it was delivered and not see its sorry state."

"Who was it?" I did not see any point in bringing Vimery's other misdeeds to his attention and pretended I did not know who it could be.

He fixed me with a pointed look, and I squirmed uncomfortably under his scrutiny. "I think you and I both know who has been giving you a hard time around here," he said, pointing a fork at me. "And in the future, I would hope you bring these transgressions to me directly. As I said before, any slight against you is a slight against me."

I nodded at his words, and after a few more minutes, we both had finished our lunch, returning to the work we had started before the meal. By the end of the day, I had finished dusting over half of the books and I could tell by Lord Dracul's expression that he was impressed with what I had gotten done for the day.

CHAPTER NINE

VALORA

Over the next weeks, I continued to clean Lord Dracul's quarters. From what he had mentioned, the other Dragon Maidens came in once a month for a day to do much needed cleaning, but that was it. And from the looks of things, a cleaning was very badly needed. Each day, I returned to the cavern exhausted, my entire body aching. But overall, I felt proud of what I had accomplished, the work helping keep my mind off my brother. I was too exhausted at the end of the day for my nightmares to plague me. Some days, Lord Dracul let me spend a couple hours in the afternoon to read books from his library, and I would do that while he continued working at his desk.

Lord Dracul eventually gave me a day off to do what I wanted. From what I could tell, this itself was abnormal—the other Dragon Maidens worked every single day with their Lords. But I was not one to question his generosity, as I looked forward to exploring the caves more. Though I had been too busy to think of Ronan, the thought of escape had never completely disappeared. Perhaps today would be the day I could find a way out. The glimmer of hope had not been snuffed out yet.

I traveled past the main tunnels, coming upon a section where they branched off that I had not seen yet. I picked one at random, not expecting to find anything interesting. As I walked, I could hear the sound of voices, the volume increasing the more I walked. Eventually, after numerous turns, I came upon a giant cavern, one that dwarfed both Lord Dracul's and the Dragon Maidens' caverns by comparison. At the top of the cavern was an opening that let in sunlight, keeping the crops scattering the cavern floor alive. People, ranging in ages from young children to the elderly, were picking a section of ripened produce, all while talking and laughing together. The only people who seemed to notice me were a few who were weeding nearby. At the other end of the cavern was another entrance where people came in and out with pails of water.

As I entered the cavern, the people closest to me avoided eye contact. They all wore the same gray clothing, similar to what the other servants in the cave usually wore, bare feet and all. I slipped off my shoes, as well, digging my toes into the cool dirt. It had been ages since I had experienced anything besides stone or rugs underneath my feet, and I relished the feeling.

A small boy raced into the cave, water spilling over the sides of his bucket. People moved out of his way, yelling at him to slow down and be careful, their voices echoing through the cavern. He paid them no heed, running full tilt in only the way a child could. He headed towards me, and I foolishly expected him to move. He was too close, running too fast, and I attempted to get out of his way, but he collided directly with me, spilling the remaining contents of his bucket onto my dress, soaking it immediately.

When he saw what he had done and noticed my clothes, his face paled, all color disappearing. "I'm-I'm sorry," he stammered. "I didn't see you."

Silence fell over the crops as everyone froze, having seen what happened. They watched us closely, their gazes trained on me, to see how I would react.

I stood and grabbed the fallen empty bucket, handing it to him. "Accidents happen," I reassured him. "But next time, you should be more careful."

He nodded solemnly at my words, remaining silent.

"What's your name?"

At my question, his face turned even whiter, making his chestnut hair and freckles stand out even more. He began to tremble, and I internally cursed myself. Of course, he thought he would get in trouble.

"Nothing's going to happen to you," I said. "It's okay, really."

"My name is Henrick," he said after hesitating for a moment, his eyes darting to someone behind me.

"It was nice to meet you, Henrick," I said, smiling widely, trying to hide my unease over the way everyone stared. "I hope to see you around. If you will excuse me, I have to go change. Bye."

As soon as I left, I could hear the cave start buzzing with talk about me.

"What's the matter with you?" I heard a woman's voice scolding the boy. "That is to be Lord Dracul's Maiden, and you just doused her with water! You could be in serious trouble!"

"I didn't mean to!" Henrick cried. "It was an accident!" I could hear the tears thick in his voice and my heart clenched at his palpable fear.

"You need to be more careful in the future. Now go get more water. Barely any got to the crops. And no running this time!"

After hearing the woman yell after Henrick, based on how her volume increased at the end of her spiel, I could only assume that he would not follow her instructions.

I walked back to the Dragon Maidens' cavern, my bare, dirt-covered feet feeling cold against the stone floors. Looking behind me, I could see a faint trail of footprints from the dirt and quickened my pace, not wanting to be caught by anyone.

No one was in the cavern when I returned, and I let out a sigh of relief. I stripped down and dropped my wet clothes in a basket to be cleaned later, changing into a purple linen dress that had cornflowers embroidered at the hem. I quickly washed my feet, cleaning them of the dirt before slipping back into my shoes. At last, I took down my braid, combing my hair before tying it back up once more. Then I sat on my bed, relaxing in solitude while I could.

The other Dragon Maidens entered the cavern about half an hour later, stopping when they saw me. The chattering amongst themselves ceased immediately and I could only assume they had been talking about me. If anything, the past couple of weeks had proven that they kept me at arms' length. Even when I tried to engage them in conversation, they only provided surface level answers to my questions. It seemed that since Lord Dracul had picked me, they all had drawn away. The openness and friendly nature they had shown me when I arrived had quickly disappeared.

"You weren't wearing that when we all left this morning," Vimery said, her tone accusatory. "Decided it wasn't good enough for you?"

The dress I had picked earlier had been a very plain cotton dress, similar to what the other Maidens wore today. I prickled at her accusation, but did not answer her, turning in my bed so my back faced her. Today, I was not in the mood to deal with her antics.

"Valora, what happened to your dress?" Alonsa asked, walking over to the basket where we discarded our clothes for the day. Servants would collect the basket the next morning and take everything to be washed. "Why is your dress soaking wet?"

I bit my lip, knowing that she would chastise me for exploring. No matter what I did, it always seemed to be wrong somehow. Only when I was in Lord Dracul's chambers did I actually feel peace—he usually complimented my work or offered other words of encouragement. There, with the Dragon Maidens, it seemed I only received comments meant to pick at all my shortcomings. I missed the gentle encouragement Alonsa used to provide.

"Valora?" she prompted once more. "Where did you go? How did this happen?"

"I had the morning off and went exploring," I admitted with a sigh.

Alonsa let out a sound of frustration, and I flinched, preparing myself for the lecture that always seemed to come.

"You shouldn't be exploring," Alonsa said in a tired voice. "The only places you need to know are Lord Dracul's rooms, his treasure hoard, and where the other Lords reside. You already know how to go to all those places, so why did you go exploring?"

"I'm tired of being cooped up in the same spaces," I said, turning to look at her. "I wanted something more stimulating to do. Is that so wrong?" When she did not answer, I flopped back on my bed. "I came across the crops and there was a small incident."

"And *that's* why your clothes are wet?" she asked, coming to sit on my bed.

I looked at her and nodded.

Once more, she let out a sigh and pushed a lock of hair out of her face. "I don't nag you to make you feel bad," she said, "but because I'm worried that you are going to make so big of a mistake that we can't help you." She placed a hand on mine. "I don't want anything to happen to you, Valora. None of us do."

I held back a snort at her words. Vimery would probably be happy to see me gone. But looking at the others, they seemed as sincere as Alonsa sounded.

I nodded. "I'm sorry for causing you to worry," I said softly. "But it can get really boring. I just wanted to find something new."

"I understand, but give it time. You'll adjust," Alonsa said.

Everyone immediately turned to the door as a gentle rustling of scales approached. Lord Dracul appeared in the doorway, his eyes passing over each Dragon Maiden until eventually stopping on me. I was surprised to see him dragon form; usually, in his chambers, he looked like a human, and I felt a strange oddness about seeing him now. From his expression, I gleaned no indication of what he thought. His silver eyes were impassive, and I could not imagine why he would be stopping by at midday. And based on the silence of the other Maidens and their shocked expressions, it was very out of character for him to be there right now. Lately, I had been having lunch with him in his chambers, even though the Maidens usually came to the cavern for meals.

"Lord Dracul!" Alonsa exclaimed. "We weren't expecting you. How may we serve you?" She and the others fell into belated bows. I remained upright, staring at him.

"Valora, come with me," he said quietly. The serious note in his tone sent shivers down my spine.

Silently, I got up and followed him to his chambers, where he transformed into his human form. I waited patiently as he began to pace, seeming to gather his thoughts.

"I heard from the servants in the garden that someone ran into you this morning," he said, his voice quiet. "Who was it?"

Silence descended on the room, as I was shocked he had heard about the incident already. I had not been planning to tell him anything.

"It was an accident," I explained at last. "There was no harm done."

I turned to go, but Lord Dracul grabbed my arm to prevent me from leaving, his ring flashing in the light. It was a light touch, but I could feel the strength he held back.

"Tell me who it was," he said. "Accident or not, they need to learn to be more careful."

"Well, I'm not telling you." I raised my chin, meeting his eyes. They glittered in anger, and I realized something. "Did you say they came and told you what happened? Why would they do that?"

"They know that if the Lords find out from our Maiden first and not them, we are less likely to want to listen to their side of the story. They told Lord Lorka, who reported the incident to me," he growled, and I was starkly reminded that even if he showed kindness to me, he was still a ferocious dragon that the others all feared. "So who was it?"

I argued back. "I'm not going to give you a name so you can punish them, not when it was an accident. They already know better for next time."

"Valora, I am going to ask you one more time, and you had better give me a name," he said impatiently. "Who knocked you over?" Steam began to pour from his nostrils, which almost looked ridiculous in his human form.

Crossing my arms, I said airily, "The name escapes me. I seem to have forgotten it."

The output of smoke intensified, but I did not allow myself to be cowed by him. Henrick was only a child.

He sighed, and after a couple more moments, shook his head. "Very well," he said. "You win."

I felt the corners of my lips curl up and did my best to quickly school my features. By the slight smirk, I could tell he noticed anyway.

"Don't be so smug," he said, trying to fight back his own smile.

I laughed, and at my reaction, he let out a chuckle. I paused, not expecting to hear such a sound from him. He was more lenient with me than the other Lords were with their Maidens, but I was still surprised he did not push the point further. I had the thought that maybe staying would not be so bad after all. As soon as the thought flitted through my mind, I squashed it.

"So I'm not in trouble?" I asked.

"No, you are not," he confirmed. "But for the rest of the day, I would like you to stay in the Dragon Maiden cavern. I don't want you getting into any more trouble."

"Yes, my Lord," I said, bowing before turning to leave, returning to the cavern to have lunch with the other Maidens.

CHAPTER TEN

VALORA

The others heard about the whole accident from Hyacinth, Lord Lorka's Dragon Maiden, who had talked with several of the workers who were present that day. After that, all except Vimery began to warm up to me a little more. I was invited to eat lunch with them. They actually talked to me. Slowly, the ice that had grown between us began to thaw. I found out more about each of them and their backgrounds. I also learned that once a year, they each were allowed to go home for a week to spend time with their families.

Alonsa came from one of the towns on the mountainside, Hilcrest, and had left behind a husband and son who, for a couple days each month, she was allowed to go see because of the town's close proximity. I could not imagine the sacrifice she had made to be there, but while she seemed to miss her family, she did not seem to regret the decision to be a Dragon Maiden.

Bethany came from a town to the east, at the furthest distance that the Dragon Lords collected their Maidens from. She was the oldest in her family, with six younger brothers and sisters. Fairly often in the evenings, she would knit some article of clothing and Lord Verhorn would send her finished pieces back with her monthly wages.

Gwen and Hyacinth, who were in fact twins, had lost their parents at a young age and had been raised by an aunt and uncle. Surprisingly, one year, they had both been allowed to be picked as Maidens, and their wages were sent to their surrogate parents. The two had not been back in several years, opting to stay in the mountains, having grown close to several of the servants there.

Vimery, unsurprisingly, remained very tight-lipped about herself, but I came to find out from the others that she had originally been picked to become Lord Dracul's Dragon Maiden. Due to an unknown incident, she had been swiftly removed from his service and became Lord Firenze's Dragon Maiden instead. Ever since then, when the other Maidens went to clean Lord Dracul's caves, she was not included in that monthly rotation. This shed a little light on why she seemed to hate me so much, but it also was not my fault that Lord Dracul had chosen me.

* * *

A week after the incident in the garden, I managed to sneak away and return. This time, when I entered the cavern, everyone stopped their work, watching me carefully as I walked through the rows of crops. If I happened to make eye contact, they quickly looked away. I felt the prickles of their stares on my back as I looked around for the boy.

One bold woman stepped forward. "You should not be here, my lady," she said. I recognized her voice as the one who had chastised Henrick. "You should leave."

"Where is he?" I asked, my eyes still searching for him. My heart quickened as I realized that Lord Dracul had probably found out who had run into me and that Henrick had been punished. "Where is Henrick?"

After a moment's pause, the woman said, "It was decided that it would be in his best interest that he no longer work in this area."

"Who decided this? Where is he now?" I demanded.

"Lord Lorka gave the order," she said, her face paling.

I realized that my hands were clenched, and I probably frightened her. Slowly, I relaxed my body and nodded.

"He's in a place where he won't run into anyone anymore."

"Did Lord Lorka order anything else?" In reality, I knew it was Lord Dracul who had made the order. I could not believe he would go so far as to punish such a young boy.

The woman shook her head. "Not that I know of."

"Then may I see Henrick?"

Everyone within earshot gaped at me.

"I guess so," the woman said. Her face showed her obvious surprise at the request. "I just don't understand why."

"I would like to talk with him," I said, my patience wearing thin. I only had so much time before I would be missed. "That's not a problem, is it?"

"Not at all, my lady," she said quickly, trying to backpedal. "I'll go fetch him immediately." She scurried off.

I looked around the cave, and everyone flinched, going back to their work. Once more, I took off my slippers and buried my feet in the dirt. Though it had only been a few days, I had missed the smell of freshly tilled soil. Kneeling, I examined a squash plant, gently probing its curling vines and the flower that was primed to soon turn into a vegetable.

After a couple minutes, I heard two pairs of footsteps padding down the corridor.

"And be sure you don't screw up this time." I could hear the woman coaching Henrick on how to behave. "If Lord Dracul hears about you messing up again, there won't be another chance."

Henrick entered the cave, walking towards me with his gaze glued to the floor. He stopped a few feet away from me. The woman who had fetched him came up from behind and nudged him, clearing her throat.

"You asked to see me, my lady?" he asked, eyes still on the floor.

"Please look at me, Henrick." I tried to make my voice as gentle as possible, to show him that he had nothing to fear. "I promise I don't bite."

Slowly, he looked up at me, shame written all over his face. "I'm awfully sorry for the other day," he said. "I promise I didn't mean to run into you."

"I know. I just wanted to talk. Is that okay with you?"

He looked to the woman, who gave him a look. "You can do whatever you want, my lady."

"Please, just call me Valora," I said, quickly growing tired of the formalities. "Come, walk with me." I moved to exit through where they had just come from, once more feeling the prickle of everyone's eyes. After a few moments' hesitation, I could hear Henrick following me. I led him a few yards into the corridor before stopping.

"Why do you want to talk to me?" he asked once we both stopped. "Are you going to yell at me? Lord Lorka and Lord Dracul already reprimanded me and I said I was sorry."

"Lord Dracul did *what*?" I asked, appalled at his words. I hoped that the Dragon Lords had not been too harsh on the boy.

"He told me that if he ever heard of me doing something like that again, I would be punished. And it's not that difficult to figure out what happens to people who don't obey the Dragon Lords."

I remained silent, although I did agree with him. They were dragons—of course it was easy to think up ways that they could punish someone. "Regardless, I'm not here to yell at you. I just want to talk."

"Why?" he asked.

I shrugged. "There's not really anyone else to talk to and I wanted to know more about you."

He looked closely at me, a suspicious look on his face. "You want something," he said, sensing there was more that I had not told him.

I bit my lip before nodding. "You're right," I admitted, figuring it was better to be honest up front. "I do want something from you. But I need information first."

"What's in it for me?" he asked, crossing his arms.

I had been expecting this, and took out a pearl necklace I had taken from the Dragon Maidens' clothing stash. "How about this?" I asked. "I can give you more once you help me."

Henrick's eyes widened at the sight of the necklace before he snatched it from me and stuffed it in his pocket. "Deal," he said, his eyes brightening. "What do you want to know?"

"Is there a village nearby?" I asked. "Where do all these servants live? Where are you from?"

"Those of us who work in the fields are from Yarstaff," he said. "It's a little further down the mountain, but not that far."

"Does everyone in Yarstaff work here?" I asked.

He shook his head. "No, but most of us do. We have people who run shops and stuff in the town."

"Do you all go back to Yarstaff every night? Do you ever get mail delivered?" Questions poured out of me, my mind whirring with possibilities. Henrick may be able to help me escape.

"Yeah, it's close enough that we go home each night," he said. He frowned slightly. "Doesn't everyone get mail delivered to their town?"

"How often?" I asked. "How often does the mail caravan stop by? And how do you leave the caves?"

He squinted his eyes at me, a frown beginning to cover his face. "You're up to something," he said. "Dragon Maidens aren't supposed to leave."

"Please, Henrick. Tell me," I begged.

"It stops by about once a month. It should be returning in three weeks," he said. "And we have special hallways we go through that lead outside. But they are closely monitored all the time by dragons."

I quietly cursed. Escaping was not going to be as easy as I thought. But I would have time to figure that out later. "Do you think I can stop by in two weeks?" I asked. "Around lunchtime? I have something that I would like to give you to pass on to the mail caravan."

He fiddled with his hands, looking at the ground now. "I guess you could," he said.

"I'll bring you something else for your trouble. And I'll have another request for you at that time." I felt bad about involving him in something like this, but I had no choice. "And you can't tell anyone about this, do you understand? It needs to remain a secret between us."

Henrick nodded. "I understand."

"Thank you, Henrick," I said, relief flooding my voice. "I will come back in two weeks at lunchtime. Don't forget!" I gave him a pat on the head before heading back through the garden, making my way to the Dragon Maiden cavern.

CHAPTER ELEVEN

VALORA

The day after talking to Henrick, when I went to Lord Dracul's quarters, he was not in his usual spot at the desk. Instead, he sat on one of the couches near the bookshelves, reading a large leather-bound book. I could tell based on the cover that it was one about tonics, I recognized it from when I had dusted the books a few weeks ago.

He glanced towards me briefly when I entered, but went right back to reading.

"Good morning," I said when he did not say anything.

He continued reading for a couple moments before shutting the book. "Good morning, Valora," he said, standing with a swish of his velvet robes. "Today, I will be working on a few things," he said, tapping the book with his forefinger, his ring glittering in the light. "I will need you to go to Lord Lorka to get ingredients for me." He walked over to his desk and grabbed a small piece of parchment, completely filled with looping handwriting.

"Yes, my Lord," I said, taking the list from him.

Our hands briefly touched and I gasped at the spark that I felt in my stomach at the contact. Lord Dracul must have felt something, too, as he raised an eyebrow.

"I will be back soon," I said, turning to go and trying to not focus on what had just happened.

A couple minutes later, I was at the entrance of Lord Lorka's cave. There was a bell outside and I rang it gently, waiting for a response. Hyacinth came to meet me, rushing from deep inside the cave. She came to a stop and stared at me, a quizzical look on her face.

"Lord Dracul needs ingredients," I said, holding out the piece of paper.

Hyacinth took it from me, her eyes scanning over the list. "We should have most of these here," she said. "But a few, I might need to send for." She gestured for me to follow her inside.

I was surprised to see that the entirety of Lord Lorka's quarters was covered floor to ceiling in foliage. Somehow, the floor was covered in grass, and vines stretched up the cave walls, with ferns and flowers spread out all over the cave. In the corner was a small waterfall, water trickling down the rocks. He had a window that shone light inside, illuminating a beautiful delphinium. I stopped in my tracks, admiring the view, and Hyacinth turned to look at me.

"I wasn't expecting to see something like this inside a mountain," I said, still absorbing the view in front of me.

She smiled. "It's one of my favorite places here," she said. "Lord Lorka takes great pride in this place and all manner of plant life. That's why he's in charge of the gardens and crops."

Hyacinth led me further inside to another room filled with shelves that were stuffed with all sorts of food. Fruits and vegetables were separated by season and there were jars of spices and pickled crops. Towards the right were jugs of juice and cider.

"Does all of this feed the entire clan?" I asked. Though it was an expansive collection of food, it did not seem enough to feed all the dragons that I knew lived within the cave system. I had not come across any except for the Dragon Lords, but from what I had been told, the rest of the clan lived deeper inside the caves. Very rarely did any of them go see the Dragon Lords.

"No," Hyacinth said, starting to pick out items that were on the list and putting them in a basket. "This is Lord Lorka's special supply of ingredients from what he personally grows. Lord Dracul prefers to use these rather than the ones harvested by the workers. He says they're better quality."

"Lord Lorka grows all this himself?" I was flabbergasted that a Dragon Lord would have time to do such a thing. Based on the size of the produce, he had great skill and care towards growing things.

"I help him," Hyacinth said, smiling at the unspoken compliment. "But it is just us two."

"That's amazing," I said.

"Thank you." A deep voice came from behind me and I spun at the sound. A man with tanned skin, cropped orange hair, and yellow eyes looked at me. He was dressed simply, wearing a beige linen shirt, rolled up to his elbows, and dark-brown pants, cuffed at his calves. Surprisingly, he was barefoot and covered in dirt. A golden hoop hung from his ear and glinted in the light of the lanterns.

"My Lord, it is a pleasure to meet you," I said, bowing. "I was talking with Hyacinth about your personal store. It is quite impressive."

He smiled at the compliment. "And what brings you here today?"

"Lord Dracul asked her to fetch some ingredients," Hyacinth said, holding out the piece of paper for him to look at.

Lord Lorka brushed past me to see the list, frowning slightly as he looked at the ingredients. "Interesting," he mumbled to himself, bringing a hand to his chin as he examined the list further.

"There are a few items that we don't have here," Hyacinth said, pointing out the ingredients in question. "I planned to fetch someone to get those from the main storeroom for me."

"There's no need," Lord Lorka said. "I will be back in a couple minutes."

He disappeared, and Hyacinth continued to gather the remaining ingredients, the basket almost overflowing.

After a few minutes, Lord Lorka returned, three small jars in his hands. "These are very potent," he warned me. "So please tell Lord Dracul to only use a small amount, around half of what he would normally use."

I nodded at his instructions, and he put the jars in the basket, making sure they were safely tucked away.

"Thank you, my Lord," I said, bowing once more. Out of the corner of my eye, I could see Hyacinth smiling at my behavior and felt a swell of pride.

"Please feel free to come back anytime," Lord Lorka said with a smile. "My storeroom is always open to Lord Dracul and his Dragon Maiden."

Hyacinth led me back to the hallway and bade me farewell. I made the way back to Lord Dracul's cave with the heavy basket, surprised at how much he had requested. I knew that he had his own stockpile of ingredients and could not figure out why he would need so much more. When I entered the cave once more, he was over by his tables, which were filled with potions and glassware, his back turned to me.

"I have everything you requested," I announced, heading towards him.

He looked up and motioned for me to set the ingredients on the table next to him. "Did Lord Lorka say anything?" he asked, looking through the basket and pulling a few items out and setting them aside.

"These three jars are very potent. You should only use half of you normally would," I said, pointing to the jars Lord Lorka had specified. "What do you need so much for anyway?"

He did not answer my question right away, continuing to pick through the ingredients. "I was running low on things," he said, checking back at his book before continuing. "There are a few tonics I would like to make over the next few weeks."

I moved to his other side to look at the book as well. "Like what?"

"There are a few potions that I want to try and combine," he said, pointing at one page and then flipping a few pages to point at another. "I'm hoping to combine these two in order to help the lingering cough a number of villagers contract in the winter months. Due to the wind, weather, and the dampness in the caves, it is not a good combination."

I raised my eyebrows in surprise, not expecting him to work on something for the humans. "That's… unexpected."

Lord Dracul looked at me. "Because why would I care about humans when I'm a dragon myself?" he asked, his mouth quirking into a smirk.

I nodded.

"Well, I want those I care for and protect to thrive," he said, picking out a couple chunks of ginger. "Are you able to cut these up into small pieces for me?"

I took the ginger and grabbed a nearby knife, beginning to chop across the table from him. Briefly, I was reminded of a time when I would help my mother prepare herbs for our homemade tinctures and a small smile crossed my lips. Quickly, my sleeves got in the way and I rolled them up to my elbows, continuing with my work. I suddenly felt the air go still and looked up to see Lord Dracul staring at my arms, at the scars left behind by the men who had attacked. Immediately, I pulled my sleeves back down, my face flushing with embarrassment. The scars were still pink; not enough time had passed for them to fade yet.

"What happened?" he asked, his voice quiet. Even though my sleeves were pushed back over my arms, he still stared at them.

"I don't want to talk about it," I said, my tone short. The last thing I wanted to do right now was relive that horrible night.

"Valora, who did this to you?" he asked, his gaze meeting mine, silver eyes smoldering with anger.

I shook my head, tears suddenly pricking my eyes. "I said I don't want to talk about this," I said, taking a couple steps away from the table. "It happened before I came here."

His face looked pained as he took a step around the table towards me. Immediately, I backed away, my thoughts once more on that night, and I felt cold, like ice had suddenly been dumped over me. I wanted to flee, to run away from this conversation, and I felt myself beginning to slip away—slipping away to somewhere deep in my mind where I could hide and not process what happened.

"Valora, I'm not going to hurt you," Lord Dracul said, holding up his hands. "But please, let me come closer." He took another step towards me, and I stepped to the side of the table, now closer to the entrance of the cave than he was. "Valora, please," he begged. "I'm sorry. I just want to make sure you're okay."

My mind raced, my breath coming in gasps as I was overwhelmed with the feelings from that night. I could feel myself starting to mentally retreat and knew I needed to get out of there before panic began to consume me. I took another step towards the entrance, and Lord Dracul cried out in alarm. That was all it took before I turned and sprinted out of the cave into the hallway. My feet flew beneath me as I ran down the corridors, through twists and turns, not sure of where I was headed. All I knew was that I needed to get away before I fell to pieces.

Finally, I found myself in a seemingly abandoned hallway and collapsed to the ground, my chest heaving. A strangled sob escaped my throat and my chest tightened painfully. I curled into a ball, shaking while I tried to escape the nightmare, tears streaming down my face. The pain increased and I clutched my arms tighter, trying to ground myself back to reality.

I was frozen for what felt like ages, unable to move, even as I heard footsteps approaching. A presence settled next to me and I felt a slight amount of comfort washing over me as they sat there, not saying anything. Eventually, the panic lessened to the point where I could breathe properly again, and I lifted my head, wiping away my tears as I did so.

To my surprise, Lord Dracul sat beside me, looking at the wall across from us. He glanced at me when I sat up, his eyes sorrowful. "I'm sorry," he apologized. "I shouldn't have pushed."

Exhaustion washed over me, and after a moment's hesitation, I leaned against him, my head resting on his shoulder. I could feel him freeze at the action, but after another moment, he relaxed, moving his hand to cradle my head. The tightness in my chest lessened further. I let out a shuddering sigh and rubbed my arms.

We stayed like that for several minutes, listening to each other breathe. Focusing on Lord Dracul's breathing helped me calm down further, and the final dregs of the nightmare washed away. Eventually, I pulled away from him, immediately missing his warmth, my chest feeling hollow. My face flushed at the thought that he had seen me in such a vulnerable position.

"I just… can't," I said, not looking at him. "It's still too fresh."

"I understand," he said, putting a hand gently on my arm. Once more, I felt the sparks dance in my stomach, but I was too drained to focus on them. "I'm sorry. I was just shocked." Lord Dracul stood and offered me a hand.

Without a thought, I took it and he pulled me upright, catching me in his arms as I collapsed against him. He held me softly for a moment, and my arms encircled his waist after several seconds, burying my face in his bare chest. He smelled like fire and wood, which was somehow comforting, even after my memories. Despite being brought there against my will, that contact, that warmth was welcomed. It had been a long time since I last received physical affection, and I suddenly realized how much I craved and missed it.

After several moments, we stepped apart. I tried ignoring the way my heart fell at the loss of contact. "Thank you," I said, wiping away a few lingering tears.

"Shall we head back?" he asked, holding out a hand to me.

I nodded and took it as he led me back through the hallways. I was surprised at how far I had gotten when I ran away. From what I knew of the caves and hallways, we were somewhere near his hoard, but it was definitely somewhere I had never gone before.

The rest of the afternoon was filled with cutting ingredients —no more reference made to my scarred arms—and crushing some of the herbs in a mortar and pestle. It was soothing to work side by side with Lord Dracul, letting my mind focus on the mundane task in front of me. I enjoyed the rhythm of our work, and that night when I went to bed, I fell fast asleep immediately.

CHAPTER TWELVE

VALORA

One day, bright and early, Lord Dracul came to the Dragon Maiden cavern to fetch me in his human form. I followed him, curious where he led me as we walked further through tunnels I had not explored before. After a few minutes, we came to a doorway. On either side was a dragon guarding the entrance. They nodded towards Lord Dracul as we walked through.

"Where are we going?" I asked at last when it seemed he would not elaborate.

"I'm going to show you where the rest of my clan lives," he said. "To give you an idea of everyone I'm responsible for."

He led me through more winding hallways before we reached another doorway. As we stepped through, my eyes widened. The cave system there was much more complex than I could have ever imagined. The doorway we just came through opened into an enormous circular cavern that stretched multiple stories high with the center completely open. I could see dragons walking around on other levels, completing their daily activities. Some were in their human forms, while others remained as dragons. There was a general volume of noise that I would expect from a small city.

I turned to Lord Dracul. "Everyone lives here?" I asked.

Smiling, pleased by my reaction, he said, "Yes, everyone except for the Dragon Lords and their Maidens reside in this area of the mountain. Different levels have different purposes. The lower levels are more residential, while the higher levels are used for the shops, workshops, storage, and stuff like that. There are also a few different spots on each level where they can fly outside if they so wish."

"Why are the Dragon Lords separate from everyone else?"

"Security purposes," Lord Dracul said. "Those guards we passed earlier? There are always two guarding the entrance to our section of the mountain, every hour of every day. Occasionally, we'll come out and interact with the rest of the clan, but for the most part, we stick to our area of the mountain. We're usually too busy for anything else."

"Are you going to show me more of what's down here?" I asked. I had spotted a food vendor a couple levels down from us and my mouth watered at the thought of skewers of roasted meat.

Lord Dracul chuckled. "I certainly can," he said.

He led me down a flight of stone steps, to the level below us. Immediately, the volume increased as we got swept up in the throng of dragons. Quickly, Lord Dracul grabbed my hand, clutching it tightly so we would not be separated.

A stall nearby caught my eye and I tugged him towards it. Willingly, he went along with me and we stopped to look at the wares.

The merchant, a purple dragon based on the color of her hair, eyed me strangely before noticing Lord Dracul. Her eyes widened and her gaze shot between the two of us multiple times before she caught herself and bowed deeply. "I did not realize, my Lord. Please accept my apologies."

Lord Dracul waved away her apology. "Do not worry," he said. "I was just showing my Dragon Maiden around the mountain. She took a liking to your stall here."

The other dragon looked at me once more and her face broke into a smile. "Your Dragon Maiden, of course!" she said, sounding somewhat surprised. "Is there anything that you fancy?"

I looked over her wares, shiny trinkets and silken fabrics. I pointed to a necklace, silver with swirls carved into it. In the center was a blue stone, the color of a clear summer sky. "This one is pretty," I said. I looked to her. "All of your wares are beautiful."

"Thank you, my dear," she said. She turned to Lord Dracul. "Will you be purchasing anything for your Maiden today, my Lord?"

Lord Dracul looked over at the necklace before nodding, taking it and a blue silken wrap. "These two, please," he said. He passed her a few gold coins and she bowed in gratitude.

"Thank you, my Lord, for your generosity."

Turning to me, Lord Dracul stepped behind me to fasten the necklace. Once he was done, he draped the wrap over my shoulders. "You seemed a little cold," he said in response to my questioning look. I realized he was right. It was chilly this deep in the mountain.

"Thank you," I said softly. "You didn't have to do that."

"It's the least I can do for my Maiden," he said with a smile.

The two of us set off again, looking into the nearby stalls and admiring their wares. None caught my interest like the first one did and Lord Dracul did not buy anything else. Once we had exhausted looking at all the stalls on this level, we went to one below, where all the food carts were. Stepping onto that floor, my nose was assaulted with all sorts of delicious aromas. My stomach grumbled and Lord Dracul looked at me, a grin splitting his face.

"We should get you some food," he said. "Is there anything in particular that you want? There's just about everything you could imagine here."

"Are there any foods that are dragon specialties?" I asked. I was curious if there was a huge difference in the cuisine. So far, the food served to the Maidens was fancier than anything I had eaten before, but it certainly was not unusual.

Lord Dracul laughed. "There certainly are, but most are known for their spiciness," he said. "There's one food in particular, but it might be too spicy for you. It usually is for most humans."

My curiosity was piqued. "What is it?" I asked.

"It's a crispy dough ball soaked in a spicy sauce," he said. "We can get one for you to try, but should probably have something as a backup."

"There were meat skewers I could see from up above that looked tasty," I said.

Lord Dracul thought for a moment. "I know where you're talking about," he said. "They're beef skewers, and are actually near the dragori stand as well."

We walked towards the two food stalls, only stopping once to grab a few sweet cakes for after our meal. Lord Dracul bought the beef skewers first, then the dragori. He handed the skewers for me to try first.

"Give this a taste before you burn off your taste buds," he said.

I took a bite, the juicy beef melting in my mouth. "It's delicious!" I exclaimed, quickly taking another bite.

Lord Dracul insisted I finish the entire skewer before trying the dragori. It was bright red and I could smell the spices, causing my nose to itch.

"Having second thoughts?" Lord Dracul asked with a smirk when he saw my hesitation as I picked up one of the fried balls.

Immediately, I took a large bite, enjoying the crunch from the crispy shell. The taste was smoky and savory, but I was unable to identify the intricate flavors. Then the spice hit. My eyes began to water and I could feel my face turning red from the heat. My tongue felt like it was on fire and as I swallowed, I felt the heat trailing all the way down to my stomach.

Lord Dracul let out a sympathetic chuckle. "I did try to warn you," he said. "Here, try this. It should help." He handed me a tall glass of thick, white liquid.

I drank the liquid, quickly realizing it was some sort of milk. Immediately, I felt a bit of relief. The milk helped with the pain from the spice, but not completely. "I guess I should have believed you," I said with a gasp, having finished the entire glass.

"Try one of the cakes too—it should help a bit." Lord Dracul took out one of the intricately decorated cakes, holding it to my mouth.

Upon taking a bite of the tiny cake, I could taste sweetness and vanilla. My family had been too poor for sweets, except maybe once a year. The flavor reminded me of the cakes they would buy when they had saved up enough for a little treat. I smiled fondly at the memory.

"That is delicious," I said.

Lord Dracul took the rest of the dragori that I had not eaten and popped it into his mouth, finishing it in one bite. I was not surprised when he had no reaction, but he smiled at me smugly. As a response, I shoved the second small cake into my mouth. He let out a bark of laughter, grabbing the third and final cake for himself before I could eat it too.

I tried to ignore the way my stomach flipped at his laugh, at how naturally we were able to tease each other. It was too easy to imagine the way we would grow closer if I stayed, how effortlessly I could acclimate to his world. I was filled with guilt at the thought of abandoning my quest to find Ronan. But maybe I could forget about that just for today—one day spent enjoying myself did not mean I gave up on my brother forever.

For the rest of the day, we wandered along the various levels with Lord Dracul pointing out different areas of interest. My favorite spot was a gorgeous fountain, encrusted with all sorts of blue and white gemstones reflecting light from nearby sconces. The whole fountain looked ethereal, and a few dragons tossed in coins. Lord Dracul said they were making wishes. He gave me a coin to toss into the fountain as well. Silently, I made my wish—that I would find my brother and be happy. I desperately hoped it would come true.

When I returned to the Dragon Maiden cavern that night, no one mentioned my two new presents that Lord Dracul had bought me. And for once, I fell asleep with a smile on my face. Lord Dracul certainly knew how to have fun, and I was blissfully happy for the first time in a long time. It was truly a wonderful day.

Chapter Thirteen

VALORA

The next day I met back up with Henrick, slipping away from Lord Dracul with the excuse that I was eating lunch with the other Dragon Maidens. Earlier, I had managed to take a piece of parchment and scribble out the message that I wanted Henrick to deliver.

The young boy waited for me, shifting from foot to foot, obviously nervous. He nodded in greeting as I approached.

"Do you know how to get out of these caves? Other than the way you mentioned the other day?" I wasted no time on greetings, my heart beginning to pound. For the last couple of days, my thoughts had been consumed with escape, running through ideas every night before I went to bed.

Henrick hesitated before nodding slowly, his eyes growing big when he realized what I wanted. "If you get caught, you'll be punished," he said. "Probably killed."

"I need to escape," I said, my voice quiet. "I was taken against my will. I have family to find. Answers that I seek. In a week, it'll be the new moon—I'm planning to escape then. In the darkness, it should be harder to find me." I held out the note to him, along with a bracelet for his payment.

He paused, staring at the note, easily guessing its contents before his gaze flicked to the bracelet. I could tell he weighed the consequences of if he got caught and implicated with helping me against the price that the bracelet would fetch.

"Please, Henrick, please help me escape," I begged. He was my only hope. I knew that everyone else was too scared of the dragons to even think of helping me. Though I hated the thought of using him, I needed to find my brother.

"It's dangerous," he said at last. "Very dangerous what you're suggesting."

"I know, but I can grab more items to pay you with," I said. "I'll make sure you aren't caught. If this somehow fails, I won't tell them you helped me. Please."

The boy considered it for several moments, my heart pounding as the time dragged on, before taking the note and bracelet, sticking both in his pocket. He stepped towards me, motioning for me to get closer. His look of apprehension did not escape my notice and I was grateful that he was willing to risk his life to help me.

"I'll see it gets picked up, and leave a pack by one of the back entrances that night," he whispered, his voice dropping as he spoke. "But you shouldn't come back here. People are getting suspicious. I've already been questioned about last time."

For the next five minutes, we talked through the logistics of my escape and Henrick gave me instructions on how to exit the caves. It was not going to be easy that night, but it was my only hope to escape and see Ronan again.

Chapter Fourteen

Valora

Now that a plan was in place, time passed slowly. I could feel myself growing restless and impatient waiting for the day to arrive, but did my best to hide my apprehension from Lord Dracul and the other Maidens. One moment, I would feel confident about the plan, and the next, I would question if it was a good idea, my mind rapidly changing on a regular basis. I could tell that the other Dragon Maidens had noticed a change in me, but so far, no one had questioned me on it, which I took as a good sign.

A couple days later, Lord Dracul was sitting at his desk when he stopped writing and looked at me where I was cleaning the bottles used for his potions. I could feel the restless energy building up within me, my foot tapping quickly.

"Valora, what is it?" he asked. "You've seemed tense the past few days."

I set the bottle I was cleaning down in the basin and turned to look at him. "I'm feeling a bit cooped up," I admitted, the first excuse that came to mind as to why I had been acting this way.

"I see," he said, a thoughtful expression coming over his face. "I suppose you have been stuck inside for quite a while." He continued to think before an idea hit him, his mouth spreading into a grin. "Come with me," he said, standing and gesturing for me to follow.

Lord Dracul led me through the tunnels, towards a different part of the caves I had not been to before. We came across a set of steps winding upwards and he took my hand, guiding me up them. The staircase stretched high up into the mountain and I was winded by the time we reached the top, where there was a small landing leading into a wall. Lord Dracul paused before the wall, pressing a hidden mechanism on the right, causing the wall in front of us to slide aside, leading outside. My mouth dropped open as he led me onto a flat stone balcony surrounded by a waist-high barrier, the wall behind sliding back into place after us.

From our vantage point, I could see the forest and the expanse of the mountain below us. We were high enough up that I could not see any animals from this height, but I could tell that the foliage had changed and fall was on its way. It was a stark reminder that it had been half a year since I was taken. Looking further up the mountain, I could see snow-capped peaks, further affirming this fact. Wind whipped through my hair. At this altitude, it was so strong it ripped my hair out of its braid. Lord Dracul moved to the edge of the balcony, and after a couple seconds, I followed him, standing at the barrier. Together, we gazed out at the surrounding area, red and orange hues filling the forest as far as the eye could see.

"I hope this helps," he said, loud enough to be heard over the wind. "This is the most I can do at this time."

I nodded, wrapping my arms around myself, not dressed enough to combat the chill of the air. Lord Dracul shrugged off his velvet robes, placing them over my shoulders, and I instantly felt warmer.

"What about you?" I asked, watching as he stood bare-chested, placing his hands on the stone barrier and leaning out over the edge of it. Immediately I was distracted and did my best to ignore his muscles. His long, deep-blue hair whipped behind him in the wind. "Won't you get cold?"

He chuckled, a low, rumbling sound that I could hear over the wailing of the wind. "I'm a dragon, remember?" he said, turning to look at me. "I don't need anything to keep me warm." Lord Dracul reached out his hands and gently placed them on my wind-whipped cheeks, warmth transferring from his touch to me. I could feel my face growing redder, though it had nothing to do with how cold it was outside.

"I suppose that's true," I mumbled, looking away from his intensely warm gaze. His eyes looked like pools of melted silver, which they resembled more often these days. I remembered the first day I had arrived, and they had looked like metallic shards, ready to pierce me. Now I felt like I could disappear into them, surrounding myself in their warmth. The thought flitted through my mind that I could always stay and continue to stare into these eyes forever.

I cleared my throat and took a step away from him, suddenly far too aware of my thoughts. This little excursion had distracted me enough, and I almost felt a pang of sadness at the thought of escaping in the next few days. Moments like that, moments of Lord Dracul's kindness, tethered me there, but I knew that I needed to move forward and continue trying to find Ronan. That familial bond, that pull to know what had happened, drove me onward, and no matter how much I enjoyed my time with Lord Dracul, it was almost time for that to come to an end.

"Are you ready to head back inside?" he asked, looking once more out at the forest.

Slowly, I nodded. Despite his robes surrounding me and the previous warmth of his hands, I suddenly felt cold, frozen by the knowledge that this would soon be ending. The thought turned my stomach to ice.

Lord Dracul walked over to where we had come from and pressed the mechanism, the wall sliding open again. Carefully, we descended the stairs, and once we reached the bottom, I handed him back his robes.

"Thank you," I said softly, trying to ignore the sadness that overwhelmed me. "I needed that."

He smiled and my heart skipped a beat. "I needed a break too. It was a pleasure to have you join me."

We walked back to his cavern, my mind in turmoil. The more time I spent with the Dragon Lord, the more attached I became. The new moon could not come soon enough. I needed to get out before I could no longer allow myself to leave.

* * *

Later that night, as I ate dinner with the other Dragon Maidens, they shared stories of their towns' fall festivities. Most had a sort of late-night fall market, filled with comforting baked goods. A couple carved squashes and traded homemade boiled sweets with other villagers. And a few others had an annual bonfire with music and dancing. The stories and laughter made me feel homesick. The fall harvest bonfire had been the last festivity I had been able to celebrate with my parents. Only a few weeks after that was when we had been attacked and my life had changed forever.

Tonight, we had spiced pumpkin tarts for dessert, the smell warm and welcoming. We all huddled together in a circle, the steam from the heated pool warming us from the mountain's chill. Gwen and Hyacinth had blankets wrapped around their shoulders. Vimery sat as far away from me as possible, avoiding my eyes as she glared at her tart.

"Vimery, you're awfully quiet tonight," Alonsa said. "Is everything okay?"

"I'm fine," the other Maiden said, her tone short.

"It doesn't seem like it," Bethany prodded.

Vimery let out a huff of frustration. "*She* gets all sort of special treatment and I'm sick of it!" she shouted, pointing a finger at me. "She breaks rules and doesn't get punished for it. And then Lord Dracul took her topside today. It's not fair!"

Alonsa let out a sigh. "She is under Lord Dracul's guidance right now," she said. "And that affords her certain benefits."

"But she shouldn't be! She's not even a full Dragon Maiden yet. She hasn't gone through the ritual!" Vimery wailed.

"Vimery, that's enough," Alonsa said firmly. "None of this is Valora's fault. You need to let this go."

The other Dragon Maiden continued to glare at me in silence. I felt the anger simmering beneath her gaze. I remained silent, knowing that any word from me and she would explode further. Though this shed more light on why she hated me, it still did not explain her immediate animosity when I had arrived.

There was a slight noise at the entrance of the cave and we all turned to look. Lord Dracul appeared in the doorway in his human form, an eyebrow quirked and his mouth set in a grim line. I knew immediately that he had heard Vimery's outburst. I stood to bow, hoping to delay any punishment he would burden her with.

"Is there anything you need help with, my Lord?" I asked.

"Valora, please come with me," he said, his voice serious. As I crossed the cavern to meet him, he directed his attention to the other Dragon Maidens. "Valora will be coming back after curfew," he said. "Do not wait up."

My stomach dropped at his words, worried about what was going to happen. Had he found out about my escape plan? I could practically feel Vimery's smirk focused on me.

Lord Dracul led me to his cavern in silence, my heart growing heavier with every step.

"Did I do something wrong?" I asked, trying to think through my actions from the afternoon and if I had done anything wrong. But nothing came to mind.

He smiled at my tone of concern and shook his head. "You have not," he said, heading up the stairs along the wall to the landing that held the telescope. "But I figured tonight would be a good night to look at the stars. You indicated your interest a while ago."

My eyes widened in excitement, he remembered my comment from months ago. "Really?" I breathed, rushing to follow him up the stairs. "I can stay up late to look at the stars?"

Lord Dracul laughed at my reaction. "Yes," he said. "You can stay up late to look at the stars. The reason I picked tonight," he said, looking through the telescope and making a few adjustments, "is there is a comet passing by later tonight. I thought you might be interested."

I nodded eagerly. "That sounds wonderful," I said.

He moved out of the way, gesturing for me to take a look, and I peered through the telescope. He had focused it on the Drake constellation, the stars forming the shape of two dragons circling each other.

"Wow," I whispered. "I've never seen it look like this before." I moved back for Lord Dracul to take a longer look.

"There's a legend about the Drake constellation," he said. "Have you heard about it?"

I smiled, knowing the answer to this question. It was one of the stories in my father's book. "There was a dragon that was so obsessed with the stars that he flew as high as he could until he joined them," I summarized.

Lord Dracul's smile grew. "That is the commonly told tale," he said. "But the story told among the clans is a little different." He paused, almost as if waiting for me to ask him to continue.

I did not want to disappoint. "Would you mind telling it to me?" I asked, sitting amongst the pile of cushions that was arranged on the landing. Lord Dracul came over and sat down next to me.

"Dragons are said to get our powers from the stars," he said. "A star fell and landed on a lizard, who absorbed its power and transformed into a dragon. And that was how the dragons were born. Each dragon is told this story as a youngling, and one of the High Dragon Lords took that story to heart. One day while he was stargazing, he saw a star falling to a location nearby. He flew to find the star and found that a special dragon had appeared directly from the star, a glowing dragon. He fell in love with her immediately. The two of them spent their days together, filled with love and happiness. Eventually, she had to return to the sky. Despite wanting to keep her by his side forever, he let her go. When she flew back to the sky, she became part of the constellation. The High Dragon Lord was so heartbroken that he started wasting away. One day as he was staring up at her in the sky, he noticed the winking of the star that was her eye. Inspired, he flew up to join her and became stuck in the sky with her. They were finally together forever."

"That's a much better story than the one I've heard," I said softly, my face heating up as he stared at me warmly. "Very romantic."

"I think so too," Lord Dracul said, his eyes molten. He was so close.

I looked away, my face on fire. There was an unexpected heat in my stomach. I thought my body was going to burst into flames. Along with that was a burning desire to touch him, feeling a pull I could not explain to be near him. Wind from the window blew in, dousing the heat that consumed my body. A shiver ran down my back at the sudden chill.

"You're cold, aren't you?" Lord Dracul asked. "Let me get something for you." He stood and went down the staircase, giving me much needed time to collect myself. My fingers fiddled with the necklace he had gifted me, giving me something else to focus on.

What felt like seconds later, Lord Dracul returned with a plush blanket and two steaming mugs. He drew the blanket around me before handing me a mug. From the smell, I could tell it was a spiced tea, quickly confirmed by a tentative sip. The warm liquid slid down my throat and I felt it re-warming my belly, though this warmth was different than the one from earlier.

"That's delicious," I said, snuggling into the blanket. "When does the comet come by?"

Lord Dracul paused, thinking for a moment. "It should be here soon," he said, standing to calibrate the telescope. "Do you want to see more constellations in the meantime?"

I stood, drawing the blanket around me to block out the cold. I looked through where he had directed the telescope next and smiled at the Mariposa constellation, one of my favorites. "I love this one," I said, staring at it for several moments before stepping back.

"It's a favorite of mine too," Lord Dracul said. "Although I think this next one is my absolute favorite." He moved the telescope once more, taking a few minutes this time to make the necessary adjustments.

With anticipation, I looked through the telescope. Immediately, tears blurred my vision as I recognized the constellation. It was the first one my father had shown me, the first one I had memorized, and one of my favorite stories. It was the Amor constellation, shaped like two hands clasping each other. My father had shown me the arrangement of stars when he told me about how he and my mother had met—they had been stargazing on the same hill. It was a pastime that they both had shared with me since I was young.

"This one is my favorite," I said, my voice clogged. "Do you have a story for this one that's different from the commonly told tale?" The tears began to fall, though I tried to hold them back. But with the anniversary of their deaths fast approaching, I was suddenly filled with lots of memories.

"No, both dragons and humans share the same story for this constellation," he said, looking curious as to why I wiped away tears. "Valora, is everything okay?"

"I'm sorry," I said. "I don't mean to ruin tonight, my Lord." The tears fell faster and I tried to hold them back.

"When it's just the two of us, you can call me Dracul. You don't need to address me by my title," he said, moving closer to me. "And you aren't ruining anything. It's fine." His voice was kind. "Do you want me to tell you another story?" He gestured back towards the pile of cushions, and I nodded, moving to follow him.

I settled back into the cushions and Dracul began to talk, his deep voice soothing. "Back before the world was created, the gods of the universe figured out how to occupy their time. They decided to create our world and busied themselves with their creations. Two of the gods loved each other dearly, but their duties took them away from each other. The daytime god, Solaris, was charged with bringing the sun, and the night goddess, Nosha, was to bring the moon, so they never got to see their love. Solaris worked with the god of the sky to create the Amor constellation so his love would be able to see the image of their clasped hands at night and know how much he loved her. Once a month, on the new moon, they are able to be together."

I closed my eyes, listening to the cadence of his voice. The way he told the story was so soothing and reminded me of my childhood, of my father reading from his book of stories by the fireplace. As the story came to a close, I opened my eyes and Lord Dracul stared at me, his eyes filled with that molten silver once again. I felt that fire begin to grow inside me once more.

"Do you feel better?" he asked, his voice soft and husky.

I nodded silently, my voice caught in my throat.

"The comet should be visible now," he said, moving away to stand.

Immediately, I felt the cold rush in from the absence of his body. He held out a hand and I took it, but he pulled me up harder than I expected, causing me to fall into him.

"Sorry," he said quietly, helping me right myself, his cheeks turning red.

"It's okay," I said, my face aflame once more.

The thought again crossed my mind that my escape could not come soon enough. I just continued to embarrass myself.

Lord Dracul moved towards the telescope, looking through it again, sucking in a sharp breath. "I found it," he breathed, standing still for several moments before moving aside. "Come look."

I stepped forward, and when I looked through the glass, my mouth dropped open. A brilliant burst of light moved through the sky, leaving behind a trail of twinkles. Never before had I seen anything so beautiful, the bright colors taking my breath away.

"It's beautiful," I breathed. It seemed almost a sin to speak any louder than a quiet whisper. I could feel Lord Dracul moving behind me, and I jumped when he placed his face next to mine, trying to look through the telescope too. "I can move so you can see more, my Lord," I said, starting to move out of the way.

His hands gently rested on my hips as he held me in place. "Dracul," he prompted.

"Dracul," I repeated, the word feeling strange leaving my lips without his title.

"There's enough room for both of us to look," he said, his voice tickling the back of my neck.

I leaned down once more to look through the telescope, trying to ignore the butterflies fluttering in my stomach. His hands remained on my waist and I felt warmth radiating from them, spreading through my body. He settled his head on my right shoulder so we could look through the telescope at the same time, but I tried to focus on breathing normally, my heart racing. This was dangerous.

We stayed still for several moments before I stepped away. "Thank you for the evening of stargazing," I said, studiously avoiding his gaze. "But I-I think I should go." I moved towards the stairs.

"Valora, wait," Dracul said. "Please." I turned to look at him, and his expression filled with confusion and sadness. "I'm sorry if I made you feel uncomfortable."

"I-I…" I was at a loss for words. "I think I need to go. Good night."

I practically ran down the stairs, heading for the cavern entrance. Dracul remained frozen on the landing, his gaze burning into me.

I was not sure what had just happened between us, something that had been building all evening, but I knew I needed to get out of there before I did something I would regret. Quietly, I ran back to the Dragon Maiden cavern and slipped under the covers, my heart beating wildly. Luckily, the other Maidens were asleep and no one was awake to interrogate me.

Chapter Fifteen

Valora

The next few days were awkward. Dracul and I did not address what had happened, preferring to keep to ourselves. We did not talk like we had been, that growing closeness suddenly froze. Part of me missed our conversations, but the rest of me was glad for the distance.

There were also rising tensions amongst the Dragon Maidens, I assumed due to the nighttime excursion, and Vimery was more volatile than ever. Rather than keeping a silent hatred of me, she purposely tried to get a reaction from me. I constantly found my things missing, and she was always there with a smirk and snarky comment.

Finally, the night of my escape arrived. I stayed awake, waiting until the other Maidens fell asleep. When the cave filled with the sounds of slow breathing, I slipped out of bed. I grabbed my satchel, filled with my family treasures and a few pieces of jewelry as payment for Henrick. Quietly, I padded through the familiar corridors, my heart pounding, until I reached an unfamiliar passage. My fingers went to Dracul's necklace and I felt a pang of guilt as I touched the stone. Silently, I repeated Henrick's instructions to myself, clenching my fists before moving forward,

"

my final decision made. I did not have time to second-guess myself. I needed to find Ronan. After a few minutes, I reached another fork, and without hesitating, I took a right. Soon after that was a left. Every so often, I paused, checking to see if anyone followed me, but I heard no other footsteps.

After a few more turns, I could finally feel a breeze on my face, my pace quickening immediately. A few more yards and I could see the night sky out of the entrance. To the left, a small pack waited for me, filled with food and other rations, along with a rope ladder leading down the cliffside. I breathed a sigh of relief that Henrick had kept his word, grabbing the pack and leaving the pieces of jewelry behind before stepping on the ladder.

I had quite the distance to climb down the mountain, glad that it was too dark to see how far up I was. It felt like ages before I finally reached the ground, and I let out a shaky breath. My steps quickened as I walked through the surrounding forest, trying to put as much distance as possible between myself and the dragon-filled cavern behind me. There was a slight feeling of hesitation, a knot in my stomach tightening the further I moved away from the mountain. My heart beat furiously that this plan had even worked, knowing that I had Henrick to thank for it. I desperately hoped he would not be found out and remained safe.

I had done it—I was free.

A scream escaped me as I felt a claw grab my arm, jerking me into the air. My head shot up, looking to see who had caught me. One of the guards stared at me, his claw digging hard enough into my arm that it drew blood.

"Thought you could escape, hmm?" he sneered. "Ever since your little stunt when you first came here, Lord Verhorn has the guards randomly check in on you every night. Tonight, when your bed was empty, we knew you were going to try and run for it."

"How?" I asked as we flew around the mountain, approaching the entrance I had first arrived through. The guard tossed me on the ground as he landed and I knew that there would be a bruise from the force of slamming into the floor. Though, I knew that was the least of my worries. He landed next to me, transforming into his human form before roughly picking me up and pulling me down the hall. His strength was definitely superior to that of a regular human and I knew this was another benefit of being a dragon.

"Lord Dracul can answer that. If he decides to let you live." He set a merciless pace, and I could barely keep up as he dragged me down the hall. I recognized the corridors we passed through, knowing that we headed directly to Dracul's chambers. He pulled me through the halls, treating me like a rag doll, before throwing me at Dracul's feet, leaving me in a sprawled heap of limbs.

I could not even bear to look at the High Dragon Lord. I could only imagine how angry and disappointed he must be. For some reason, I could not figure out which of those thoughts bothered me more. The guard left the room, leaving the two of us alone. There were no witnesses for this, and fear began to stir in my heart.

"Valora, look at me," he said. I could tell by the tightness of his voice that he was livid.

I bit my lip and closed my eyes for a moment before lifting my head to look at him. He was in his dragon form, his silver eyes stormy, and I fought the impulse to look away.

"Why would you try to escape?" Dracul demanded, smoke escaping his flared nostrils in his fury.

"I—" His anger frightened me and I could barely speak. Though he had always said he would not hurt me, right now, I was not so sure that he would not kill me on the spot.

"*Why?*" he roared. "Why did you try to escape?" I could see the betrayal in his eyes and a spike went through my heart.

"I need to find my brother and talk to him," I said hoarsely. "I've wasted enough time here. If I don't go, I'll possibly miss my chance of finding answers forever."

"What answers do you seek from him?" His voice grew louder and angrier the more he spoke.

"To find out what he did that I deserved to get these!" Venom laced my voice as I drew up my sleeves to reveal the numerous scars lining the entirety of my arms. I grew tired of his anger. If he was going to punish me, I would rather he do it sooner than later. "And these!" I pulled at the back of my dress, revealing more of the jagged scars, the fabric ripping at my ferocity.

Dracul paused in shock upon seeing the scars, his silver eyes widening. After realizing what I had done, I hastily pulled my sleeves back down, covering the scars once more. I fiddled with the back of my dress, trying to fix it, but I quickly gave up as there was no way to close it. It was too late anyway—he had seen almost everything.

"What happened?" he asked quietly, his anger subsiding. Based on his expression, he was thinking back to those weeks ago when I had cried.

"I don't want to talk about it," I said, knowing that I had already given away too much. Previously, he had only seen a fraction of my scars, and now, he had seen almost all of them.

His face turned soft for a moment, before returning into a fierce scowl. "I don't know what to do with you," he said. "Time and time again, you try my patience. And with this recent turn of events… I don't know how I'm going to convince the other Lords to let you stay."

"Then just roast me!" I threw my hands up in the air as I shouted. Even though I wanted answers, I was so tired of feeling like a burden to everyone. Too many times, I had been so close, yet was still so far from answers. Not to mention the swirling wheel of shame, switching from feeling guilty about leaving to wanting to stay. "Just roast me and make it easier on everyone!"

From the look on Dracul's face, I knew he was not expecting that answer. "No, I will not be roasting you, Valora."

I turned away from him, unable to stare at the tenderness that entered his eyes, but he reached out, using a single claw to gently turn me back towards him, his gaze serious once more.

"I just need you to understand the severity of what you've done."

I stared at him. "I do know what I've done," I said. "But the risk was worth the opportunity to see my brother again."

Dracul shook his head. "How long has it been since you last saw him?"

Once more, I could not meet his eyes, knowing that my answer would not be sufficient. "I haven't seen in him a long, long time. It's been over three years," I admitted. It had been almost two years since my parents had been killed, and Ronan had left home a year before that. The question I had asked the guard earlier came back to me. "How did you know I was going to escape tonight?"

He sighed heavily, as if he did not want to answer the question. After a few moments, I was certain he would not answer, but he surprised me. "We intercepted the note you gave to Henrick," he said.

My heart skipped a beat as I suddenly worried for his safety.

"He was not punished, don't worry," Dracul said, seeing the look that crossed my face. "But he has been reassigned and you will no longer be able to see him."

"How long have you known about this?" I asked, my mouth suddenly dry.

"About a week, as soon as you gave the note to Henrick. You were not as sneaky as you thought—a few of the other workers raised their concerns to us," Dracul said. He looked very tired all of a sudden, and I realized how much of a burden this must have placed on him this past week.

The other night came to mind and I wondered if that was somehow his way of trying to convince me to stay, to prove that there was something there for me. It made me wonder if it had just been a ruse or if he really felt the way he had acted. An unexpected tenderness had grown between us, and now my mind spun, wondering if any of that had been real.

"Go back to the other Maidens. I will figure out how to deal with you in the morning."

I nodded, turning to go. Right now, I would not think about what was going on between us. I had bigger problems at the moment.

"And Valora," he said, making me pause. "If you are ever caught outside your chambers again at night, you will be killed. That, I can tell you for certain."

I remained silent, only bowing before returning to the chamber.

The other Maidens were awake and stared at me in shock, having expected Lord Dracul to kill me, or at least punish me in some way. Not that I blamed them—I had expected the same.

CHAPTER SIXTEEN

VALORA

The next morning, when everyone woke up and got dressed, the cavern was filled with prickly silence. Everyone avoided looking at me. My face burned as I dressed, embarrassed that I had been caught and now everyone knew about it. But the heat in my face was nothing compared to the wriggling pile of snakes in my stomach.

Before breakfast even arrived, Lord Dracul showed up at the cavern entrance in his dragon form. Without being told, I followed him, knowing that my punishment had been decided. I did not say any goodbyes, and as soon as we departed, I could hear the other Maidens begin to whisper. Dracul led me to a part of the caves I had never been to, through many twisted corridors, almost maze-like to get to our destination. There was a small opening in front of us, only big enough for one person to squeeze through. I looked to him, not understanding what I was to do.

"It has been decided that the Whispering Pool will decide your fate," he said. If I was not mistaken, he sounded almost resigned, his voice deep with exhaustion. He must have stayed up all night discussing with the other Lords. "You will remain in here for three days. I will return at the end of that time and then we shall know your fate."

"How will I know what the decision is?" I asked, taking a long look at the dark opening.

"The Whispering Pool will either kill you or let you live," he said. A coldness settled throughout my body at his words. "If it deems you worthy, you will be allowed to remain my Maiden." His jaw clenched, and I could not tell whether or not he wanted me to live.

"Why is it called the Whispering Pool?" I peered inside, but the cave was too dark to make out anything.

"You'll find out soon enough," Dracul said. "Now you must go."

I bit my lip before entering the unusually small opening. It seemed even smaller than it looked. If Dracul had tried to enter in his human form, he would have barely fit inside the doorway, as I had to hunch over and turn to my side to squeeze in. Turning, I watched as he moved a rock in front of the entrance, sealing me inside. Tentatively, I opened my mouth to say something, but immediately closed it, dread filling my entire body as the rock cut off my last remaining tie to the outside world. Now I was truly alone.

A small window shed a little light into the cave. My new home for the next three days was quite spacious. It was nowhere near as big as the Dragon Maiden cavern, but big enough for four or five people. At the far end of the cave was a small pool with water trickling down from an opening in the rock. Slowly, I approached it, apprehension building in my chest. From what I could tell, it seemed normal, but I got the foreboding sense not to touch or drink the water. After staring for several moments, I retreated back to the other side of the cave, settling down for what was sure to be a long wait.

Hunger gnawed at me throughout the day as I examined the rocks nearby, memorizing their size and shape. By late afternoon I was thirsty and while I eyed the pool of water, I dared not approach. My thoughts were filled with Dracul's disappointment and I cursed myself for not being more careful in my escape. A few times I dozed off, only to awaken at the wind rattling outside the cave.

Night fell, by what I could tell from the small window. Uneasiness draped over me as I tried to find a comfortable position to go to sleep. After a while, I heard a sound coming from the end of the cave and felt my body jerk awake. A strange humming seemed to be emanating from the pool, but I was too frozen with fear to approach it. Through the window, a thin sliver of light came from the moon, illuminating the water, which seemed to glow. The humming grew louder and louder until it reached a deafening roar, and I cringed at the volume. With the humming, the water began to bubble, growing in intensity. Suddenly, the noise stopped and the water shot towards me. I managed to hold back a yelp as it formed into the rough shape of a person. They stopped mere inches from my face and stared at me with eyes that seemed both empty and limitless.

"Who are you?" the being asked, still intensely holding my gaze. Their voice contained what sounded like thousands of other voices. They barely spoke above a whisper and I had to strain to hear what they said.

"My name is Valora," I said, struggling to keep my voice even. Somehow, I knew this would be the entity that decided my fate.

"Valora." The being tried out my name, flexing their mouth as they spoke. "What brings you to the Whispering Pool?"

"I was told this was my punishment for trying to... steal something," I lied. For some reason, I did not want to reveal the true reason I was locked there—something held me back. "That the Whispering Pool would decide if I live or die."

"Ahhhhh, so the Dragon Lords are too lazy once again to figure out a person's fate," the being mused, pulling away to pace a couple feet away. "How many days do I have this time to decide?"

"Three," I whispered, my mind whirling too fast for me to comprehend my own thoughts.

"They're feeling unusually generous. Interesting." They paced more, and it seemed like they were not going to say anything else.

"Excuse me," I said, gathering up my courage to continue talking as they turned towards me. "How exactly do you decide if a person lives or dies?"

In one swift movement, the being was once more a couple inches away from my face. I jumped, not expecting the speed and fluidity of their movements. "It all depends," they said. "For most, it takes mere moments to decide if they will live or die. You seem more difficult. This will be interesting. Yes, very interesting," they muttered to themselves. "I might very well need the full three days to decide."

They stared at me for several more minutes, their limitless eyes piercing into my soul before whooshing back into the pool. I watched the water's surface, waiting for them to suddenly reemerge, but I was alone until sunrise.

* * *

Wind howled through the cave the second night, passing through the window and unseen crevices in the rock. I was huddled in the corner, trying to keep warm, when the figure emerged from the pool, less explosively this time. Instead, they quietly rose from the water and stepped down, their footsteps sounding like the trickling of water on rock.

"Good evening, Valora," they said, keeping away from me this time, yet I could feel their eyes closely watching me. "Are you cold?" Their voice was mocking.

"What do you think the answer is?" I snapped. Though I knew if I wanted to stay alive, it was best not to anger this being that controlled my fate, I had been cold all day and did not want to answer stupid questions. I had already slept very little due to shivering all day.

"My, my. We are in quite a mood, aren't we? If you're like this all the time, I can imagine why the Lords didn't want to deal with you," the being said. Though they had no facial expressions, I could tell from their voice that they were certainly gleeful this evening. "That means we should be able to have a little fun tonight."

I glared at the figure, continuing to shiver. "The temperature will continue to drop," I said. From my time outside, with both Dracul and my escape, I knew that fall had arrived, and it was only a short while before winter would be there. "If this continues, you won't get the choice to kill me. I'll freeze to death." I shifted, wanting this thing to stop enjoying my severe discomfort. Hopefully, if I reminded them that I could freeze, they would have no choice but to keep me alive until they made their decision.

The being tsked in disappointment. "Well, that won't do at all. I get to choose," they said. "Now let's get you warm." They snapped their fingers and a flash of fire appeared in their hands. "Come over here. I'll keep you warm."

I moved closer as instructed, a sigh escaping me as immediate warmth flooded my body when I held my hands over the small flame. It reminded me of when Dracul had warmed me up the other night and I batted away the memory. Just as I got comfortable, the figure jerked the fire away and instantly, I was cold again.

"For now," they said, shaking a finger at me. "If you behave, I will keep you warm." They brought the fire back and the heat flowed into my body, warming me quickly.

"Thank you." I knew I would have to tread carefully tonight to stay on the being's good side—and in the fire's vicinity.

"Now, how did you get here?" they asked.

I frowned, not knowing where to begin to answer the question. "You mean why I ended up *here*? I told you that yesterday."

Once more, the fire disappeared. "We both know you lied about that," they said so matter-of-factly that my heart skipped a beat in fear. "So how about you tell me the real reason? You can start with how you became a Dragon Maiden. How you were chosen." The flame returned.

My eyes flew to their face, the reflection of the fire rippling in the pools of their eyes. "I wasn't chosen," I snapped. Everyone fawned over how it was a privilege to be chosen, but I'd never felt that way. "I was kidnapped, taken. I'm not even from the town I was taken from. I was just passing through."

They backed away from my vehemence, clearly surprised by my sudden anger. "Why were you passing through?"

I opened my mouth, then closed it, trying to think of an answer.

"No more lies," they warned.

"I was looking for my brother. He left home and did… something. I'm not sure what." I paused, preparing for the rest of the story. "I think that whatever he did, some men came in retaliation. They killed my parents and left me for dead. I was searching for him when I was taken."

"Which means you never found out what he did," the figure said.

I nodded.

"And what did you do to end up here?"

A sigh escaped me. "I've become too comfortable here, so I escaped to try and find him. Instead, I was caught and the boy I had given the note to got caught as well."

"What did Lord Dracul think?" They laughed harshly at the look of surprise that overcame my face. "You think I didn't know you are his Maiden? So what did he think?"

"I'm not entirely sure," I admitted. "He seemed… disappointed, I guess. Betrayed? He's hard to read sometimes."

The figure began to shake with laughter. "That he is," they said. "And what do you think he wants my verdict to be?" They leaned closer to hear my answer.

I gulped, noticing the increasing severity of the questions. "I would hope he would want me to live," I said softly. "We've had good moments despite… everything."

"Very interesting," they said. "That is the end of my questions for tonight. I will leave the fire to keep you warm."

They moved away, taking the fire with them, and a chill entered my body once again. They knelt on the ground and whispered a few words. The flame spread slightly to make a nice blazing fire.

"That should keep you warm until tomorrow night," they said, before whisking back into the pool.

I jumped at the suddenness of the action before huddling by the fire. At least I wouldn't spend one more night freezing on the floor.

* * *

On the third night, as I watched the sun set and the moonlight begin to stream through the window, my stomach was in knots. I felt nauseous.

Like the previous two nights, the being rose up and stepped from the pool, the water forming their body glimmering in the moonlight. "Tonight is the night," they said, rubbing their hands together. "Tonight, I'll decide whether you live or die."

"You don't need to sound so excited," I said dryly, clenching my hands together to concentrate on something other than the sick feeling in my stomach.

They smiled. "Tonight, we will do things a little differently. You may ask me one question."

I jerked back in surprise. "Really?" I could not fathom why they were giving me this opportunity, what they could gain from this.

"Yes. You may ask me any question you wish and I will give you the answer. My knowledge spans far and wide, so ask your question."

The question burst out of me without a thought. "What do you call yourself?"

"What?" They pulled back in surprise, then leaned closer to peer into my face.

"What do you call yourself?" I repeated.

"You could ask me any question and that's the question you pick?" they asked. "You could ask me about your brother and I would give you the answer."

"I'm sure," I said. "If I'm going to be killed by you, I might as well know your name."

"No one has ever asked that before," they said. I could not quite tell in the light, but it almost looked like the figure frowned. "I just wasn't expecting the question." They took a few steps away from me.

After a few moments, when they did not seem like they would respond, I asked, "Are you going to answer my question?"

"Oh, sorry," they said, still seeming distracted. "My name is Kessland."

"It is nice to meet you, Kessland," I said, bowing my head in greeting.

Wind blew through the cavern, and I shivered at the cold. The fire Kessland had created last night had disappeared sometime in the afternoon.

They looked my way before shifting towards me with wooden movements, still disoriented by my question, and held up a flame once more. "Here you go."

"Is it really that surprising?" I asked after a couple minutes of silence.

Kessland looked at me. "I guess so, yes," they said. "I don't think anyone throughout the ages I've been here has ever asked or known my name."

"That sounds lonely," I said, feeling sympathy for them. I knew a little of what that loneliness felt like. Sometimes it was so strong I thought I would be swallowed whole by the emotion.

"It isn't all bad," Kessland said. "There are fish and other creatures in the waters I inhabit. I spend time with them, though they aren't much for talking."

"How often do the Lords send people to you to judge?" I asked. "Is that the only time you get interaction?"

"It's about every decade or so," they sighed. "But most times, it is a cut and dry case and they just want me to dole out the punishment. Rarely do I get opportunities like these." They flashed me a smile, but I could sense a sadness underneath the expression.

"Have you always been like this?" I asked. Kessland seemed somewhat starved for companionship, no matter how much they had tried to convey a façade of malicious delight at determining my fate. "I've never encountered anyone like you before."

Kessland puffed up at the compliment. "Of course, you haven't," they scoffed. "I don't think there's another like me in the entire world. I was born long before the dragons, before your kind even existed. I swam through the deepest depths of the oceans to the corner of every creek. I have been part of the water since water existed."

"How did you end up here?" I breathed the question.

They drooped now, deflating in front of my eyes. "Due to the cause of their creation, the dragons have powerful magic," they said. "Especially the power of the High Dragon Lord that is passed down to each successor. Ages ago, they discovered me, what I could do, and captured me, locking me here to do their bidding. So now I have no more adventures, no more exploring."

A flash of anger shot through me at the story. How dare the dragons lock up another innocent being? It was bad enough they took humans and threatened them into submission, but it sounded like they had been doing this for generations.

"That's horrible," I said in a choked voice, trying to keep a lid on my temper.

Kessland's eyes shot to me and they grinned wickedly. "Yes, it is," they said. "But you have gotten more than enough information out of me for one night. Why don't we turn to you?"

"What do you want to know?" This was my last night. I was willing to do anything I could to help my case, to survive.

"How have you liked your time here with the Dragon Lords?" they asked. "With Lord Dracul?"

My heart thumped at the question, unsure of why Kessland asked such a thing. "There have been good and bad things," I said slowly, trying to organize my thoughts. Kessland nodded in encouragement, and I continued to talk. "The other Dragon Maidens—mostly Vimery—have been very standoffish since I joined, but that's slowly been getting better. Although after this, I don't know what will happen."

"And what about Lord Dracul?" Kessland's voice was a whisper, thousands of voices asking me what I thought of the High Dragon Lord. "How have things been with him?"

"He's hard to read," I said softly, beginning to look away.

"You said that already," Kessland said. "What else?"

"He-he's very nice to me," I stammered, my face beginning to flush. I stared up at the ceiling, willing my cheeks to go back to normal. "When I talk back to him, he doesn't get angry, but he tells me not to do that in front of anyone else, so on some level, he cares. He's comforted me when I've been upset. And about a week ago, he…" I trailed off, trying to gain the courage to say the words. "A week ago, I think we shared a… moment. He let me stargaze with him and he told me stories. It was… it was a wonderful night." My voice dropped so I could barely hear it. "It was almost enough to make me not want to leave."

"Interesting." Kessland's voice did not give away what they thought, and I looked to them, my cheeks still flaming in embarrassment. "I'm glad to hear that he treats you well," they said after several moments of pause. "You have been through enough in your short years."

I bristled a bit at the slight. "I've been an adult for a few years now," I said.

Kessland chuckled. "I know, but to a being as old as I am, your lifespan is just a second of time for me."

The light inside the cave began to brighten, and I knew my time was almost up. The sun would be rising shortly and Kessland still had made no move to kill me. But I had at least made it this far.

"Are you going to let me live or not?" I asked. "Dawn is almost here."

"I've known since the first night that I was going to let you live," Kessland said. They smiled gently. "But I've been lonely for the past few years. I thought it would be nice to have someone to talk to."

"You mean *tease*," I said, relief flooding through me at the verdict. "And you couldn't have told me the first night?"

Kessland grinned. "Nope," they said. "I thought I would see what kind of person you are, to see if I was correct. To see if the future I foresaw for you would come true." They came forward and kissed my forehead. "Be careful, Valora. The Dragon Lords *will* kill you if you try to escape again."

"I know," I said. "Thank you for your concern, Kessland."

They stood, walking back towards the pool. "Valora," they said, putting one foot in the water. "The road ahead is going to be difficult, but I think you'll like how your ending will turn out." A mischievous grin split their face. "And while you're at it, you should ask Lord Dracul what *dragaria* means." With that, Kessland disappeared back into the pool.

With Kessland and their fire gone, the chill in the air swarmed me, settling into my bones. I went to huddle in the corner, hoping that someone would come get me before long. Just as I began to doze off, I heard the sound of the stone in front of the cave fly back with a horrible scraping sound.

"Valora?" I heard Dracul's voice shouting as he sprinted into the cave in his human form. "Valora?" To my surprise, he sounded concerned. His long hair was askew and his robes were falling off his shoulders.

"I'm over here, Lord Dracul," I said.

He spun at the sound of my voice, spotting me in the corner. Relief immediately filled his features and he ran over to me, pulling me into his arms. "Oh, thank goodness," he said. "I was worried the verdict would be…" He could not finish the sentence as he clutched me tighter.

My arms slowly encircled him, and I realized he was shaking. Dracul pulled back and I could tell that he had not slept these past three nights based on the circles under his eyes and the emptiness in his cheeks.

"Everyone thought Kessland would choose to kill me, didn't they?"

"Who's Kessland?" Dracul frowned at my words.

"The Whispering Pool!" I exclaimed. "And you sent me in here betting I was going to die!" I stood in my frustration and swayed from the upward rush of motion—a mix of my adrenaline leaving me and the past three days of no food made me woozy. The room spun slightly.

Dracul steadied me with his hands. "I hoped you weren't going to be killed, but I knew it was a possibility. It was the only option the Lords would consider other than killing you outright. I had no choice." I could tell by his tortured gaze that he spoke the truth. He had been tormented with the possibility of me dying.

"Then I suppose you had no other option," I said, smiling slightly. If that was what he'd had to do, then he truly had no choice. But looking at the man in front of me, I could tell that he would not willingly send me into danger.

"We need to get you food," he said, moving to help me out of the cave. "Let's do that and then you can rest. I'm sure spending the past three days here have not been the most restful."

CHAPTER SEVENTEEN

VALORA

Dracul led me to his quarters, where papers and books were strewn everywhere, covering almost every visible surface. I could only imagine what he had been through the last few days if the state of his quarters and his body were any indication. He let out a mighty roar which was surprising to hear from his human form, and a servant girl came running into the room looking terrified.

"Yes, my Lord?" she asked, trembling.

"Bring me food," he growled. "Lots of it."

"Right away, my Lord!" She scampered off.

Dracul let out a sigh, and his entire body seemed to droop. Deep in his eyes, I could see his exhaustion. At a brief glance, a few plates of uneaten food sat on his desk and I guessed that he also had not eaten in the past three days.

I walked over to the couch, clearing away the papers and books before sitting down and patting the spot next to me. "Come here, my Lord," I said gently.

Without a word, he stumbled over and collapsed onto the couch. I took his shoulders and laid his head in my lap. Slowly, I stroked his hair, pulling my fingers through his mussed, long locks. His eyes watched my face as I massaged his head, rubbing his temple and the crown of his head.

"I told you to call me Dracul when it was just us two," he said softly, his eyes beginning to tug closed.

"Well, right now, you just need to rest," I said. "From the state of things, it looks like you did not take care of yourself while I was gone."

His head began to fall to the side before he jerked himself awake, his gaze frozen on my face.

"Shh," I said, continuing to massage his temple and brow. "I will be here when you awake, I promise, Dracul. For now, just rest."

Once more, he closed his eyes, and soon, his breathing turned even.

Soon after he fell asleep, a couple servants entered the cave, their arms laden with platters of food. I motioned them to clear off the nearby table and set the food there, holding a finger to my lips to signal them to keep quiet. They nodded, silently completing their task before scuttling off.

I continued to run my hands through his hair, slowly working out the tangles.

* * *

After half an hour, Dracul began to writhe in his sleep, making small sounds of distress. I tried to massage his head more, to comfort him, but the dreams were too much as he began to thrash around on my lap. His face scrunched in agony and moans of anguish escaped from him. My heart split at the sight of him in obvious pain, but no matter what I did, it did not help.

Soon after his nightmare began, he shot awake, sitting up on the couch. His head spun to look around the room, his entire body relaxing when he spotted me. It was at this moment I realized what he had been dreaming about, and warmth filled me. Dracul truly had been worried about my well-being. His affection for me was genuine.

He lifted a hand towards me, cupping my cheek, and I leaned into it. A small gasp escaped him, almost a sigh, and I could see the relief in his face.

"I told you I would still be here," I said, smiling gently.

"I know, I just…" He trailed off, unable to finish his sentence.

"Food arrived while you were asleep," I said, gesturing toward the table. "I'm guessing you haven't had a proper meal in a few days. You should eat something."

Dracul rubbed the back of his neck sheepishly. "I actually ordered that for you," he said. "I know you haven't eaten since you've been in the Whispering Pool."

I moved towards the table and prepared two plates of food. "Let's eat together then," I said, placing one of the plates in his hand. "What kind of Dragon Maiden would I be if I allowed my Lord to starve?"

We ate in silence for several minutes before I remembered what Kessland had told me before disappearing. "What does *dragaria* mean?" I asked.

Dracul immediately started choking on the bite he had been eating, coughing for several moments until he could catch his breath. "Where did you hear that term?" he asked, his face paling.

"It was something Kessland said I should ask you," I said, frowning over his reaction. "Is it bad?"

He shook his head. "No, it's not bad," he said. "But now is not the time to discuss that."

I gave him a look.

"Please Valora, trust me. I will eventually tell you what it means, so please don't look for answers elsewhere. And please do not ask any of the other Maidens or Lords what it means either." He fixed me with a serious gaze, and I nodded. I had already betrayed his trust by trying to escape. I was not about to push this topic any further.

"I will wait," I promised.

Dracul sighed with relief before continuing to eat.

Once we were both done, he sat next to me on the couch again, fidgeting slightly.

"Do you want me to stroke your hair?" I asked, somehow knowing what he wanted.

He nodded. "Yes, please," he said.

We stayed silent as I ran my fingers once more through his cobalt-blue tresses, occasionally pausing to massage his temples. The silence was surprisingly comfortable, and I felt myself relaxing, too, as we listened to the sound of the other breathing. Eventually, I could feel myself drifting off, my hand slowing to a stop. I was vaguely aware of Dracul moving to maneuver me to lay down instead, his hands combing through my hair the way I had done for him. At last, I was able to drift off to a restful sleep.

Chapter Eighteen
Dracul

Since I had received the news that Valora planned to escape, my heart had been broken. In the end, despite my best efforts to show her my feelings, to prove that there was something worthwhile for her with me, she still felt compelled to leave. Our evening of stargazing had affected her, and I could tell she was beginning to notice how I felt about her. Maybe I'd come on too strong and driven her to leave, but deep down, I knew her justification of finding her brother was true. Her loyalty to him overrode any feelings she harbored for me, and that fact stung my pride.

That night had been almost perfect. She'd eagerly listened to my stories, stories I wanted to share with her. There had been many times I wanted to gather her in my arms and kiss her, even though it was too early for that. But as we had gazed at the comet together, she had not shied away from my touch. That alone had given me the hope that she would maybe choose to stay—until she had fled. Her face had been flushed and she'd stumbled over her words. I knew she felt something towards me. But in the end, she had still decided to leave.

The decision to leave Valora in the Whispering Pool for three days fully cleaved my heart in two. By then, I knew it was too late to reveal her as my *dragaria* to the others. The Lords would only assume I was making excuses to keep her out of trouble. Even though I had been angry she had deigned to escape, they had been *livid*. Most of them, with the exception of Hiram and Lorka, had clamored for her immediate execution. She had committed the gravest sin a Dragon Maiden could by abandoning her Lord. Only Lord Hiram's point that she had not fully taken the oath had quieted their calls for her death.

From the moment I had sealed her in the Whispering Pool, my true hell had begun—never knowing whether she lived or not, how the creature in the Whispering Pool treated her, not to mention the rapidly dropping temperatures. I had kept my word that the boy, Henrick, had not been punished, but with each passing moment of imagining her in there, I had to fight the urge to find him and tear his head off. He had helped her escape, allowed her to leave—my *dragaria*! Only the thought of her reaction when she found out—if she survived—stayed my hand. I could all too easily imagine her look of disappointment and despair when she realized what I had done.

The other Lords went about their days like nothing had happened, but I was unable to. I could feel my already short temper snapping at any minor inconvenience. The servants brought me food, but their mere presence irritated me. How dare they be there when she could not? From time to time, the Lords checked in on me, their constant nagging driving me insane. Their visits increased in frequency the longer time went on, checking to see if I had eaten, if I had slept, if I was fine. I could not stand it.

Verhorn had made the mistake of saying that it was a mercy we'd sent her to the Whispering Pool, that if this was how I was going to act then maybe we should have just killed her on the spot. I had thrown him against the wall, steam flowing out of my nostrils, a murderous rage slipping over me. Three of the other Lords had to pry me off him, and after they left, I had trashed my quarters, throwing papers and books everywhere. What was the use if she was not there? I convinced myself I could still feel her presence so the Whispering Pool must not have killed her. But on the third day of no sleep and no food, I knew I was delirious. I could not face the thought of her death.

I paced in front of the stone hours before sunrise, waiting for my chance to open the cave. Due to its design, I could not hear anything happening within the Whispering Pool, a fact that made me crazier than I already was. Hiram had stopped by briefly, but when he saw my face, he returned to his quarters. I knew I looked insane, a true madman, but I did not care.

Finally, when it was time for the cave to be opened, I threw the stone aside, rushing inside to see her. I hoped she was alive—she *needed* to be alive. If Valora was dead then I would tear this mountain apart stone by stone, crushing everyone inside it and turning everything to ash.

When I found her unharmed, I immediately felt myself coming back to life. She was mine once again, and now I stroked her hair in my quarters, hardly believing that she was lying on my lap. Surprisingly, she did not shy away from my touch—in fact, she seemed to relish it. My fingers trembled with emotion as I stared at her face, her serenely beautiful face. I knew that I could never let her go again. Just this once had almost ruined me, and I was so afraid of what monster I would turn into if she was not by my side.

"You are my *dragaria*," I whispered to her sleeping face, hardly believing that the Whispering Pool, Kessland, had told her to ask. "It means I am wholeheartedly yours, now and forever." I lifted a lock of her raven hair to my lips and kissed it. "And you are mine."

Chapter Nineteen

Valora

I awoke to the soothing feeling of fingers running through my hair. My dreams had been pleasant—not that they had stayed long enough for me to remember—but I awoke feeling relaxed and happy, something I had not felt in a long time. Opening my eyes, I saw Dracul staring at my face, a tender expression on his. He smiled when he noticed me looking at him.

"Did you have a nice rest?" he asked.

I nodded and started to sit up, but he gently pushed me back onto his lap, continuing to stroke my hair. "Not yet," he murmured. "Just a little longer."

It seemed that whatever wall had been between us when I had gone into the Whispering Pool had somehow crumbled. I had never seen Dracul look this vulnerable before. Usually, he focused on his work or was busy with his potions. The only time that had come this close was the night we stargazed together, but even that did not compare to was happening right now.

"Are you feeling okay?" I asked.

He frowned slightly at my question. "Yes," he said. "Why do you ask? Are you feeling ill? Was it the food?"

I shook my head. "No, but you seem… different," I said.

Dracul chuckled and I could feel the reverberations from where I laid. "I have never had a Dragon Maiden before," he said. "And I've gotten used to you. I think this experience made me realize what I gained when you came here, and I don't want to lose that." He placed a hand on my cheek, lightly cupping my face. "Now that you're back, I just want to bask in this moment." His eyes turned molten silver again, and I felt that knot in my stomach tighten once more, moving lower down my body.

I placed my hand over his. "I'm not going anywhere, Dracul," I said.

The Whispering Pool had changed me. Somehow, after speaking with Kessland and not taking the opportunity to find out more about my brother when I had the chance, I had let that part of myself let go. Seeing how much Dracul truly cared for me, I would rather spend my time here with him than try and find what would surely be disappointing answers from my brother. He had abandoned us and did not care about the consequences of his actions.

The hurried footsteps of a large creature rapidly approached Dracul's quarters, and I sat up, looking towards the entrance. Dracul turned as well, and together, we saw a giant gray dragon enter the room. Two twisted horns sprouted from either side of his head, spiraling back towards his shoulders. His deep-brown eyes surveyed the two of us before he transformed in a cloud of smoke, turning into a hunched old man with gray hair, long embroidered black robes, and a wrinkled face. I openly gaped, never having seen a dragon this old before. He must be one of the oldest in the clan, if not the world.

"Lord Hiram," Dracul said, gesturing to one of the nearby chairs covered in papers. "What can I do for you?"

Lord Hiram walked towards us, pausing briefly to swipe all the papers off the chair before sitting down, a tired sigh escaping him. "The past few days, you've been… preoccupied," he said, his eyes glancing towards me briefly. "But now that your Maiden has returned unscathed, we have events we need to discuss."

Dracul crossed his arms, his mouth forming a thin line. "Is this about Borthen again?" he asked tiredly.

Feeling as though I should not be sitting while the two talked, I stood and walked to get drinks for them. From what it sounded like, this would be a serious conversation. I went to one of the back rooms, fetching a bottle of dragon-red wine, one of Dracul's favorites, and two goblets. As I came back, I could hear Lord Hiram's raised voice.

"You need to take him seriously, Dracul!" he said. "Borthen is actively trying to gain the other clans' favor so they can overthrow you!"

"Which he has been trying to do since I took the title, and has failed every time," Dracul said calmly.

I approached with the bottle and goblets, filling both.

Dracul took one from me, swishing the liquid around the cup before taking a sip. "The Starfire clan has gained more members in the past few years, I'll give you that, but nothing that could rival the strength of our army."

Lord Hiram held up a hand, refusing the offered glass of wine while glaring at Dracul. "Regardless, they have been a thorn in our side for decades. You need to go to Borthen to make peace with him. This has gone on long enough." He gave Dracul a beseeching look. "As your advisor, this is the best decision to keep peace among everyone. Firenze's forces have noticed strange movements from their side of the continent."

Dracul remained silent, shooting me a glance before looking back at Lord Hiram. "I will take your concerns under advisement," he said. "And I will speak with Lord Firenze myself to receive his opinion on matters." He stood and walked towards his doorway, holding the curtain open. "Thank you for stopping by, Lord Hiram. Unfortunately, I have other matters to attend to."

Lord Hiram looked at me, an unintelligible expression in his gaze. "I'm sure you do," he said under his breath, so quiet that I almost missed it. He walked towards the doorway, bowing to

Dracul. "Thank you for listening, my Lord," he said. "Please call on me if you need my counsel on this matter."

"I will," Dracul said curtly, letting the curtain drop behind the older dragon. He came back to the couch and slouched into it with a sigh, passing a hand over his face.

"Is that something you need to be concerned about?" I asked, coming to refill his glass.

Dracul took another long drag from the goblet. "I'm not sure," he said, his fingers tapping the side of it. "Hiram is the eldest dragon among all the clans. He doesn't come with concerns unless they are well-founded." He took another sip of wine. "I just wish he had picked another day to do so, not when you've just returned."

I set the bottle down on the table and began to start picking up the papers. "Well, if you were distracted for the past couple days, I could see why he would come to you now," I said. "It sounds like it might be an urgent matter."

"I'll have to talk with the other Lords in the next few days," Dracul said. "And maybe arrange a visit to Borthen." He let out a sigh. "But traveling to the Starfire clan before winter is hardly something to look forward to."

"How far away is the Starfire clan?" I asked. I had vague knowledge of where it was located on the continent, but did not know any specifics.

"It's about a day's flight," he said. "And Borthen is the most pigheaded of the clan Lords to deal with. He's always wanted to be High Dragon Lord and was livid when I was picked instead. Ever since then, he's been trying to undermine my authority. Luckily, his schemes are pretty easy to thwart." He finished his glass and set it down.

I had continued to pick up papers while he spoke and had cleared off an area by the bookshelf, stacking all the papers in a single pile. "What do you want me to do with these?" I asked.

Dracul looked at them dully. "I want to just burn them," he sighed. "But I'll spend tomorrow organizing all of them." He looked out the window, realizing that night had started to fall. We had spent the day eating and sleeping, taking the time to relax. "You don't need to do anything else tonight. You can head back if you want to," he said.

I hesitated at his words, not quite wanting to go back to the Dragon Maiden cavern yet. By now, word would have spread that I had survived the Whispering Pool and I was not ready to face the other Dragon Maidens, their judgments, their questions.

He sensed my hesitation. "You don't want to go back yet?" he asked with a knowing smile.

I shook my head. "Not particularly."

"If you want to, you could stay here for the night," he said.

"Really?" I asked, flabbergasted by the suggestion.

Dracul shrugged. "I'm the High Dragon Lord," he said. "If I say it's all right, then it's all right."

"Where would I sleep?" I asked.

He pondered for a moment before his expression brightened. "You can sleep up here," he said, bounding up the stairs to the landing where the telescope was. I followed him and he pointed to the pile of cushions. "This is okay, right?" he asked. "I can get you blankets."

I remembered how comfortable the cushions had been during that night and nodded. "This is perfect," I said, sitting down and settling into the softness.

Dracul left and quickly returned with two plush blankets, wrapping me in them. "These should keep you warm throughout the night," he said, finishing tucking me in.

I snuggled further into the cushions and nodded. "I'll be warm enough," I said. With the fire going in the cave and the blankets, I should be plenty warm.

"Good," he said, looking at me warmly. I felt myself flush under his gaze. "Don't hesitate to call for me if you need anything," he said. A look came over him and he leaned forward, brushing his lips on my forehead. "Good night, Valora," he said before going back down the stairs.

I was glad that the room had darkened—based on the heat coursing through me, I knew my face must be crimson. My heart raced as I thought back on the day, on everything that had happened. Despite the exhaustion settling in my limbs, it took a long time before I fell asleep, my brain going too fast for me to succumb to sleep.

CHAPTER TWENTY

VALORA

The next morning, I woke to raised voices—Dracul and someone else were arguing. Their voices echoed through the landing, reverberating in my head as the two went back and forth, escalating more as the conversation went on.

"It's against protocol!" I vaguely identified Lord Verhorn's voice in my sleepy haze. "She is to be in the Dragon Maiden cavern every night!"

"She is my Dragon Maiden and if I decide that she can spend the night in my quarters, then she can." Dracul's tone was even, but his voice was loud.

"She just received punishment for trying to escape. She shouldn't be spending any time outside of the cavern!" Lord Verhorn screeched. I could only imagine what he would look like in his human form—cheeks red and his eyes bulging. "Don't you see what kind of message this sends?"

"Why does that matter?" Dracul's voice dropped so dangerously low, I had to strain to hear him.

I could tell Lord Verhorn could sense the danger he toed, as he paused for several moments before responding, his voice much quieter this time. "Lord Dracul," he said diplomatically. "I know you are High Dragon Lord and that you are afforded more liberties with the rules, but you might give the other Dragon Lords the wrong… impression if you continue to favor her so."

I sat up at his words, my face flushing at what he implied. Though there was a certain closeness to the relationship Dracul and I shared, that line had not been crossed. Last night, I had not even thought about the implications of staying overnight in Dracul's quarters and could only imagine the insults or insinuations Vimery would throw my way.

I shimmied my body closer to the edge of the landing so I could watch from my perch.

Dracul stepped towards Lord Verhorn. "You should choose your next words very carefully," he growled.

Lord Verhorn visibly paled and took a small step backwards. "I'm just warning you to watch how you behave, my Lord," he said. "Having her stay here overnight gives the wrong idea. There are rumors already swirling around about how you've given her special treatment. I would hate to see your leadership skills brought into question because of this."

I swallowed at his words, thinking back to what Lord Hiram had said yesterday. If news got out outside the Shadowvale clan, it could give more credence to Borthen's claims that Dracul should not be High Dragon Lord. I did not know what went into being High Dragon Lord, but it sounded like Borthen would not be a good fit for the position. Though I was glad that Dracul seemed to have good Dragon Lords surrounding him, looking out for his reputation, I did not like the insinuations Lord Verhorn made.

"Your advice has been heard," Dracul said in a strained voice. "I will take it under advisement."

Lord Verhorn heard the dismissal in his tone and bowed before leaving the room in a swirl of robes. Dracul muttered to himself before walking over to his desk and collapsing in his chair, his hand on his forehead. After a few moments, I stood and slowly descended the stairs, my gaze trained on Dracul.

He glanced up when my feet hit the floor, a sad look on his face. "You heard all that, didn't you?" he asked.

I nodded. "Most of it, yeah."

"I don't want you to pay Verhorn's words any heed," he said, waving his hand.

"Based on what Lord Hiram said yesterday, it sounds like I should stick strictly to the rules," I said, fidgeting with my hands and averting my eyes.

Dracul stood and walked towards me. "Do I make you uncomfortable?" he asked.

I did not answer, my gaze focused on my feet.

"Valora," he said gently.

I looked up, staring into his molten eyes that always seemed to set my body on fire.

"Do I make you uncomfortable?"

"No," I said. "But I don't know if we are the same as the other Dragon Lords and the other Dragon Maidens." I paused, trying to choose my words carefully. "Dracul, I don't want to be the reason that others are questioning your leadership."

His eyes were impossibly kind as he took my hands, fire spreading further through my body. "I can handle any rumors they throw my way," he said. "I am High Dragon Lord. That's not a title that's easily rescinded—I inherited the position from my father and the other Lords agreed with my appointment. And as High Dragon Lord, I am afforded more privileges than most. Everything is going to be fine, I promise."

I slowly pulled away, fighting the urge to continue holding on to his hands. "Regardless, I should probably go have breakfast with the other Dragon Maidens," I said. "I'll have to face them sooner or later. I might as well get it over with."

Dracul nodded, taking a step away. "I will work on paperwork in the meantime then," he said.

Feeling awkward at this wall I placed between us, I left, taking my time heading back to the Dragon Maiden cavern. I could feel a pit in my stomach, only imagining the tension that would be there when I entered. Everyone was chatting as I walked in, and from the snippets I caught, I could tell they talked about me.

A hush fell over the room, all eyes focused on me. Looking at each Maiden, I could see clearly on their faces that any trust I had built in the past months had dissipated completely. I hung my head, walking over to my bed and sitting on it. I did not want to be the first one to break the silence, only imagining what they would say.

Vimery was first with her scathing remarks. "Did you have fun kissing up to Lord Dracul?" she sneered, her face twisting into an unpleasant expression.

A quick glance at the other Maidens, and I could tell she voiced their unspoken opinions.

"I don't know what you're talking about," I said, staring her down. "I do my duties as a Dragon Maiden should."

"Most Dragon Maidens don't try to escape and live," Vimery shot back.

"Valora, why did you try to escape?" Alonsa asked, holding a hand up to Vimery as a signal to be quiet.

I looked at my hands, gently touching my sleeves where my scars lay underneath. "I don't want to talk about it," I said quietly. "I've already addressed this topic with Lord Dracul."

"Is it true you were sent to the Whispering Pool?" Bethany asked, her tone somewhat excited.

I nodded. "I was there for three days," I said.

Gasps filled the room.

"Barely anyone who goes there comes back alive," Hyacinth said. "The Lords must be furious."

"Are you going to remain Lord Dracul's Dragon Maiden?" Bethany asked, inching closer towards me.

"She broke one of the most sacred rules. Why would *she* get to stay?" Vimery scoffed. "Especially as Dragon Maiden to the High Dragon Lord?"

"Well, the Whispering Pool decided not to punish her," Bethany said. "Isn't that enough proof for the Lords?"

"I will be remaining as Lord Dracul's Dragon Maiden," I confirmed, aiming my response at Bethany.

Out of the corner of my eye, I could see Alonsa and Vimery exchanging a look.

"Why?" Vimery spat out with such venom that I was taken aback. She stepped towards me, practically spitting in my face. "Why does he still want *you*?"

I stood and faced her, staring her down. "Your guess is as good as mine," I said quietly. "But you've been nasty to me since the moment I got here without any reason for it."

"You tried to escape," she hissed. "Abandoned your post. You don't *deserve* to be his Dragon Maiden. I knew you weren't going to work out."

Her words stung. I felt them deep to my core, knowing that she was right. I did not deserve to be by Lord Dracul's side, not when I had abandoned him. The thought prickled against my pride and I could barely hold back the words that spilled out of me.

"And you think *you're* better than me?" I asked.

She looked surprised that I finally fought back rather than letting her insults go.

"At least I still try to be better, try to do my best to serve him. You're just hateful and rotten. If he had you serving him, he would be more disappointed in having you than me as his Maiden."

To my surprise, Vimery's eyes filled with tears and she turned, fleeing the cavern.

The rest of the Maidens stared at me in silence, shock on their faces. Alonsa gave me a withering look before moving to go after Vimery. The other three continued to stare at me until I felt like I needed to defend myself.

"She's been antagonistic to me since day one," I told them. "I know you've seen that much. Until now, I've kept my silence. I've kept the peace all while she's insulted and tortured me."

The three looked at each other, exchanging a look. I could tell there was more history there that I did not know about, but I did not want to wait around until one of them decided to deign me with an answer.

"I originally came here for breakfast, but I don't think I'm hungry anymore." Spinning on my heel, I left the cavern, leaving silence in my wake.

Just outside the cavern, I bumped into Lord Dracul. "My Lord," I said, bowing. "I did not expect to see you here."

"I heard everything you said," he said, mirth gleaming in his eyes. "You certainly gave her a dressing down."

"I'm sorry if you heard all that, but I was sick of how she treats me," I explained.

"Oh, I certainly understand," Lord Dracul said. "As I've said before, to disrespect you is to disrespect me. I've been waiting for you to finally stand up for yourself."

"You've known what's been going on this whole time?" I asked, flabbergasted that he would not step in.

"It was a test to see if you had the guts to stand up for yourself or not," he said. "And you passed." His smile grew before he gestured me to follow him to his cave.

"You were just testing me this whole time?" I said. I could not believe he had been sneakily watching from the sidelines.

"As I said, it was to see if you would stand up for yourself. The Dragon Maiden of the High Dragon Lord needs to put boundaries in place with the other Maidens. Vimery certainly was not an easy opponent, but she was a good lesson for you," he said.

When we arrived at Lord Dracul's cave, I immediately set to work picking up the scattered papers and books, organizing as I went. I briefly glanced over the paperwork as I sorted it into piles, quickly realizing that the issue with Borthen and the Starfire clan seemed far more dire than Lord Dracul had alluded to. More than once, I took several moments, my eyes scanning over the papers to glean more information on the issue. From what I could gather, it seemed that Borthen had been reaching out to other clans more frequently, bringing up concerns with Lord Dracul's leadership and amassing more military forces. My heart skipped a beat when I read the words, *He is beginning to pull more humans to his cause, willing to sacrifice them to reach his goals.*

"My Lord," I said after reading a few more papers that said the same thing. "This issue with the Starfire clan seems to be quite serious."

Lord Dracul looked up from his desk, frowning slightly as he saw the sheaf of papers in my arms. "Bring those here," he said, reaching a hand out. I brought them to him, and he quickly scanned the documents. "I'm not too concerned," he said at last. "Like I said, he's been trying to do this for years." He fixed me with his gaze. "And I thought I told you to call me Dracul."

I bowed my head, feeling the need for formality. "I understand, my Lord," I said. "I'm sorry for my question."

He leaned his elbow on the desk, resting his chin on his hand. "What about the other part?" he asked. I knew he would not like my answer.

"My Lord, for now, I think it best that I address you by your title," I said.

A look of despair briefly crossed his face before he could fix his expression. "I understand," he said. "If that is what you wish, then I won't push further."

He went back to his paperwork, and I could not ignore the pang in my heart at his saddened expression, but the closeness rising between us was growing dangerous.

Chapter Twenty-One

Dracul

For the next few months, my days were spent attending meetings with the other Dragon Lords. Once again, they expressed concerns with Borthen's behavior, citing it as suspicious and inflammatory. While I agreed the Starfire clan's actions were a cause for concern, I did not think it warranted the level of alarm the other Lords thought it did. Most of the time, my meetings were with Lord Hiram and Lord Firenze, receiving updates on Borthen's military actions. Lord Firenze assured me that our forces were ready for any attack from the Starfire clan, so I was not that worried. The Lords I had appointed were good at their jobs, though they did have a tendency to worry more than they should. Eventually, we decided that I would visit the Starfire clan in the spring with Lord Verhorn and Lord Firenze to examine the situation up close.

Usually, in the afternoons, I was able to spend time in my quarters to complete any paperwork, but Lord Verhorn and Lord Noxus would typically barge in with some other concern about how the clan functioned and whether our financial status was in a good spot. This was one of the reasons I hated winter—I could not easily escape the cave to avoid their questions. My only saving grace was that I could stay near Valora while they brought their concerns forth. And even though she pretended to be occupied with her tasks, I could tell she listened in and learned a lot in the process. After they left, she would wait a while before asking her own questions about what had been discussed. She had really started to take an interest in the clan activities.

I knew Lord Lorka had a good hand on our crops and distributed food to the human villages that did not have enough to survive the winter. Thanks to his talent and effort, our clan always had more than enough, so we were easily able to spare food to help those less fortunate. His reports were always the easiest to read and the ones I had to worry the least about.

After her punishment, Valora threw herself into her duties more than ever. She made sure to stick strictly to the rules and had maintained that wall she had put up, much to my disappointment. I still felt the pull to her, to my *dragaria*, and I knew based on the way she would pause at times that she could feel the pull as well. The distance she put between us hurt, and it was an effort not to push aside all boundaries and embrace her. Her interest in the activities of the clan gave me hope that we would be able to move past this, but there was a new stiffness to our interactions now. At least the fact that she had been following the rules without issue made it easier for the other Lords to approve of her going through the oath ceremony to become an official Dragon Maiden. I hoped to tell her about it soon, but felt anxious as to what her reaction would be.

* * *

One afternoon, I came back from my morning meetings to see her dusting the bookshelves once again. She certainly seemed to love the books, taking any spare moment she had to read them. From what I could tell, she loved the books about herbalism and flowers, eagerly devouring the pages of information. As I watched, she took a book from the shelf and sat down on the couch, beginning to read.

I slowly crept behind her. "What are you reading?" I asked, popping up over her shoulder. I got a small feeling of delight as she jumped, her face flushing.

"My Lord, I wasn't expecting you!" she exclaimed. She slammed the book shut, but not before I saw it was one about dragon history. Interesting.

"You thought you could slack off in your duties?" I teased, raising an eyebrow.

"No!" she said, moving to put the book back. "This one just caught my eye, is all."

I moved swiftly, plucking the book from her hands before she could put it away and flipped through the pages. "What exactly were you hoping to glean from this?" I asked.

"It doesn't hurt to learn more," she said, looking at the floor. From her reaction, I could tell she was embarrassed for an unknown reason, but could not figure out why.

"I'm not mad about this, Valora," I said softly, bringing the book over to her and placing it in her hand.

She blushed harder as our hands touched, and I was glad to see she was not totally unaffected by my presence. There was hope for us yet.

"I just wanted to tease you."

"I know," she said, still avoiding my gaze. "I just wanted to know more about you—I mean, about the clan," she suddenly corrected herself.

A laugh escaped me as I sat down on the couch, patting it for her to join me. "You can ask me anything," I said. "What do you want to know?"

She sat down at the other end of the couch, much too far away for my comfort, but I stayed in my spot, not wanting to make her uncomfortable. She fidgeted with her hands for a few moments before finally looking at me, her face red. "What exactly is my purpose?" she asked. "Why do Dragon Maidens exist?"

Her question surprised me. "Well, long ago, dragons realized if they formed a pact with a human, they would become stronger.

No one knows the exact reason behind it, but there is a philosophy that a pact of trust and understanding between the two ruling species of the world helps garner hidden powers of each. Dragons are known for unlocking additional powers after accepting a Maiden, so that honor is only reserved to the Dragon Lords."

"And why didn't you pick one until me?" she asked. "You're…" She trailed off. "I don't even know how old you are, but surely it's been a long time?"

I chuckled. "I'm around ninety in human years," I said, and her eyes widened. "Which is considered young for a dragon. Lord Hiram is many centuries old. I am the youngest High Dragon Lord in recorded history, having assumed the title twenty years ago. But around age fifty, I could have appointed a Dragon Maiden."

"So why didn't you?" she asked.

Shrugging, I said, "I hadn't found the right one yet and it didn't seem like an urgent situation to focus on."

"I'm sure our short lives also make it difficult too," she said. "You would have to keep finding new ones to replace the old ones."

"Not necessarily," I said.

Her eyebrows furrowed in an unspoken question.

"A Dragon Lord taking on a Dragon Maiden tends to elongate both of their lives. But in most cases, a Dragon Maiden dies because they either broke a rule too grievous to be allowed to survive or they are killed off by an enemy of their Dragon Lord in an attempt to weaken them."

"Having a Dragon Maiden is really that important to be strong?" she asked, her voice quiet.

"For some, yes," I said. "I've heard that when losing a Dragon Maiden, a Lord is overcome with overwhelming pain, and any strength he gained from her is immediately sapped. If a Maiden is killed at an opportune moment, a Lord could effortlessly be killed, which is not an easy feat."

"How many Maidens has Lord Hiram been through?" Valora asked. "Alonsa's stories make it sound like she's only been one for the past twenty or thirty years."

"He's been through more than most," I said, nodding at her question. "Over the centuries, there have been many attempts made on his life, but he's managed to escape every one of them. Unfortunately, the same cannot be said for the Maidens that he's had. And at his age, as long as the Maiden can perform her basic duties, he does not care who it is. Some of the other Lords are pickier about who they choose as their Maiden."

"Like you," she prompted, a smile crossing her lips in pride. My heart skipped a beat and I wished I could see her smile like this all the time.

"Like me," I said, mirroring her smile.

I noticed her quick intake of breath, and a flush crossed her cheeks. "So have you felt any stronger since you chose me?" she asked.

My smile fell. "Since we haven't exchanged the oath, you are not officially my Dragon Maiden yet," I said, and a slight frown crossed her face. "A ceremony needs to take place to seal the bond between the two of us before I gain that additional strength. Instead, I have this ring that makes me stronger, even though it doesn't grant me any special power." I gestured to the blue ring that I constantly wore.

"Why haven't we done the ceremony?" Her voice was small as she looked away.

Immediately, I could tell she felt insecure. I reached a hand over, grasping hers. She looked at me, and I could see the glimmer of tears in her eyes. Holding back a sigh, I knew I would have to choose my words carefully. I did not want to hurt her needlessly.

"Usually, there is a trial period to ensure that the candidate has what it takes to be a Dragon Maiden," I said. "And then the Lords vote on the decision. The Dragon Lord with the potential Maiden has the largest share of the vote. Being High Dragon Lord, the decision comes with a lot more weight."

"And I'm sure that my escape a few months ago didn't help in that consideration," she mumbled.

I wanted to tell her that she could be my Dragon Maiden, that the vote had turned in her favor, but for some reason, I held back. I wanted to somehow know that she was truly ready, that she was willing to go the extra mile to be with me, that she wanted this as much as I did. Though her escape had been recent, I hoped that she would do something soon to show me that she wanted to be my Dragon Maiden, that she had what it took to be in my life.

She let out a sigh. "I guess I'll just have to work harder to prove that I'm worthy," she said, a gleam shining in her eyes.

"I look forward to seeing what you show me," I said, giving her hand a small squeeze of encouragement.

Chapter Twenty-Two

Valora

Now that spring was on its way, the caves were a flurry of activity. On a daily basis, I ran back and forth between Lord Dracul's and the other Lords' caves, passing back papers and summons for meetings. The High Dragon Lord had grown busier over the past few months, worry about the Starfire clan's activities causing a stir among the populace. As I passed by the human servants, they'd whisper about the problem and what it would mean if Lord Dracul was overthrown.

More dragons from the main part of the caves started to appear more frequently, as well, delivering updates to Lord Firenze, Lord Hiram, and Lord Dracul. They always appeared in their human forms, as moving around the corridors as dragons would easily cause congestion due to the frequency of people around nowadays. The dragons were easy to spot because of their eyes. Most were unusual colors, or their hair would give away their true identity. Because of the bustle, Lord Dracul and I did not have much time alone anymore, and I was unable to ask him more questions, instead having to glean information on my own.

I hoped that my efforts since my escape would prove that I was ready to be a Dragon Maiden and go through the ceremony, but after that initial conversation, neither Lord Dracul nor I mentioned it again. The other Dragon Lords eventually warmed up to me, finally greeting me when I stopped by to drop off papers or missives. This gave me hope that I was making progress with them. Deep down, I knew that becoming a Dragon Maiden would mean finally turning my back on trying to find my brother and receiving answers, but I found that the more time I spent with Lord Dracul, the more the need for answers lessened.

The other Maidens began to thaw in their iciness towards me, following their Lord's attitude, except for Vimery. There was still tension in the cavern, but it had lessened considerably in the months following my escape. Finally, they spoke to me again and I knew we had reached a tenuous peace. Continuing to do my job well would put me further into their good graces, any misstep would destroy the friendliness we built. Once more a flicker of hope began to grow. I wanted us to be friends, especially if I continued to stay here. And the longer I stayed, the desire to stay by Lord Dracul's side grew.

* * *

One morning while I ate breakfast in the Dragon Maiden cavern with the other Maidens, they all suddenly gasped and fell to the ground, bowing. My back was to the door, and I turned, somehow knowing who was there. Lord Dracul stood in the doorway in his dragon form, his silver eyes trained on me. For a few moments, we stared at each other before I sank into a bow. When I stood, I noticed an eager brightness in his eyes.

"How may I help you, my Lord?" I asked.

"Come with me," he said, motioning me to follow.

I looked back at the other Maidens, and they shrugged, equally as confused as me.

He kept up a fast pace as we navigated the corridors, so I had to walk briskly to keep up with him. Servants and dragons alike jumped out of his way, bowing in respect as he passed by. I could feel their eyes staring at me as I followed closely behind, nodding in acknowledgment.

"Where are we going?" I asked. I could sense an excited energy about him and was curious as to what he was enthused about. Rarely did he have this type of attitude, especially lately, with all the paperwork and meetings.

We reached the entrance of the cave where I had first arrived, a place I had not been in ages. Lord Dracul knelt down, settling his bulk on the ground and moving his wings to the side. He glanced at me with bright eyes, which seemed to sparkle in the crisp morning air.

"Get on," he said.

"Excuse me?" I could not believe what I was hearing. Did he want me to ride him?

"Get on my back," he said. "We're going flying."

"*Flying?*" The incredulous words left me.

By his smug grin, I could tell that he was serious. "Climb on. There should be a spot you can sit between my shoulder blades," he directed me. "You've been very busy the past few months. I figured we could both use a break."

I scrambled onto his back and settled in the spot he had mentioned. Surprisingly, it was a comfortable seat, as if nature had intended for people to ride dragons. The few spikes protruding from his back in front of me looked perfect for steadying myself, and I held on to one tightly. He shifted slightly, and I gasped at the feeling of him underneath me, how my body moved with him.

"Ready?" Lord Dracul asked, turning his head to look at me.

"I suppose." Anxiety settled in my stomach, forming a hard knot. I knew this would be quite different from the first time I flew with a dragon and was nervous as to what this would feel like.

With a powerful launch, we were in the air. My heart dropped to my stomach as the ground quickly grew further and further away. My knuckles turned white as I gripped the spikes in front of me tightly, trying to remember to breathe. The wind flew past me, pulling at my hair and my clothes. It took everything within myself to keep from screaming in fear. As I looked at the swiftly distancing ground, it suddenly hit me how easily it would be to fall off and plummet to my death.

Lord Dracul chuckled and I felt the rumble underneath me, sending a heat to my abdomen. "You can relax. I won't let you fall," he promised. I could barely hear him over the wind. Quickly, he settled into sailing at a steady altitude.

After several minutes, I began to calm down, my heart rate slowing as I got used to flying. With much effort, I loosened my grip on his spikes, now holding them firmly rather than with a deathly tight hold. Surprisingly, I even began to enjoy myself, looking at the landscape below and the fluffy clouds in the distance. Never before had I seen the land from this vantage point, up this high. It was amazing how beautiful and serene everything seemed.

We flew around for a couple hours, Lord Dracul taking time for a few dips and dives, seeming to enjoy my squeals of surprise every time. I could sense the way his body moved to prime his tricks, and could prepare myself in response. Together, it truly felt as if we moved as one.

The fluffy group of clouds that had been closer to the horizon at the beginning of our flight had darkened quickly and the wind had picked up before we realized. Not to mention we had traveled quite a distance from the mountain in that amount of time.

"Lord Dracul?" I shouted into the wind. "I think we should start heading back now. It looks like there's going to be storm."

"We should be fine for a little while," he said. "But we can head back now if you want."

"Yes, please," I said, tightening my grip once more as the sudden blustering wind threatened to blow me off his back. "I don't feel like it's a good idea to stay out here much longer, my Lord."

As soon as the words left my mouth, ice-cold rain began to come down. Lord Dracul spun around in the air and began to head back to the mountain. On our way back, the rain intensified and the wind blew harder. Instinctively, I drew closer to Lord Dracul to lessen the force of the wind hitting me, closing my eyes as the rain pelted my face.

"How much farther?" I shouted into the wind to be heard, beginning to shiver from the cold. My clothes were drenched and offered no protection from the wind.

"We're still quite a distance away," he shouted back, turning his head to talk. "I hadn't realized how far we had flown."

A huge gust of wind suddenly surprised me, ripping me from his back. My eyes flew open as I felt myself suddenly falling, plummeting towards the ground. A rushing sound filled my ears and I was acutely aware of pain in my hands from getting pulled from Lord Dracul's spikes. But that pain paled in comparison to the paralyzing terror I felt from falling.

"Dracul!" I screamed as my heart pounded in fear, reaching up towards him as if that would save me. "Dracul!"

He swooped down and caught me gently in his claws. My body shook, both from adrenaline and the cold. Using one claw to shield me from the rain and the other to support me, he clutched me to his chest. I settled against his claws, gripping one of them tightly. This way was much more comfortable than the first time I flew.

"I've got you. You won't fall," he repeated over and over, a quiet chant that filled me with relief.

Despite the shelter in his hands, I could sense the storm worsening. I burrowed closer into his claws, my heart pounding furiously. Thunder rumbled overhead and I could see flashes of lightning in the distance.

"I'm going to land and find shelter. I don't think we can continue to fly safely in this weather," he said.

A gust of wind veered him off course, proving his point, and I gasped in fright. Dracul began to dive towards the ground, and

I clenched his claws at the sudden movement. I could sense his head moving, scouting for shelter, but it was a couple minutes before he found a small cave in the distance. He glided down as gently as possible in these worsening conditions into the small, cramped cave. Carefully, he set me down before following me in. His bulk took up most of the cave and he looked around before transforming into his human form. To my surprise, his human self was soaking wet as well, his robes dripping, rivulets of rain tracing down his bare chest, and I had to stop my eyes from following them.

I sat down on the hard ground, drawing my legs close to my body to conserve warmth and make space. Even with just the two of us, the cave was still cramped.

"I'm sorry. This didn't turn out like I expected," he apologized, sitting down next to me. "Are you okay?"

"I'm fine." I began to shiver, soaked from the rain and cold from the wind. Now in this damp cave, sitting on the cold, hard ground, the tendrils of the fleeing winter seeped into my body.

"You're cold," Dracul observed. "Wait here."

He got up, taking off his robes to hand to me before realizing they were wet and setting them on the ground. Turning, he left the cave for several minutes before returning with an armful of wood. Carefully, he placed everything into a pile on the ground before transforming back into his dragon form, blowing a fireball to start a blazing fire. Then he settled at the front of the cave, blocking the outside wind.

I inched closer to the new fire, savoring the warmth as it spread through my body. Slowly, I could feel the iciness that had settled deep within my bones beginning to thaw. Winter might not be willing to give in to spring just yet, but the warmth of the fire was enough to make me forget. Just as I felt closer to normal, a bone-chilling gust of wind blew through the cave. Not even Dracul's bulk could block everything. My clothes were still soaked from the rain and I shivered violently, the fire not enough to warm me up.

"Come here," Dracul said, shifting slightly to make room for me. I moved closer to him, but stopped, still a few feet away. "Come closer," he said. "Lean against me. You'll get warmer, I promise."

I hesitated for a moment before following his instructions, and leaned against his side. A sigh escaped me as I immediately felt warmer. The warmth from a dragon's belly was more than enough to keep a person from freezing to death. Last night, I had slept restlessly, and my eyes began to drift closed, lulled to sleep by Dracul's rhythmic breathing and warmth. Shifting into a more comfortable position, I barely caught Dracul's self-satisfied smile before my eyes tugged shut completely.

CHAPTER TWENTY-THREE

VALORA

The next morning, with the tendrils of dawn peeking into the cave, I awoke to the gentle rumblings of Dracul snoring. I had to fight a smile as I stood and stretched, noting that it still poured outside. My stomach growled, and was answered by a much louder grumbling from Dracul's stomach. His snoring paused for a moment before he rolled over, then it resumed, and I let out a small chuckle.

Determined to find some sort of food for both of us, I set out into the rain. A few minutes into my exploration, I found a small cropping of dandelions and chickweed. I gathered the entire batch, stuffing my pockets full. What I had found was really all I could hope to forage in this part of the woods at this time of year.

When I arrived back at the cave, Dracul was already awake and looking out into the forest for me, his expression turning to one of relief when he spotted me. He had transformed back to his human self and had his arms crossed, looking very dry.

Upon reentering our shelter, I shook my head, trying to dispense of the extra water that had gathered during the downpour, though it did not do much to help.

"I didn't know where you had gone," he said. "I thought you'd use this time to try and escape like you did before." His tone was light, but I could tell that he really had been worried by the way he had been pacing.

I ignored the comment and sat down, pulling the greens from my pockets. "No, I went to get breakfast." I separated everything into two piles, making sure Dracul's pile was bigger before looking at him. "That's what a Dragon Maiden does, right? Makes sure that her Lord is well fed? I know this isn't the usual fare you're used to, but I thought it would be enough to take the edge off your hunger." I took a small handful of the dandelion greens and began to eat them, trying to ignore the slightly bitter flavor.

Dracul sat down next to me, beginning to eat what I had gathered. The two of us were quickly done with the small amount of food.

He looked outside. "The weather is still too nasty for us to fly back," he said, taking in how the trees bowed in the wind. "We're just going to have to wait out the storm."

A crack of thunder proved his point, rumbling close by overhead.

I sighed, leaning against the cave wall, thinking about how close we probably were to a town where I could find information about my brother. I had spotted multiple on our flight, and from my estimations, one would be close, though not close enough to brave the storm.

Dracul leaned against the wall as well, looking at my expression. "What is it?" he asked.

Wistfully, I said, "We're just so close to a town. If I could get information on where he is…" I trailed off, not letting my thoughts go further.

"Why do you want to know where your brother is so badly?" Dracul asked, his voice soft. We both knew he tread on unstable ground, based on what had happened during our last conversation on the topic. I could tell he did not want to push me too far with his questions.

"He left our family, and about a year after he left, some men came." Though the last time he had asked about my scars had been disastrous, now that we were stuck in a cave with nothing else to do, the story came pouring out. And I felt I could trust him, that he had earned the right to know now. "They murdered my parents and forced me to watch. Afterwards, they turned on me." I drew up my sleeves, revealing the scars.

Dracul stared at them, a look of disgust on his face, but I could somehow tell it was not directed at me, but rather the men who had done this.

"They tormented me and said it was in retaliation for something my brother did. They set the house on fire, and once they left, I set out after him, determined to find answers." I looked to Dracul, meeting his silver eyes, which were filled with sympathy and kindness. "I want answers. Why did they come? What did he do? What did he get himself into? The day I was taken, I was on my way to find him, only a few days behind. But instead, I was brought to you, and every hope I had at ever catching him disappeared."

To my surprise, I felt empty at this notion rather than feeling angry or the need to cry. At that point, I supposed I was all cried out over my parents' deaths and what had happened to me. It was something I had finally accepted and was ready to begin moving on.

Dracul seemed surprised at my reaction, but placed a hand on mine. "I'm very sorry," he said quietly.

"I don't know what I would have done if I found him anyway. But that's why I had Henrick take a letter to send to contacts I have, to see if I could find out where my brother went next. And that's why I tried to escape that night." I looked away, unable to keep eye contact. "But I know better now and I've accepted that I'll never know. I've accepted my life now and even look forward to seeing what being by your side will bring." I could feel determination flowing through me, the strength that I had relied upon these past months to not crumble and give up. My life might have taken a different path than I had been expecting, but I truly looked forward to whatever was next with Dracul.

He looked at me, a glimmer of pride in his eyes. "You've transformed from the trembling girl who was tossed at my feet those months ago," he said quietly. "And in that time, with the proper training given to you and the change I see in you, you are now ready to become an official Dragon Maiden."

His words shocked me, and I felt a charge of energy slice through my body. "Are you serious?" I asked softly, as if any louder would dissolve this illusion.

"Very," he said, bringing a hand to my cheek and smiling. My heart began to beat faster.

I leaned against his shoulder, looking outside. "How much longer do you think it's going to rain?" I asked, my mind whirring with this news.

"Who knows?" the Dragon Lord replied. "It could stop within the next hour or tomorrow."

As it turned out, later that night, the storm stopped, but Dracul decided it was too late to fly back. Once more, I fell asleep against his stomach, which warmed me to the core, my dreams pleasant and filled with light and laughter. I looked forward to what the next chapter would bring.

CHAPTER TWENTY-FOUR

VALORA

Though there had been shock and horror—mostly on Lord Verhorn's part—that we had been caught in the rain and away for almost two full days, preparations began immediately for the ceremony where I would take the oath and become a Dragon Maiden. Besides the actual ceremony—which to my surprise happened in front of the entire clan—there would be a grand feast afterwards where all the dragons and humans celebrated. The evening would be filled with food, drinks, and dancing. It sounded very exciting, and due to the fact that the last ceremony had happened five years ago with Bethany's induction, the caves were filled with a flurry of enthusiasm and anticipation.

The ceremony was planned to take place on the full moon, which was a few weeks away. The other Dragon Maidens had begun working on my dress, which was made up of flowing midnight-blue fabric. Each one worked on a different section, embroidering the fabric with silver thread, filling the dress with swirling designs that started at the bottom of the dress, lazily spinning upwards. Every time I saw it, my stomach filled with butterflies. It was breathtaking.

At last, the day before the ceremony had arrived and I busied myself with tasks to distract myself from the giant event that was occurring tomorrow, an event that would change the trajectory of my life forever. Dusting the books was an easy task, though not needed, as I had already done so last week, but I tried to focus, to keep the panic from rising within me.

"Tomorrow is the ceremony," Dracul said as he entered the cave. He had just finished a meeting with the other Lords, ensuring that all the final details were in place. "And you will finally become my Maiden."

I nodded silently at his words, continuing to dust, unable to meet his eyes.

"What's wrong?" He approached. "You were so excited before."

He was not wrong. Just last week, I had been prancing around excitedly, waiting for tomorrow to come. I remained silent, continuing to dust, and I could feel his apprehension growing behind me, prickling the back of my neck. At last, I paused my dusting, but still could not face him.

"It's such a life-changing moment," I said, my voice trembling. "What if I'm not cut out for this? What if I really mess up? What happens? I'll be your first ever Maiden, and I might be a complete disaster."

Dracul leaned forward, taking the cleaning rag from my hand and pulling me towards the couch, motioning for me to sit down. My eyes darted to him and watched as he knelt in front of me, his gaze level with mine.

"You will not be a disaster," he said calmly. "And I'm assuming you heard rumors from the other Dragon Maidens about why I have not picked a Maiden?"

Silently, I shook my head. Even when I was on good terms with the other Maidens, we never were close enough for them to gossip with me. They would not want to risk the rumors getting back to Dracul.

"Regardless, the reason I have not picked a Maiden until now is that I have never found any that I felt was qualified to do the job required of them. You are the first one that I feel is ready."

"But what if I'm not? What if your confidence has been misplaced?" The words rushed out of me before I could stop them.

"Then we will work through the problems together," he said. "I do not make this decision lightly, I hope you know that. I would not have picked you if I did not think you were ready. But you are, Valora. Do not doubt yourself, not when you have come so far."

"It's hard, knowing that so much is expected of me," I said softly, tears pricking my eyes at his kindness.

"My expectations have not changed from the first day, and you have risen above and beyond them time and time again," he said, his silver eyes gleaming. "Please believe me when I say that there is nothing to fear from becoming my Maiden, and that you will be fine."

"What about the fire?" The words spilled out, referencing the part of the ceremony after exchanging oaths where Dracul would have to bathe me in his dragonfire. That part of the ceremony was what I felt most nervous about. "Won't it burn me?" Though he had told me this hundreds of times, I needed to hear it once more. After the ceremony, his fire and heat would be unable to burn me.

"If the Lord does not truly believe that she is the Maiden for him, then the woman will burn," Dracul said, repeating what he had told me previously. "I *do* believe in you and that you are to be my Maiden. You are worthy of this title, worthy to be the High Dragon Lord's Dragon Maiden. And tomorrow, everyone will see what I saw in you that very first day."

"And what was that?" I whispered.

"Originally, you were just going to be another tribute to be added to the workforce in the gardens," he said. "But I saw something in you, especially when you tried to jump, even though you were scared and knew there was no way to escape. I saw that look in your eyes when I caught you—don't deny it," he said when I opened my mouth protest. "I saw that determination that you would get whatever you wanted, no matter the cost. And when I decided to keep you on, imagine my surprise when you turned out to be vastly different from any other Maiden I've trained before. You were not afraid to speak your mind, to stand up for yourself. There is a bright flame inside of you, as bright as any flame a Dragon Lord could create. And it was this flame that made me know you were different, that you were meant to become my Dragon Maiden."

"Really?" I asked, my cheeks flushing at his flattery.

"Really," he said, smiling. "Now, are you still worried about the ceremony?"

I smiled brightly. "If my Lord has no worries about this, then how can I?" On an impulse, I leaned forward and kissed his cheek, pleased at his look of surprise. "Thank you," I said softly.

He touched his cheek. "You're welcome."

* * *

That evening, I bathed while the other Maidens finalized décor in the hall where the ceremony would be held. When I finished, Alonsa brushed my hair until it shone before tying it up to be perfect for tomorrow. The other Maidens excitedly talked about the banquet and feast after the ceremony. I let myself get excited along with them, trying to push down the bundle of nerves that always lurked in the corner of my mind. Stories of previous ceremonies and feasts were shared, and I could imagine what tomorrow would be like.

Sleep did not come easily. I stayed awake for what felt like hours while the others slept soundly around me. Worries, fears, and excitement for tomorrow flitted through my head, each thought more overpowering than the last. I tried to empty my mind, to calm the storm, but it took a while before I finally drifted away.

* * *

The next morning, I awoke bright and early, nerves churning in my stomach the instant I awakened. I got up, worried that I would vomit, but the feeling quickly passed, though the butterflies attacking my stomach still remained. All the other Maidens were still fast asleep, light snores radiating throughout the room. I could see the lanterns on the wall gently starting to illuminate, indicating that it was almost time for everyone to wake up.

Despite knowing that everything had been meticulously prepared yesterday for the ceremony, I changed into a simple dress, planning to double-check that everything was in place. Silently, I treaded through the caverns, knowing I broke the rules by doing so by being out of bed unsupervised at this time of day. The cavern where the ceremony would be held was gigantic, with enough room for all the dragons in the clan, along with spots for the Dragon Lords and their Maidens along the main aisle leading up to a dais where the ceremony would take place. Slowly, ever so slowly, I walked across the length of the room, imagining it filled as it would be later today. At last, I was at the other end of the room and took a deep breath, taking in the dais.

"Not having second thoughts again, are you?" A familiar voice sounded from the entrance.

I spun to face Dracul, knowing that I was caught in the act of actively breaking the rules. He smiled before walking towards me, closing the distance between us. My heart pounded, his blue scales glimmering spectacularly in the lantern light.

"No," I said quickly as he approached. "I just couldn't fall back asleep. I was too nervous."

He raised an eyebrow.

"But I'm not having second thoughts."

"That's good to hear," he said. "I wouldn't want you running off again."

My smile faltered as I was reminded of how stupid I had been. Of course I would be caught. It had not been a well-thought-out plan. "Trust me, I'm not foolish enough to try again," I said. "It was a mistake before." It now irked me whenever someone brought up my failed escape attempt. Mostly it was Vimery, but I hated to be reminded of when I had despised being brought there, after all of Dracul's kindness and patience.

"You've accepted your life here now," he observed, and I nodded at his words. He took a few more strides until he was in front of me, and before I could register the change, he was in his human form. "I hope you enjoy living here," he said. "But if you prefer, I will let you go."

I sucked in a breath, shocked at his words. "What?" I whispered, unable to make myself believe him.

"I will let you go," he repeated. "And you can find your brother and the answers you seek." He smiled, but I could see the sadness in his eyes, the agony he felt. It made my heart squeeze in pain.

"Why now?" My heart beat rapidly, and I thought back to our conversation yesterday. "Are you rethinking your decision for me to be your Maiden?"

"My opinion of you remains the same," he said. "But I've been thinking. You've already been through so much. There's no reason for you to be tied to a life you don't want. If you want to leave, you are free to go."

Silence filled the cave, oppressive with anticipation. Just when I had accepted my life, Dracul gave me the choice to leave. The chance to leave was right there, within my grasp, but I knew that I might never find my brother. I had already spent a year looking for him when I had been captured.

I was touched that Dracul was giving me the choice to do what I pleased. Looking in his eyes and seeing the chagrin, I realized that he already assumed that I would leave. My choice was instantly made. Over the past months, I had grown fond of the Dragon Lord, and I was not sure what my options would be even after I found my brother. It was not like I could ever return home anyway. It no longer existed.

"Thank you, but I think I'll stay," I said softly.

Dracul's eyes widened at my words, and he picked me up, spinning me in a circle, clutching me tightly. My heart pounded as I hugged him back, and I could feel the rapid beating of his heart too.

"Are you sure?" he whispered, as if his words would break this illusion. "It was all you wanted before. Don't you want answers?"

"I've accepted that I may never find answers," I said, pulling away so he could see my face. "And I find that to be perfectly fine. I would rather stay here and be your Maiden."

"But—" I could tell that he was convinced I would have taken the opportunity to leave.

"Lord Dracul, I have made my choice. I thank you for giving me the option to leave, but I am going to stay," I said firmly, a smile tugging at the ends of my lips.

My decision had been made. I was not going to change my mind, nor have any regrets about the path I had chosen.

"Really?" It was really quite amusing to see the Dragon Lord at a loss for words for once.

"Yes. I'm afraid you'll just have to be stuck with me."

A smile twitched on his lips, and soon, Dracul beamed. "I am very glad to hear that," he said, relief flooding his voice.

"I should go get ready," I said, moving to walk past Dracul, but stopped right next to him. "Thank you very much," I said quietly, hoping that he could hear the emotion in my voice. "I really appreciate what you did."

"And I appreciate you for staying," he said.

I nodded before rushing back to the cavern. The other Maidens were sure to be awake now and I needed to get ready for the ceremony. My footsteps were weightless as I ran back to the cave, a lightness settling in my heart that had not been there before.

CHAPTER TWENTY-FIVE

DRACUL

I watched Valora skip away before shaking my head. She never failed to surprise me. "Never in a million years did I expect her to stay," I muttered to myself. I was not sure what I would have done if she had wanted to leave. Letting my *dragaria* go would have been torturous, but if that was what she wanted, I would be unable to deny her.

An older gray dragon emerged from the shadows. "Then you shouldn't have given her the choice," he said, wisdom echoing in his voice.

I turned to face Lord Hiram, watching him approach. As he neared, he transformed into his human form, too, fixing me with a look.

"To what do I owe this pleasure?" I asked. "Normally we do not see you out of your caves unless it is to lecture me on something."

"Today is a special day, is it not? Not every day does the High Dragon Lord pick a Maiden," Lord Hiram said. "If you thought she was going to leave, why did you give her the choice?"

I knew I should feel offended that he had been eavesdropping, that he had heard everything, but for some reason, relief flooded through me. "She's been through so much, I did not want her to be stuck here if she did not want to be."

"If word got out about this, the other Lords would start to question your leadership abilities. It would give Borthen more ammunition to overthrow you," Lord Hiram warned. "You better make sure that no one hears of this."

"I trust Valora not to say anything," I said.

The older dragon examined me for a moment before nodding.

"What would you suggest I do?"

"Dracul, I have seen a few High Lords come and go, including your father," Lord Hiram said. "I was a friend and supporter of his, just as I am with you. I do not want to see your reign end too soon like his, and I want to make sure you minimize any damage she could do to you."

My gaze sharpened at his words and I looked at him, trying to judge how much he knew.

"I've seen the way you look at her. You've grown fond of her. There's nothing wrong with that, except for the fact that you treat her differently than the other Lords treat their Maidens."

"I'm the High Dragon Lord. I'm not held to the same standards as the others," I said. "And while they might not act the same way towards their Maidens as I do towards Valora, I know they are attached to theirs as well. I'm doing nothing wrong." I was not sure if I was trying to convince Lord Hiram or myself. Based on his look, we both knew that what I felt for Valora was not typical.

"I'm not saying that you are," Hiram said quickly. "I'm just letting you know that you need to be careful of your behavior. Since she's arrived, your actions have been closely watched. None of the other Lords would have even *thought* about making such a headstrong girl their Maiden. Your abilities to do what's best for the clan are remarkable, but I want you to be aware of everything so you can make sure you're not overstepping bounds. Dracul, you are the youngest High Dragon Lord we've had in history, and no one questions your brilliance when it comes to protecting the clan. Your methods are different, but effective. However, your youth does not help you among the older Lords, not all the time. Whispers are already beginning to cultivate, and I just want you to be careful." His eyes softened as he pleaded with me. "Please don't let her be your undoing."

My heart stopped at his plea. Valora was my *dragaria*, my strength. She could never be my undoing. I would not allow it.

"I won't," I said. "I'll do my best to make sure no one questions me as a leader. My fondness for her is not clouding my judgment to lead the clans."

"Good," Lord Hiram said, placing a hand on my shoulder. "Now, you should go prepare for the ceremony as well. There's still much to be done."

"Thank you for your words of wisdom," I said, bowing my head in respect. "It's nice to know I have a friend looking out for me."

Chapter Twenty-Six

VALORA

By the time I arrived back at the cavern, the other Maidens were already awake and getting ready for the day. All had eaten breakfast and were dressed in their outfits for the ceremony, their dress colors matching the scale color of their Lords.

"Valora, where have you been?" Alonsa asked. "You know you aren't supposed to be out so early in the morning."

"Isn't it obvious?" Vimery sneered. "She thinks that just because she's going to become Lord Dracul's Maiden today, she's allowed to do whatever she wants and get away with it."

I chose to ignore Vimery's comment, walking over to grab my bowl of eggs and sausage. "I woke up early and couldn't go back to sleep," I said. "I went to make sure that everything was in place for today. Besides, Lord Dracul was with me."

Alonsa tsked in disapproval. "You really need to stay here until breakfast is served, Valora," she said. "Just because you're becoming an official Maiden today doesn't mean that they become less lenient on you when it comes to following the rules."

"I know," I said, beginning to eat my breakfast. "I just thought—"

"You thought *what*?" Vimery snapped, her face turning red in anger. "You thought that since you're Lord Dracul's favorite that you can do anything you want? It's amazing how narcissistic you are."

"What is your problem?" I stood, facing Vimery head-on. "Why do you hate me so much? I have done nothing to deserve your anger."

Vimery glared at me, slowly growing redder by the moment. "You just get away with *everything*!" she hissed. "And I'm absolutely sick of it! The others are, too, but they're just too nice to say anything." She stalked out of the room, not even waiting for a response.

I turned to the others, my mouth agape. "I don't even—"

"She's right, Valora. You can't keep acting as if you can get away with everything," Alonsa interrupted. "You have been acting as though the rules don't apply to you. And that reflects poorly on us because it seems as though we didn't train you properly. It also reflects poorly on Lord Dracul. He *chose* you. That is a great honor. And your actions can undermine him as a leader."

I was taken aback by Alonsa's lecture and by the nods of agreement from the other Maidens. Shame filled me as I realized they were right—to an extent, I had relied on Dracul's influence to bend the rules.

"I'm sorry," I apologized. "But that still doesn't answer the question of why Vimery hates me so much."

Alonsa sighed, and it was clear she did not want to answer. Instead, Gwen spoke up.

"Originally, she was to be Lord Dracul's Maiden," she said, repeating what I already knew. "But after a few weeks, it was obvious he was displeased with her. Instead, Lord Firenze took her and she's never been able to get over how Lord Dracul rejected her. I imagine she feels resentment that you were picked over her when you're a stranger to our ways and have the tendency to break the rules, whereas she followed all of them. It stings."

"Oh." Suddenly, everything clicked into place. Never had I imagined that to be the reason behind Vimery's anger.

"Well, come on, we have to get you ready," Alonsa said, motioning for the others to help dress me.

The midnight-blue dress they had worked on was magnificent, the flowing silver embroidery perfectly matching Dracul's eyes as it slowly spun its way up from the hem. There were a few small, clear gemstones sewn in, creating a sparkle depending on the angle of the lighting. Truly, it was the most elegant thing I had ever worn. The sleeves were long enough to cover my scars and the skirt fell in folds to the floor. Dracul had fireproofed it a few days ago for the ceremony so it would not burn.

"It's beautiful. You all did a wonderful job," I breathed as I spotted my reflection in the mirror.

Alonsa moved behind me to fasten my necklace, the one Dracul had bought for me at the market those many months ago.

The four Maidens nodded at the compliment, moving to work on my raven hair, pulling it into an intricate up-do. I clenched my hands, my nerves beginning to act up. Each woman took a strand of hair, plaiting them within each other to create an elaborate weave.

When Alonsa's eyes met mine in the mirror, I asked, "Does it hurt?"

"Each Maiden has her own experience, depending on her relationship with her Lord," she answered as she brushed out a few tangles. "Some feel nothing, while others feel excruciating pain." Her words did nothing to comfort me.

"Mine tickled," Bethany spoke up.

"It felt like pins and needles all over my body," Gwen added.

"Vimery's hurt quite a bit," Hyacinth said quietly as she tweaked one of the braids. "She had to fight back tears."

"There," Alonsa said, fitting the final pin into position. "You're ready."

"Is it time yet?" I asked. Butterflies took over my stomach and I could feel my palms becoming clammy.

"Someone will fetch us when it's time," Alonsa said.

I let out a shaky breath. It was so close now.

"It will be fine. Just a short ceremony and you're officially a Dragon Maiden."

"Were any of you nervous?" I asked.

"No." Vimery's sneering voice came from the entrance of the cave. I whipped around to see the scowling Maiden. "I was assured that it wouldn't hurt. By Lord Dracul, no less. Well, he lied, because it was the most excruciating pain I've ever felt." With each word, she stalked closer and closer to me. "But I was instructed by Lord Firenze that if I cried out, he would kill me. It's what awaits anyone who lets on how much it actually hurts. If anyone tells you otherwise, they're lying." Her voice had dropped to a menacing whisper, her piercing green eyes trained on mine.

A servant girl raced into the cavern, stopping suddenly when she noticed the standoff. "They are ready for you now," she directed to the room in general.

"Come on," Alonsa said to us when no one started to move. "They're waiting for us."

In the procession, I was last, following Alonsa's lead. Once we reached the cave I had been in not long ago, the other Maidens entered first, walking down the aisle to stand next to their respective Lords, who lined the aisles in their dragon forms. From my vantage point, I could see that the room was absolutely filled with dragons, all their eyes trained on me.

Lord Dracul stood at the end of the room at the dais, waiting for me. As our eyes made contact, I felt an invisible string fall into place, tying us together. I could feel the heat of eyes on me as I began to walk towards him, praying that I would not trip. The distance between us felt impossibly long, but with each step, I could feel the string tying us together shortening. At last, I was before him, craning my neck to see his face as he stood at his tallest height.

"Valora Marchton." His voice boomed throughout the room, and I flinched slightly at his volume. Now that I was before him, staring into his eyes, the nerves that had been threatening to overwhelm me began to fade. "You are here today to pledge to become my Dragon Maiden. You will do any task I ask of you, and in return, you will be under my protection from any danger, be it man or beast. I will have your loyalty and obedience, and in return, you have my trust and confidence. Knowing this, do you pledge yourself to become my Maiden?"

Without hesitation, I said, "I solemnly promise to be your Dragon Maiden until the end of my days."

"Then the final act to consecrate this pact is to bathe you in fire," Lord Dracul said. He opened his mouth, and I braced myself for the part of the ceremony I had been dreading most, forcing my eyes to stay open.

As a stream of flame erupted from Dracul's mouth and enveloped me, I jumped slightly at the impact, not sure what to expect. What surprised me the most after I got over the initial shock was the pleasant warmth of the fire. It was not painful or uncomfortable, and within the flames, I felt at peace. They reminded me of when I fell asleep against Dracul's warm belly. Because of his earlier fireproofing, the dress did not burn and my hair remained unburnt as well. After a few seconds, the flames turned to a deep blue. A gasp sounded throughout the room, as if they had never seen such a thing before. Based on the look on Dracul's face I could guess he had not expected that either. After a full minute of bathing me in fire, Dracul stopped, and I beamed out at the room.

"I present to you Valora Marchton, the High Dragon Maiden of the High Dragon Lord," he formally announced, using my new title.

The Lords dipped their heads in respect to Lord Dracul's decision, while the Maidens curtsied to me, their new leader in terms of rank now that I was High Dragon Maiden. Together,

Dracul and I walked down the aisle, past the other Lords and their Maidens. I made sure to make eye contact with each Maiden and smiled, receiving a smile in return. When I got to Vimery, the other Maiden smiled back, but it was a chilling smile that sent a shiver down my back. I knew she was not yet done making me suffer.

"See? I told you there was nothing to worry about," Dracul whispered as we walked to the banquet hall.

I smiled, but did not say anything as the other Lords trailed after us, knowing that they strained to hear what I had to say. Now that I was officially a Maiden, I would be even more harshly judged than before.

We entered the chamber where the feast was to be held. Though I had initially felt relief that the ceremony was over, my stomach churned. Everyone's attention would be focused on me and I was unsure if I would be able to eat. The servants had done an excellent job preparing the food and setting it out, the tables absolutely stuffed with all sorts of meats, pastries, potatoes, and roasted vegetables. Each table even had an entire platter of dragori, easily identifiable by the bright red coloring.

Lord Dracul led me to one of the tables at the end of the hall, the head table, with the other Lords and Maidens following us. All the dragons who'd attended the ceremony filed in, as well, filling the remainder of the tables. Everyone stared at the head table and I realized that they were waiting for Lord Dracul to take the first bite.

He transformed into his human form, and to my surprise, rather than the usual robes and pants he wore, he wore tailored gray trousers, a fitted long-sleeve white shirt, and a navy waistcoat. Glancing at me for a moment, he took the leg of the turkey in front of us and lifted it to his lips, taking a bite and swallowing. A cheer rang out as he gave a nod of approval and everyone else began to eat as well, piling their plates high with food. I grabbed a small amount of turkey, potatoes, and roasted green beans, though my plate was nowhere near half as full as what the other Lords consumed.

To my surprise, many who feasted transformed into their human form, while others remained as dragons as they ate, the dragon ones hungrily gobbling down their fare. The other Lords at the head table transformed to their human forms, following Lord Dracul's example.

"What happened in there, Lord Dracul?" asked Lord Noxus, a midnight-black dragon who oversaw finances. In his human form, his deep-umber skin glowed under the lights, and his ebony locks fell past his shoulders. Sunset-orange eyes stared out at the room, assessing everything. Through my interactions with the Dragon Lords, he was the one I had met with the least. "I've never seen the fire turn colors before during the ceremony."

"I'm not sure," Dracul admitted, taking another bite of food. "I have to say, I was completely unprepared for it myself." He turned to his left, speaking to the dragon right next to him. "Lord Hiram, have you heard of anything like this happening before?"

A look passed through Lord Hiram's eyes, but it was gone so quickly that I thought I had imagined it. "I'll have to do a bit of research," he said. "But I will let you know when I find something."

The rest of the meal passed smoothly, chatters of conversation filling the hall. I was able to eat a few bites of food, enjoying the delicious flavors the chefs had created. After the meal, a number of musicians filed in and set up in a corner of the room. Tables were moved, making way for a dancing area in the center of the room. By this time, all the dragons had transformed into their human forms and stood around the dancing area, waiting for something.

Lord Dracul stood and held out his hand to me. "Are you ready to dance?" he asked.

My mind went blank. "We have to dance?" I asked, hesitantly taking his hand. I'd known that dancing was involved after the ceremony, but I was not aware that I would be required to dance. The small amount of food I ate settled like a stone in my stomach.

"It is customary for the Lord and his newly inducted Maiden to kick off the dancing," he said with a gentle smile. "I didn't tell you because I figured you would panic even more than you already were."

The Dragon Lord led me to the center of the dance floor. I could feel all eyes on us, burning my skin. He guided my hand to his shoulder, settling his on my waist, and kept our hands clasped together. Everywhere he touched, I felt fire spread through my body.

"It's going to be fine," he whispered. "Just follow my lead."

The music started up in a jaunty tune and Dracul began to move. I stumbled, tripping over my feet, trying to follow his nonverbal cues. A couple steps went by without issue before I tripped again, and I could feel my face heating in embarrassment.

"You're doing fine," Dracul murmured. "Left, back, right, forward. There you go, just like that."

I finally was able to follow him and relaxed slightly as the music went on. At one point, Dracul gripped my hand and spun me around. I was able to continue following him after that, and I beamed, proud of myself. He smiled encouragingly at me.

Finally, the song came to an end and I curtsied while Dracul bowed. He led me from the dance floor while others flooded in, eager to frolic as the music started up again. The other Lords led their Maidens for a customary dance while I watched on the sidelines with Dracul.

"You did very well," he leaned over and whispered to me.

"I was like an animal learning to walk for the first time," I said. "I stumbled all over my feet."

He let out a low chuckle. "Regardless, you did well with no training," he said. "We can practice more later, if you like."

At the end of the second song, the other Maidens swarmed me. They had all completed their obligatory dance and were now free to do what they wanted. Lord Dracul had mentioned that sometimes other dragons would ask the Dragon Maidens to dance, but he stayed nearby so no one would ask me, sensing that I did not want to embarrass myself.

"You did magnificently," Alonsa said, coming forward to give me a hug.

I beamed at the compliment while the others echoed similar sentiments.

"Though your dancing needs work," Vimery snorted.

My face flushed, but I had no rebuttal. She was correct.

"She did fine," Dracul said quietly, his tone a warning for Vimery to behave.

She paled, not having noticed him before, and bowed her head. "Yes, my Lord," she said. "I apologize for my comment."

He huffed and looked out towards the dance floor, but I could tell his attention was still focused on me. Every once in a while, his eyes darted towards me, checking to see how I was doing. The music rose in tempo, and I could see the dancers speeding up to match the music, their colorful outfits swirling around the floor.

"I'll have to take lessons from you sometime," I said to Vimery. "You looked wonderful dancing." She and Lord Firenze had glided around, easily dodging the other dancers.

"Thank you," she muttered, her cheeks reddening slightly before walking away.

"What did the fire feel like?" Bethany asked, leaning in close for my answer. "The changing color was so unexpected! Did it hurt?"

At this point, I could tell Lord Dracul's full attention was on me, standing unnaturally still at Bethany's question.

"It felt warm and welcoming," I said. "A pleasant heat, no pain or anything."

At my words, his shoulders immediately relaxed. I was surprised that he had been worried about how I would feel in the fire. He had seemed so confident earlier today.

"That's amazing!" Gwen exclaimed. "That means you two have a close bond! You'll be an amazing Dragon Maiden, Valora!"

"I hope so," I said, suddenly feeling overwhelmed. The music, the crowd of people, and this new responsibility became too much for me to process. "If you'll excuse me, I need to step out for a moment."

The other Maidens shifted out of the way, moving to the side of the dance floor to watch the dancers. Immediately, Bethany and Gwen were asked to dance by two younger dragons, and smiled as they eagerly accepted. My feet took me to outside the cavern, where I was able to breathe in the cool, fresh air. I had not realized how stuffy it had gotten inside.

"Is everything okay?" Dracul's voice came from behind me, and I spun to face him, not expecting him to have followed me.

"I needed some air," I said. "I was just getting a little over-whelmed."

"You did wonderfully today," he said, putting his hands on my shoulders. Once more, I could feel heat spreading from his hands throughout my body. "I'm sure you must be feeling relieved that it's all over now."

"I am," I said. "I'm looking forward to what happens next." I heard a cheer coming from inside, and a smile crossed my face. "I'm sorry for my dancing earlier. I've never had much need for it before."

"You were perfectly fine," he said. "But if you want to practice any time, I will gladly dance with you."

We could hear the next song start, its melody floating out to us in the hallway.

"If you want, I can teach you a little now." He held out a hand to me.

Without hesitation, I took it, my face flushing from the warmth rushing through me. Dracul was firmer in his move-ments this time, his nonverbal directions easier to follow as we danced in the hallway. It also helped that this song was slower than our first dance together. At one point, he pulled me close so our bodies were flush against each other, and without thinking about it, my head moved to lean against his chest. I could hear the thumping of his heart and closed my eyes, comforted by the sound. We danced in silence, each of us enjoying the presence of the other.

The song came to an end, and I pulled away, suddenly conscious of my actions, my cheeks reddening. The two of us stared at each other for several moments, neither one wanting to break the silence, the magic of the moment that had just been between us.

Dracul cleared his throat, his cheeks redder as well. "That was much better than before," he said, his voice low and husky. "We should head back inside now." He held out his hand to lead me back in.

The rest of the evening, I remained on the sidelines, watching the dancers swirl around the dance floor. Towards the end of the night, when most participants had left to go to bed, Dracul escorted me back to the floor to dance one final time. This time was a very slow dance—a waltz, he told me—and he kept me close the whole time as we moved to the music. The other Lords brought their Maidens out for a final dance, as well, and with that, the festivities were complete.

When the Maidens returned to the cave, we all collapsed into bed, exhausted from the day's activities. I curled up within my blankets, a smile on my face. The ceremony had been a success and I was now officially a Dragon Maiden.

Chapter Twenty-Seven

VALORA

After being officially inducted as a Dragon Maiden, my daily life did not change much—only now, when I spoke with the other Maidens, I could feel them giving more weight to my words. And when passing other humans in the corridors, they would bow their heads out of respect for my new title. Overall, I could feel a new presence of attention on myself and I was not sure how to feel about it. My daily tasks remained the same—continuing to clean and deliver correspondence to the other Lords.

Dracul acted like he normally did, and it was a relief, something familiar that I could slip back into. We worked together on brewing more of the potions that he was experimenting with. He would have me prepare ingredients or read steps from one of the many books to him. Now he even gave me additional time to read on my own, and would discuss any questions I had.

Despite daily life going back to normal, there were more whispers in the caves now. Borthen's forces made very bold moves. It was glaringly obvious that he was preparing for war. Lord Firenze and Lord Hiram stopped by Dracul's quarters almost on a daily basis now, taking up most of his day for discussing next steps. From what I overheard about their conversations, they soon had to discuss with the other Lords about what was to be done.

It took a couple weeks before a strategy meeting was held. I prepared the cavern where all the Lords were to meet, one of my new duties, and I wanted everything to be perfect. There was a room adjacent to the ceremonial hall, big enough for all the Lords in their dragon forms. It was mostly filled by a grand table, and ornate sconces lit up the room. The overall atmosphere was somber as the Lords met. I was allowed to remain to ensure refreshments were always available—each Lord had a goblet filled with cider and a plate full of meats in front of them.

"We're here to discuss the Starfire clan's egregious actions as of late." Dracul started the meeting off, his voice clipped. I could tell the past few weeks had been getting to him, he grew increasingly worried with each passing day. "Lord Firenze, please provide an update on what your scouts have found."

Lord Firenze, a brilliant crimson dragon, nodded. "From what we can tell, Borthen has gained human forces from both ours and Grathal's borders," he said. "He's been able to entice them with false promises of greater prosperity."

"We have not been able to gather taxes from those towns on our side of the border for several months now," Lord Noxus interjected. "Those towns provide us with lumber, stone, and crops that we do not grow here."

"Our food reserve is in a good spot," Lord Lorka said. His orange scales looked like fire in the sconce light. "If we do not collect from those towns, we will be fine for many months."

"Regardless," Lord Firenze said, looking at each of the Lords, "it does not change the fact that Borthen is trying to overthrow Lord Dracul. He has also been going to Grathal, where he has amassed an army of dragon mercenaries as well."

A small outcry at this news rang throughout the room.

"Lord Hiram," Dracul turned to the oldest dragon in the room, "have you come across a situation like this before? How would you recommend we proceed?"

Lord Hiram drew his claws together, thinking over his answer. "I would recommend we go visit Borthen, at least hint that we know what he's up to, and try to negotiate another treaty with him. If that fails then we will need to call on Lord Fangburn to enlist the Twisturn clan's forces and bring Borthen down."

There was silence after his words. The severity of the situation was not taken lightly by the Lords and I could see each of them considering Lord Hiram's words.

It was several moments before Lord Dracul spoke. "I will go see Borthen," he said. "And have Lord Firenze and Lord Verhorn accompany me."

There were murmurs at his announcement.

"Lord Hiram," he said, directing his attention to the gray dragon, "I want you to remain behind to keep an eye on Borthen's movements in Lord Firenze's absence, in case he tries to attack while we are away. If you see any movement, I want you to go to Lord Fangburn and enlist his help."

"Yes, my Lord." Lord Hiram bowed his head.

"Does anyone have any criticism on this plan?" Lord Dracul looked at each of the Lords, who all shook their heads. "Then we have an agreement. Lord Firenze, Lord Verhorn, we leave first thing tomorrow morning." He stood and swept out of the room.

I ran after him back to his quarters. When we got there, he transformed into his human form and slumped against the wall.

"I hoped it would not come to this," he said softly, and for the first time, I noticed dark circles under his eyes. This problem had been bothering him this whole time. He had hidden his worries well.

"How long do you think you'll be gone?" I asked. Worry began to gnaw in my stomach as I watched him walk over to his desk.

He sat down with an exhale of air and stared at the papers, beginning to move them around. "Hopefully it will only be a day or two at most," Dracul said, sorting the papers into a few different piles. "At worst, a week."

"Will your other duties be fine in the meantime?" I asked as I watched him.

"I'm organizing papers for Lord Hiram and you to take care of while I'm gone," he said, looking to me and smiling. "This pile is for him to take care of, and this pile is for you." He pointed to two of the piles, leaving a third one unassigned. "The last one can wait until I get back."

I walked to stand next to him, taking the top sheet of parchment on my pile and looking at it. From what I could tell, it looked like a sort of staff assignment sheet. "What's this?" I asked.

"You'll be in charge of scheduling different servants for specific days," he said. "Creating the schedule of when they'll work. Everybody gets two days off every fortnight."

"You've been handling this all this time?" I asked, aghast. "I thought Lord Verhorn would cover this task."

Dracul chuckled. "He usually does," he said. "But he'll also be going to with me on this trip, so I'm passing it along to you. Lord Hiram can help you if you get stuck on anything. I trust you can handle it." He stood and yawned. "Now if you'll excuse me, I need to get some sleep before the trip tomorrow."

"Do you need me to pack anything for you?" I asked, suddenly not wanting to leave him. The knot deep in my stomach pulled me towards him.

"I'll be fine," he said, leaning forward and absentmindedly kissing my forehead. "I'll see you tomorrow before I leave."

He turned and walked back to his bedroom, not seeming to realize what he had just done. But the spot where he kissed me burned and I knew my face was bright red, a heat pooling in my core. Unbidden, the thought that I wished he had kissed my lips instead flashed through my mind and I gasped in shock. I took several minutes to slow my breathing and clear my thoughts before heading back to the Dragon Maiden cavern.

Worry gnawed at me all throughout the night.

* * *

The next day, I awoke bright and early, preparing to bid farewell to Lord Dracul. Vimery and Bethany got ready as well, as they were to join me in saying goodbye to their respective Lords, Lord Firenze and Lord Verhorn. The three Dragon Lords waited for us in their dragon forms, at the entrance I had originally arrived through, almost a year ago. Vimery and Bethany went up to their Lords, wishing them goodbye, and I approached Dracul, suddenly feel self-conscious.

"It'll be only a short while," he said, smiling softly. "I'll be back soon, I promise."

I gulped past the lump in my throat and forced a smile on my face. "I know you'll do great," I said, trying to keep the tears from my voice. This was the first time we would to be apart since I had arrived. Already, I could feel an emptiness growing within me.

Dracul leaned forward and nuzzled my hair with his snout. "As will you," he said. "Don't worry. All will be well."

"Good luck," I said as he walked to the entrance, his wings spread, ready to take off. Lord Verhorn and Lord Firenze quickly followed, and us three Maidens watched until they disappeared on the horizon.

"What are you two up to for the rest of the day?" Bethany asked, turning to Vimery and I.

"I have cleaning to do," Vimery said, marching off towards Lord Firenze's cave. Since the ceremony, her patience for my presence had dwindled to be nonexistent.

Bethany watched her go before turning to me, waiting for my answer.

"I have paperwork to focus on," I said. "What about you?"

"Lord Verhorn wants me to clean his hoard," she said, her eyes sparkling. "Usually he has other tasks for me to do so I don't have time. It'll be nice to have it all perfect and polished when he returns."

"Have fun," I said as she ran off. Her enthusiasm made me chuckle slightly. I had not seen her so animated about her duties before.

With both Vimery and Bethany gone, I walked to Lord Dracul's quarters, to the paperwork that awaited me.

CHAPTER TWENTY-EIGHT

VALORA

I did my best to follow Dracul's instructions, trying not to worry and quell the rising ball of nerves that had taken up residence in my stomach. Each day that passed, each hour that ticked by, my anxiety only grew, the feeling of unease becoming unbearable. Even the paperwork he had left behind did little to distract me from my concern. I had finished it all by the end of the second day, delivering the applicable papers to each of the remaining Lords.

Multiple times, I stopped by the entrance where Dracul and the other Lords had departed, watching for any sign of their return, to no avail. The remaining time, I tried to keep myself busy, making Dracul's quarters spotless and from time to time, I would try to struggle through the books I had been eagerly waiting to read. But my focus was gone, my thoughts always turning to Dracul. I had not expected to miss him as much as I did, his absence gnawing at me. I felt a coldness with him gone. I had grown to rely on his warm presence more than I had realized. Each day, I prayed for his safe return, that everything would turn out fine, but deep down, I had a fear that something was wrong.

At the end of the week, I finally acknowledged my worry, allowing it to overtake me. I sought out Lord Hiram for his advice. If the Dragon Lords could go to him for counsel, could I not as well? Dracul seemed to trust him, so I should be able to as well. My feet swiftly took me to his chambers. I knocked on the door and entered without waiting for Alonsa to answer. Both were in his office, Alonsa looking shocked to see me.

"What may I do for you?" Lord Hiram asked as he looked up at me over a pair of glasses hanging at the end of his nose. Both of us knew that what I did was against protocol, but I could think of no other alternative, I could not wait. He motioned to Alonsa, and she bowed before leaving us alone.

"Lord Dracul left over a week ago and he has not returned," I said, kneading my hands in worry. Once I realized what I was doing, I forced them to my sides, where they instead fiddled with the fabric of my dress. "Shouldn't we be worried? Is something amiss?"

A brief look of worry passed over Lord Hiram's features, but it was gone so quickly that I barely had time to register the expression. I knew what I had seen, and my anxiety only grew. This wise Dragon Lord was just as worried as I was, and the thought gave me no comfort.

"He is fine. He took two very capable Dragon Lords with him when he left," he said with a false confidence. I could see past the façade. "I'm sure they have everything under control."

"But what is taking so long? Lord Dracul said it should only take a few days," I said.

"Lord Dracul probably got caught up talking with friends he hasn't seen in a long time," Lord Hiram said, shifting uncomfortably in his chair. I could hear the lie in his voice. "Don't worry. Just go about things as usual, Valora. He'll turn up soon enough and you'll see that all this worrying has been for naught." He looked to the door, an obvious cue that the conversation was over.

I bowed low. "Thank you, my Lord, for your kind words," I said before leaving, the knot of worry only growing.

For the next few hours, I stayed in Lord Dracul's chambers, organizing his potion ingredients for what felt like the thousandth time. My hands shook, and I eventually had to stop or risk breaking the bottles containing the ingredients. My duties for the day were over and I was at a loss for what to do. I was unwilling to go back to the Maiden cavern just yet, not wanting to deal with the prickly silence. The Lords' departure and absence had made the whole cave uneasy, and the longer they were gone, the more the uneasiness grew. I could not stand to be in a room with the others just yet, having to quell my own fears and worries so as not to alarm them. Not to mention, Lord Hiram's words had done little to comfort me. It was obvious he was worried, too, which meant something had to be wrong.

* * *

Once more, I decided to go to the entrance of the cave to resume my vigil. Before the sun set, rain began to fall from the skies, limiting my vision. Suddenly, over the sound of the rain, I began to hear the beat of wings and my heart quickened as two dragons flew back, a third supported between them. My heart sped up as they approached, recognizing the middle one as Dracul, his head slumped as he was carried through the air. At last, he was back, but from the looks of things, he was not in good shape.

Moving out of the way, I followed Lord Firenze and Lord Verhorn as they hastily flew in and pulled Dracul to his quarters. They set him gently on the floor before stepping aside for me. With the three of them in their dragon forms, there was now very little space left in the cavern.

"Can you fix him?" Lord Verhorn asked, his eyes bright with worry.

I stepped around him to assess the damage and gasped in shock. "What happened?" I asked quietly, taking in the sight in front of me. Never had I ever imagined seeing anything like this in my life.

Dracul was bleeding heavily, one of his wings ripped almost all the way to the bone. There were other cuts and scrapes along his body, one even across his eye.

He opened the uninjured one and stared at me. "Things got a little out of hand," he explained, smiling slightly at his joke. The smile quickly disappeared as he grimaced in pain, letting out a groan.

At the sight of his pain, I was spurred into action. "I'm going to need a lot of towels, warm water, healing herbs, a needle and thread for the wing," I ordered, pushing up my sleeves.

I rushed to the potions area in the back of the cavern to grab the supplies I would need while the two other Lords summoned their Maidens to assemble the other items. The women immediately disappeared after delivering the supplies. I could see by their faces they did not like seeing the High Dragon Lord in such a state. Lord Firenze and Lord Verhorn stayed to observe my work, while Lords Hiram, Noxus, and Lorka were summoned. The rest of the Lords transformed to their human forms to allow more space in the cave. Dracul was the only one who remained as a dragon.

I thoroughly cleaned the big wounds I could see, the ones that would become infected if I did not tend to them right away, covering them with the healing herbs and bandages. I was grateful to lean on the experience I had gained spending time by Dracul's side, learning the practical properties and uses of various herbs.

At last, I turned my attention to the wing, feeling overwhelmed by the need to stitch it. It was such a vital part to a dragon. From the looks of the injury, I was unsure if Dracul would ever be able to fly again.

"I'm going to do the best I can to patch it up," I told Dracul, his eyes trained on me the whole time. "Your other wounds should heal just fine. Your wing on the other hand... I can sew it up, but there will be a scar, and I'm not sure if you'll be able to fly with it."

"As long as you can get it to the scarred state, I can fix it the rest of the way," Dracul said, grimacing at the pain. "Just do what you have to do."

"It's going to hurt a lot. You can't move," I warned, taking the sterilized needle in hand and beginning to thread it. "Promise?" I asked when he did not respond.

"Promise," he grunted.

I took a deep breath. "Here we go," I said quietly, more to myself than anyone else. I started at the beginning of the injury, at the base of the wing, and began to sew the wound shut.

Dracul closed his eyes in pain and growled his disapproval.

"I'm sorry," I apologized, continuing to make small, even stitches. "But it needs to be done."

Slowly, agonizingly, I stitched the wound closed, focusing on the task at hand and forcing myself to ignore Dracul's rumblings of pain. After what felt like hours, I finished, tying off the thread and wiping my brow. I placed more herbs along the seam to help the wound heal faster, hoping all would be well.

"Done," I said triumphantly.

Dracul craned his neck to view my handiwork. "Not bad," he said. He looked at the other Dragon Lords. "You may go now," he dismissed them. "Firenze and Verhorn, get your wounds checked out as well."

I had not noticed that the other two were injured. They had scrapes and cuts along their faces and bodies, but it seemed as though Dracul had taken the brunt of whatever attack they had been through.

After the Lords left, I began to gather the supplies and started to clean myself off.

Dracul shifted behind me. "Valora?" he asked, his voice quiet. "Thank you for your help." He smiled, though I could see the pain in his eyes.

"It's a Dragon Maiden's job to care for her Lord, is it not?" I asked, turning back to wash my hands thoroughly in the basin of water. They were filthy and I felt like I would never be clean again, the blood soaking my skin reminding me of that day.

"It is, but this is beyond the call of duty," Dracul said.

I turned to him, sensing there was more he wanted to say.

"I would like to ask a favor of you," he said, resting his head on the ground, his eyes level with mine.

"Yes?" I asked when he did not elaborate.

"I prepared a room for you in my quarters before I left, since you and the other Maidens had a falling out," he said. "I was hoping you could stay and keep an eye on me throughout the night. Just in case something happens."

I dried off my hands, my mind whirling. "I don't mind," I said. "And it'll make it easier when I have to change your bandages in a couple hours anyway."

"Very well," Dracul said. "You can go gather your things and bring them here if you wish."

Rushing back to the Maiden cavern, my thoughts were a in whirl. Obviously, something had happened at the negotiations with the Starfire clan. Dracul was severely injured. I was glad he had made it back alive, but I had never expected this level of injury.

The other Maidens had gathered already, and all looked up when I entered, their faces tight with worry.

"How is he?" Alonsa asked.

"He'll survive," I said, going to my bed to gather my things. "But it will take time for him to recover from his injuries."

I almost missed the Maidens exchanging a look as I finished gathering my meager belongings together.

"Where do you think you're going?" Vimery asked accusingly, blocking my path as I started to leave. "Planning on leaving again?"

"No," I said tersely, not feeling like wasting time arguing with her. "Lord Dracul has prepared a room for me in his cave and asked that I stay there with him instead of here."

Everyone's mouths dropped open at my announcement.

"That is unheard of," Bethany said quietly. "He's never done something like that before."

"He's never had a Maiden before, has he?" I countered, seeing the accusatory looks the others gave me, knowing the assumptions they made. "He's injured and I'll have to tend to him throughout the night." I stepped around Vimery and continued to walk out. "I'll see you all later. Good night."

There was no response, and I knew now that I was a complete outcast to the group. They probably would still treat me with respect due to my status, but any chance at getting closer to any of them was now completely gone.

When I returned to Dracul's chambers, he was in the same spot where I had left him lying on the ground. "Do you have all your things?" he asked, glancing at the lonely pack in my hands, the one I'd brought with me when I first arrived.

"Yes," I said, moving to check the bandages to ensure all was well. "Everything looks good," I said in relief. He raised an eyebrow, and I acquiesced, "Well, as good as they could look considering the circumstances."

"Then you may retire for now," Dracul said.

"What about you?" I asked. "Are you going to lay on the floor all night?"

"At the moment, I have no other option," he sighed. "I'm too injured to move much right now and I can't transform into my human form without disastrous consequences to my wing."

I walked to the landing and grabbed cushions and blankets, moving them in place under his head. "You can at least have something plush to sleep on," I said as he looked at me quizzically. After he was settled, I moved to sleep on the couch nearby.

"Valora, I have a room for you," he objected as he saw me laying down on the couch.

"I will stay here," I said firmly. "I'm not leaving you alone, not now."

He gave me a kind gaze, his eyes melting once more, and I felt a heat slice through me. "Very well," he said, moving to grab a blanket with his teeth and dragging it over my body. "Good night."

After several moments of silence, I spoke. "Dracul?" I asked quietly, hoping he had not fallen asleep just yet.

"Yes?" he asked after a prolonged pause, his voice sleepy.

"I thought you said that when you got a Dragon Maiden, you would become stronger," I said. "But you still got hurt. Does that mean I'm not a good Dragon Maiden?" My voice broke.

Dracul's face came into view to look at me. "Oh, Valora," he said gently. "It's not that. I actually lasted longer than I would have without you, which just goes to show you how bad the fight was. If I did not have you as my Dragon Maiden, I would be dead now."

"Really?" I asked, shocked at this confession.

He nodded. "Yes."

I paused before asking my next question. "Have… have you unlocked any special powers yet?" I asked, looking at my hands. "I know you said it doesn't happen every time."

He leaned in close to me. "I can fly faster now," he said. "Much to the chagrin of the two Lords who came with me." He blew my hair affectionately. "We'll have to go flying again so I can show you how much faster I've gotten."

I smiled at him. "You need to get better first before we can do that," I said.

"A good night's sleep will help with that," he said. "Good night Valora."

"Good night, my Lord."

I quickly fell asleep. Now that Dracul was back, my anxiety had lessened considerably, despite the state he had returned in. Throughout the night, I would awaken, checking on his bandages and finding his condition unchanged. Once, I needed to change them, but otherwise, everything seemed stable. He snored as I fell asleep, a gentle, rumbling sound. I slept deeply. Now that my Lord had returned and was in my care, I could relax.

* * *

The next morning, when I checked on Dracul, I found him in a very different state from the night before. His normally cool scales were warm to the touch and I was unable to wake him, no matter how hard I tried. Thinking quickly, I gathered spare rags and doused them with cold water, laying them on his body to hopefully get his fever down.

"What's going on?" Lord Verhorn had stopped by. I could tell he was puzzled by my suddenly frantic actions.

"He has a fever," I explained. "His body is trying to rid itself of any infections he may have."

"It would be in your best interest that he does not succumb to these wounds," Lord Verhorn said, leveling me with a stare. I gulped at his words, feeling the murderous intent rolling off him. "Otherwise, a new High Lord will be picked and I doubt he would want to keep you around. Remember that."

"I will, thank you," I forced out the words past a suddenly very dry throat.

A little while after Lord Verhorn left, Lord Lorka paid me a visit. He had with him a basket of herbs and a couple vials of potions which he set down on one of the tables. Slowly, he approached Dracul, his keen eyes taking in the state of the High Dragon Lord.

"I heard from Lord Verhorn that he's taken a turn for the worst," he said, giving me a sympathetic smile. "I thought these might be able to help. Lord Dracul may be the expert when it comes to potion-making, but I know a little bit."

"Thank you," I said quietly, walking over to take stock of the ingredients he had brought. "Is there a doctor or anybody who could help him? More than I can?"

Lord Lorka ran a hand through his hair and let out a sigh. "Lord Dracul has shown more interest than most in the healing arts. He's usually our de facto doctor," he said. "For the most part, dragons don't get sick, and typically our injuries aren't serious enough to require a lot of treatment. There hasn't been any fighting between the clans in generations, even though everyone still maintains their own armies. It's something that has just kind of… died off."

"It doesn't seem like any of you had good enough reasoning to plan ahead for something like this," I said, pursing my lips. I grabbed one of the potions Lord Lorka had brought, and he helped pry Dracul's mouth open enough so I could administer it.

"Typically, a Dragon Lord's Maiden gives him enough strength to prevent injuries like this." His words stabbed me, reminding me that I was not enough. I was the Maiden who'd tried to escape. "I don't mean that how it sounds," he said quickly upon seeing my expression. "But usually, the only way to hurt a Lord is to kill his Maiden. Rarely do we become injured like this."

I nodded at his words, and together, we watched for any sign of improvement. Lord Lorka stayed longer than I expected, but eventually, he returned back to his cave, though not before telling me to call him if I needed any additional ingredients.

After he left, I continued with my ministrations, checking different areas of Dracul's body, ending with his stomach. If he had not bathed me in fire, ensuring that he would never burn me, the heat radiating off his stomach would have blistered my hands. On a normal day, the heat from his belly would fill me with warmth, but now, it could probably boil a pot of water in mere seconds.

Tears entered my eyes. I was not sure what to do next. Lord Lorka's potion did not seem to have helped at all. "Please don't die," I begged him. "Please don't."

The only thing I could think of to bring his temperature down was to keep reapplying cold rags, but otherwise, I had no clue what to do. Placing the rags on his stomach caused the fabric to hiss and steam from the extreme heat. After an hour, I began to search the cave, looking for any ideas of how to save him. On a table in the potions area rested a large book, one that had not been there the night before. It laid open to a specific page, and I walked over to read it.

I examined the book, gasping at what lay before me. I glanced quickly to Dracul before turning back. It seemed that before the High Dragon Lord succumbed to his fever, he had been looking for a way to heal himself. He must have known what was wrong with him. On the page before was a brief explanation of what had happened, a list of symptoms, and at last, a cure. All those hours of creating his own tinctures and potions, studying medicine, had paid off. My blood ran cold as I realized what I had to do, what was required of me. Scrawled in a very unsteady hand were the words *I understand if you can't do it.*

There was no question. Of course I would do it.

Taking a deep breath to steady myself, I rushed around the cave to gather the ingredients necessary for the cure. I followed each instruction to the letter, chopping, mixing, boiling, and stirring the concoction. At last, I got to the final step—the worst step. For the cure to work, the Lord's Maiden had to put her hair in the mixture, as well as a large amount of blood. Quite easily, I cut off a hank of hair and dropped it into the mixture, turning it a light-purple color. However, it was the blood that made me panic. As I held the knife to my hand, I began to tremble. The emotional scars from my past were not as gone as I had hoped.

I looked over to my Dragon Lord, took in how labored his breathing was, and knew that I had no choice. He would die if I did not do this. Before I could change my mind, I ran the blade over my hand and squeezed the blood into the cauldron, gasping at the pain and memories that flooded my mind. The drops sizzled as they hit the boiling liquid, changing it to a dark blue that matched Dracul's scales, as the book said it would. After squeezing my hand multiple times to ensure enough blood was in the potion, I bandaged it haphazardly before scooping out the potion into a nearby goblet.

Quickly, I went to Dracul and worked to open his mouth. In his unconscious state, his teeth were clenched shut. Carefully, I opened his mouth slightly and reached past the razor-sharp teeth, pouring the potion in so he swallowed it. My adrenaline rush swiftly left me and my body began to crash, exhaustion overwhelming me. I collapsed next to Dracul and began to stroke his snout, wishing for a noticeable change. After several minutes with no change, I began to despair, feeling sick to my stomach.

"I did everything correctly," I whispered. I looked to Dracul and pleaded, "Please, don't die." Tears pricked my eyes at the thought of him dying, of how I would have failed him, one more person in my life. I had been unable to save my parents, and now, with the opportunity in front of me, I was unable to save Dracul too. The pain was too overwhelming. My heart felt as though it split in two. Just as I had been worried about—I had grown too close and too fond of him.

"Just don't die," I breathed, tears beginning to trail down my cheeks, my hand still on his snout. I pulled my knees to my chest and buried my face to muffle my cries as I began to sob harder. The book said he should have begun to improve by now. Obviously, I was too late, and now he was going to die.

I did not register at first when the snout beneath my hand began to move slightly. In between my sobs, I felt him move, and when I realized what was happening, my head snapped up, met with two kind silver eyes watching me. Ones that I thought I would never see again.

"Don't cry, Lora," he said gently, bringing forth a claw to carefully wipe away my tears. My heart stuttered at the nickname, at how easily the endearment slipped from his lips. His eyes darted to my hand and clouded slightly. I could see that he was upset over what I had to do to save him. "I'm sorry about that," he said. "I can heal you, if you would like."

"But… but you need to get better." My mind struggled to accept that he was still alive, that I had done it. That I had saved him. "You need to rest."

He smiled at me. "Thank you for what you did," he said. "Though I wish there had been another way, I wish you didn't need to mutilate yourself for my sake."

"I was lucky enough to spot the book you left out for me." I waved away his concerns. "I wasn't sure what to do next."

Dracul's gaze was tender as he stared at me. "I knew you'd be smart enough to figure it out," he said.

I stood and stared at him, trying to realize that he was alive—to calm my heart. Since he had returned, it had become a constant source of pain, seeing him injured. Suddenly, I felt the overwhelming need to embrace him.

I rushed to him and encircled my arms around his neck. "I thought you were going to die, Dracul," I said, my voice muffled by his scales. "I was so worried."

A scaly arm wrapped around my body, holding me close. "I'm going to be fine, Lora," he said. "One of my wounds had been poisoned and I did not realize it at the time. But a potion concocted by my Maiden, containing her blood, is enough to overcome any poison and any ailment. It's an old remedy that only a few know." A small smile graced his lips. "When Borthen injured me, I don't think he realized I have an official Maiden, otherwise he wouldn't have dared to try such a bold move."

Suddenly conscious of the heat growing within me, I pulled back, my face flushed. "I should look at your other injuries," I said. "To make sure they are doing fine."

Keeping my gaze averted, I moved to check his other wounds, feeling his watchful eyes focused on me. I was unable to hide my shock as I pulled up the bandages and found the wounds almost completely healed.

I looked up at Dracul, my mouth open. "How?" I asked.

"The blood of a Maiden has a very interesting effect on her Lord," Dracul explained. "Because of our bond, that potion you made can heal my injuries, even the more serious ones." He moved his wing to show me that it was almost completely scarred, the bloody mess from the night before completely gone. "Could you remove my stitches?" he asked.

Mutely, I moved to do as he asked, shock overloading my brain into complete silence. I could not believe the power my blood held for Dracul, how it could have so many uses. Carefully, I removed the stitches, noticing Dracul wincing at the foreign feeling. Quietly, I apologized, and at last, all the stitches were gone. I cleaned the area to ensure no residue remained. After a quick once-over of all his wounds, I started putting the supplies away.

"There's still more potion left," I said, earnestly not looking at Dracul. "We should save it in case you need it again." I found a few empty vials and moved to the cauldron to bottle up the remaining potion. Dracul moved his tail, and I found my path blocked.

"Valora, look at me," he said gently, so gently.

After a few seconds, I did as he asked, my heart beating rapidly. Ever since he had awakened, I had made a fool of myself, first by crying and then by hugging him. Dracul used his tail to herd me, and I was forced to take a few uncertain steps closer.

"Why the sudden change?" he asked. "Does it make you uneasy to know that your blood has such fantastic powers?"

I nodded silently, hoping he would drop the topic, but he could see right through me.

"There is no reason to be embarrassed over how you acted."

I blushed furiously as he correctly guessed what had been bothering me.

He leaned closer. "It's nice to know you care," he said. Carefully, Dracul reached out a claw and gently took my hand, pulling apart the messy bandage to reveal the cut I had suffered. "I'm going to heal this now," he said, his voice instructing me not to argue.

Slowly, he let out a steady stream of fire over the injury, not burning me, but I could still feel the unpleasant intensity of the focused heat. After a long minute of expelling the fire, he stopped and examined my hand before showing it to me. My mouth dropped open. The cut had completely disappeared.

"Is this another thing that has to do with the bond between us?" I asked.

"Yes." Dracul nodded. "Your blood can heal me, and my fire can heal you."

"Oh." My mind raced. I examined my hand for several more moments before looking back to him. "Dracul, what happened? How did you get hurt?" I asked. "You said something went badly."

He let out a sigh and moved his tail so I could finish filling the vials with the remaining potion. "We went to negotiate with Borthen," he said. "He was obviously not pleased to see us, but nothing seemed amiss at first. After a few days, it was apparent that negotiations had not gone anywhere, but we decided to try a couple more days before leaving. Our last day, his soldiers attacked us, accusing us of stealing. I think he hoped to kill me so he could take over the clan. And that's how I became injured. Firenze and Verhorn tried to defend me, but the sole focus of their attack was on me."

"What's going to happen now?" I asked. "When they find out that you're fine, aren't they going to come here?"

"No," Dracul growled. "Because we are going to take them by surprise and get rid of Borthen once and for all. We've had too many troubles with him, and once he's out of the way, I'll be in charge of his clan." He did not sound happy about the fact, more chagrined, and I knew that he was only doing his duty as High Dragon Lord.

I reached over and gently patted his neck. "Is it bothering you to have to do this?"

"I wouldn't say I'm looking forward to it," Dracul said. "But he has become too much of a threat, so it's my duty to do this."

I remained silent. There was still so much I did not understand about draconic politics, even after observing Dracul for the past months. I could only hope that whatever plan he had in mind would work, that he would be able to successfully take down Borthen with little issue.

CHAPTER TWENTY-NINE

VALORA

Over the course of the next week, Dracul met with the other Lords to plan a battle strategy, as well as sent messengers to Lord Fangburn asking for the Twisturn clan's help in attacking Borthen. The other Lord replied immediately that he would devote his forces to the effort, and arrived within two days, along with his officers. From the brief glimpses I got of these visitors, Lord Fangburn was a teal-blue dragon with yellow eyes, while his three officers were maroon, yellow, and brown dragons. They had immediately followed Dracul into the battle room upon their arrival.

Everyone planning the attack holed up in a room for many days, rarely taking time to sleep as they debated the best course of action. Borthen had committed a grievous act in attacking Dracul, but the fact that he had slowly been building up his forces meant that they would need to tread carefully. Finally, a date was decided for the battle. Almost all of Dracul's armed forces would set out. Only a few would remain behind to protect the caves and human servants. Maidens were to remain behind for their own safety as well. Once more, I would be separated from Dracul, a fact that made my heart ache.

"Don't worry. I'll bring along the potion you concocted," he said gently after I expressed my concern in private when he had one of his very rare breaks.

He had healed marvelously over the past few days, any scarring completely disappearing with another small dose of the potion. Now, he was even able to transform into his human form without issue, and his wing had made a full recovery. Two days ago, he had taken me along for a quick test flight around the mountain. It had been exhilarating how fast he was able to fly now.

"And I'll have the other warriors defending me as well," he added.

"I know, but last time you left, you almost died," I said, unable to shake this new fear that something else bad would happen. Last time I felt like this he had returned injured and with that memory so fresh in my mind it was hard to shake the sense of dread. I took his hand and squeezed it. "I don't want that to happen, Dracul." Tears pricked my eyes.

He put a hand to my cheek. "I need to do this, it's my duty as High Dragon Lord," he said. "And if I don't, next time, Borthen might come here and find you. If that happened, I don't know what I'd do, Lora." At every opportunity he got, he used the nickname he had given me, and it filled me with warmth.

I leaned into his hand. We had grown closer since he had returned and I had started to pull down the walls I had put between us. Something deep down in me told me that our relationship was not typical for a Dragon Lord and his Maiden, but I was too frightened by the prospect of losing him to keep those boundaries in place. If something were to happen, I wanted to soak up every single moment we could share together.

"I know," I said softly. "And I know you're capable of taking care of yourself, that this time you're going with hundreds of others to fight. But I can't help but worry about you."

Dracul leaned forward and kissed my forehead, something he had started doing more to ease my worries lately when we were alone. "I will return, Lora," he promised, staring at me with those lustrous silver eyes. "And after Borthen is gone, there's something I want to tell you."

"Why not tell me now?" I asked, somehow feeling that it was important. "Why wait?"

He hesitated before shaking his head. "No, it needs to wait," he said firmly. "It will be worth the wait."

"I will trust you then, Dracul," I said, leaning forward to kiss his cheek.

For the rest of the evening, we stayed in each other's company, relishing the other's existence before Dracul would leave for battle tomorrow. I did my best not to dwell on what was to come.

* * *

The next morning, I accompanied the other Dragon Maidens to where the army was to depart, to wish our Lords farewell. Lord Fangburn had left in the early hours of the morning to gather his forces. The Twisturn clan would rendezvous with Dracul just south of Borthen's borders. Already, the cavern where the army gathered was packed, as everyone was in their dragon form, covered from head to tail in armor. Dracul had left his quarters a little while ago to have his armor assembled.

Last night, Dracul and I talked for hours before drifting off in each other's arms. It had been disappointing to wake up and swiftly realize that he would be leaving shortly, and I had to fight back my tears. I needed to stay strong for the other Maidens and dragons. I could not show my weakness. Already, I could feel his absence and the pit of emptiness in my stomach.

The Dragon Lords were lined up at the entrance of the cave and each Maiden went to bid her Lord goodbye. Dracul leaned his face close to mine so we could talk quietly without anyone listening. In my peripheral vision, I could see the other Lords doing the same.

"I will return, Lora," he said. "We will communicate through messengers so the other dragons left behind should be able to tell you what's going on."

I placed my hands on either side of his face, moving so our foreheads touched. "You will be safe," I said, making it sound more like a certainty than an order. "You will return to me, Dracul."

To my surprise, a light emanated from between our touching foreheads and gasps filled the cavern. I pulled back, shocked at what happened. Dracul's forehead still glowed, and I could only assume mine was, too, based on a warmth I felt.

He looked at me, his eyes first showing his surprise before he started grinning. "My dragons!" he bellowed. "Fortune smiles down upon us. We have been blessed by the stars! This light is the blessing that will lead us into battle. Let us be off!" He gave me a smile before taking off into the air.

The warriors cried out in support before they took off as well, following their Lord into battle. I pressed against the wall to protect myself from the pull of their wings. And with that, the cave was empty except for the other Dragon Maidens.

"What happened?" Gwen asked. "What was that?"

I could feel the warmth fade from my forehead, and knew the glow was gone. We all looked to Alonsa, as she was the eldest.

She shrugged. "I'm not quite sure," she said. "But we have work to do. Just because our Lords are not here does not mean we can slack off in our duties."

The other Maidens nodded and we dispersed, heading to our respective Lord's quarters.

On my way back, two humans approached in the corridor, their bright hair color indicating they were dragons. I frowned slightly. To my confusion, they looked able-bodied enough to have gone with the rest of the army. They even had armor on.

"They already left," I said. "If you're going to join the army, you should hurry up."

The two exchanged a look before turning back to me. "Oh, we aren't with the army," one said, his orange eyes containing a look that made my stomach drop. He had a scar on his lip that added to his sneer and his greasy burgundy hair was unkempt.

"Then what are you doing here?" I asked. "This corridor is off limits except to those who have approval." Dracul had told me only Lords and their Maidens were given free rein to the corridors leading to his quarters. The way these two waltzed about made me wary of their intentions.

Both took a few steps towards me and I backed away, sensing that something was wrong. Very wrong.

The one with shorn, dark-green hair smirked. "We're here for you, of course," he said.

At his words, my body froze, my heart pounding. I turned to run, to call for help, but they jumped forward. Quickly, I dodged the attack, taking a few more steps backwards. A shiver sliced down my back as I realized that the insignia on their armor was not familiar to me. These must be Borthen's men.

"We'll be kinder if you come quietly," the burgundy-haired man said.

"I will not be going with you," I said with false confidence. I looked around, but there was nothing nearby I could use as a weapon. As dragons, even in human form, they held the physical advantage over me. But maybe I could make enough noise for someone to come to my aid.

The green one came towards me again and I ducked past his outstretched arms. Belatedly, I noticed I was now stuck between the two of them and a sinking feeling overcame me as I realized they toyed with me. I would not go down without a fight.

I lunged towards the green one, not giving him time to approach me again. He let out a shout of surprise as we both collided with the wall and fell to the ground. I began to punch him, hitting wherever I could, and he grunted in pain.

"You stupid... wench. Hold... still..." He struggled to speak as he attempted to grab my hands, but I was faster.

Adrenaline coursed through me, focusing my attention on the dragon in front of me. I had completely forgotten about the burgundy dragon until I felt a hard smack across the head. As darkness began to overtake me, I hoped someone had heard the struggle.

I should have screamed.

CHAPTER THIRTY

VALORA

I awoke with a pounding headache and my vision was foggy for several moments. Looking around, I took in my surroundings. I was in a fairly large, domed enclosure, with a large opening at one end. A rough blanket lay underneath me and to my right was a pail of water and another bucket that I could easily guess its purpose. Slowly, I moved towards the opening, pausing to check for any movement. I looked out and my heart dropped. The dome I was in was attached to the wall of an enormous cavern, high enough up on the wall that if I was to try and jump, I would surely perish. Along the walls of this cavern were other domes similar to mine, but from what I could tell, they all seemed empty. Sconces lined the walls, two on each side of every dome to light up the cavern. At the bottom was a large entrance leading to a hallway.

As I took in my surroundings, trying to figure out where I was, a bronze dragon entered the cavern, his eyes going straight to me. His mouth morphed into a smirk and I scrambled backwards into my dome as he began to fly towards me. When he reached the entrance of my dome, he transformed into his human form, stepping in with me. His skin was bronzed, his hair a reddish-gold hue, and his eyes were a glittering gold as he stared at me hungrily. To my dismay, he only wore pants, and I looked away, wanting to crawl as far away from him as possible.

"So you're Dracul's Maiden, huh?" he asked in a gravelly voice, swaggering towards me.

I said nothing, continuing to look at the wall. My skin crawled as he got close enough to grip my face, forcing me to look at him.

"I was talking to you," he said roughly. "And I expect an answer when I ask you a question, is that understood?"

"Yes," I whispered, fear flowing through me. The coarseness of his eyes instilled a primal fear in me. I knew how easily he could kill me and he showed no restraint in his gaze. More than ever, I wanted Dracul to be there. "I'm Lord Dracul's Maiden."

He let out a harsh laugh. "I can't believe the bastard finally got himself one!" he crowed, pushing me away. "I never thought he had it in him. If I had known, I would have tried something different to off him."

My heart stopped at his words. "You're Borthen?" I asked in disbelief.

His brows furrowed into a thunderous frown. "Watch it! That's *Lord* Borthen to you," he growled. "Your precious Lord may have stolen everything that was mine, but I will *not* have you disrespecting me." I bowed my head, and he cackled. "Oh, if only he could see how easily you submit to me," he said. "I would love to see the look on his face once he realizes what I've stolen from him."

"What do you want with me?" I asked, attempting to keep a tremble out of my voice.

Borthen stepped towards me again and I flinched, much to his delight. "It was a shock finding out that he had a Maiden," he whispered, once again coming close to my face. I could feel his breath stir my hair. "But once I realized what happened, I immediately started my plan to kidnap you. That way, he will feel as helpless as I did when he stole everything from me."

"Are you going to kill me?" I asked.

He shrugged. "Maybe," he said. "And maybe not. Either way, you will be good bait to get Dracul to come here for you. Sources say he's *very* attached to you." His eyes darted up and down, surveying me. I hunched myself into a smaller ball, disliking the look in his eyes. "Yes, I can see why," he murmured, licking his lips.

Once more, I looked away, feeling sickened. "Lord Dracul didn't steal anything," I said loudly, surprising myself. A quick glance at Borthen and I could tell he was surprised too. "He was rightfully picked as High Dragon Lord."

Borthen laughed once more. "Is that what he told you?" he asked.

Slowly, I nodded, a sinking feeling filling me.

"What a pack of lies! There is a special ring that unlocks a Lord's power without a Maiden," he said. "Something that would be very useful for a High Dragon Lord with no Maiden. Usually, a High Dragon Lord is not inducted until he has a Maiden, but he falsely claimed he had this ring. A few years ago, I actually found it in our clan's vaults. When Dracul found out, he sent humans to come and steal it for him. He knew I would never hand it over willingly. These humans ingratiated themselves to me and I welcomed them in with open arms. For almost a year, they worked enthusiastically for me until one day, they gained access to the ring and stole it away." He stopped to laugh. "Even though I couldn't get revenge on Dracul, I was able to get revenge on those humans."

His words had an edge of truth that I did not want to believe. "What did you do to them?" I breathed, unable to speak any louder.

Borthen's face twisted into a wicked smile. "I sent my men to their homes to kill their families and burn their houses," he said quietly, leaning his face towards mine.

I could feel all color drain from my face, feeling lightheaded.

"And your brother was one of the men who stole from me, Valora Marchton," he hissed.

My blood ran cold.

"How ironic that your brother's work for your current Lord happened to be the reason that your parents were killed."

Tears streamed down my cheeks. "You're lying," I said in a choked voice, but by his eyes, I could tell he was not.

He tsked at me, shaking his head in mock sadness. "Poor little Valora," he said in mockery. "I wish I was." Borthen turned to leave now that he'd had his fun with me. "I will see you tomorrow," he said before jumping out of the dome. I could hear the flap of wings as he transformed midair.

All I could do was collapse into sobs, my heart breaking at the truth. After all this time, after all my travels, I finally found out what happened in the cave of my Lord's greatest enemy. And the fact that Dracul was the reason behind my trauma made it hurt all the more.

CHAPTER THIRTY-ONE

DRACUL

We flew north, meeting with Fangburn's army along the way. With both sets of forces, we were at least six hundred dragons strong, more than twice Borthen's forces. The glow from Lora lasted well into the afternoon and I felt lightened by its presence, proof that her hope and goodwill was with me.

The plan was to split into three units—my unit to take on Borthen's forces head-on, with Firenze's and Fangburn's units to take both flanks. A horn sounded as soon as we passed into Starfire clan territory, raising the alarm, and I grimaced. Soon, we would have enemy dragons headed our way and the bloodbath would begin. Despite the fact that these dragons fought for Borthen, they were still considered my people and I did not want them injured.

One thing I gave Borthen credit for was his forces were well organized. His army's response time was surprisingly swift, and soon, we were in all-out war. The smell of fire and burning hide filled the air, cries of fallen dragons trailing off as they reached the ground. Several of his warriors headed towards me, but the dragons I had on my side dispatched them quickly. Anyone who made it through, I killed without much issue.

It was a flurry of action, and trying to make way towards the Starfire Mountains was slow progress. Human archers assembled on the ground, located at strategic points in the mountains. They were able to shoot down a good number of my dragons. I gritted my teeth. It seemed Firenze's reports of Borthen recruiting a large number of humans had been correct.

Swooping low, I let out a giant stream of fire, bolstered by the idea of returning to Lora. The rest of my unit aimed their fire at the mountain, trying to reach the hidden archers. Screams from the humans echoed against the rocks as they burned. To my surprise, we were able to quickly finish them off. Our numbers simply overpowered Borthen's forces, even with the advantage of the human archers.

Nowhere did I see Borthen—the coward decided to remain in his cave, it seemed—but soon we had defeated his army. Only a small number of his warriors were allowed to flee as they flew back to their cave. We set up camp at the foot of the mountain, keeping an eye out for any further attack. I made sure to have a messenger head back to our lands to deliver the news to the other dragons and Lora that we had been victorious and tomorrow we would continue our onslaught. The sky had begun to darken and my forces needed rest from the long journey and fighting.

*　*　*

I was sitting at a campfire with the other Lords enjoying our dinner when a messenger came rushing up to me, whispering something in my ear. Immediately, my heart dropped, my pleasant mood from earlier disappearing. The other Lords could see the look on my face and knew something was wrong.

"What is it?" Fangburn asked.

The others leaned close to hear my answer.

"Borthen's kidnapped Valora," I said, hardly believing my words. "His men snuck into our mountain and took her."

"Your Maiden?" Fangburn asked. "The one you just inducted? Just leave her. There'll be plenty more like her." He waved his hand, unconcerned with the news I had just shared.

The other Lords from my clan exchanged a look, Hiram looking the most perturbed by this news.

Without thinking, I leapt at Fangburn, throwing him to the ground. All the other Lords around the fire jumped up as I began to pummel him, punching whatever bit of flesh I could find.

"She's not just a Maiden!" I shouted, my voice carrying far across the camp. "You watch your tongue. I ought to rip it from your face!" I continued my onslaught, and the others seemed too hesitant to pull me off him.

Fangburn managed to grab one of my fists, spitting out blood. "If she's not just a Maiden, then what else is she?" he coughed out. "You have the ring, you have no need for a Maiden anyway."

I let out a feral cry, yanking my fist free and punching him once more. "She's… my… *dragaria*," I said in between punches.

Immediately, I felt strong hands pulling me off Fangburn, and turned to punch whoever stopped me, only to stop short at the sight of Hiram holding my shoulder, his eyes kind.

"I knew it. That was why your flame turned blue and the glowing happened earlier today," he said gently.

I felt a cold realization wash over me with what I had done. I had attacked my ally. I turned to Fangburn, ready to apologize.

He stood and wiped the blood from his face, spitting on the ground. "Your *dragaria*, huh?" he asked with a cheeky smile. "She must be someone very special then. I've never heard of a *dragaria* being human before."

From behind me, I could hear whispers and murmurs making their way through camp. My outburst must have been loud enough for everyone to hear. I looked up the mountain, where Valora most likely was. Right now, I would not have been surprised if somehow Borthen found this information out. My anger had been out of control. I could only imagine how he would use this as a pawn in his sick game.

"Lord Fangburn, I'm sorry," I said, the words stumbling to come out.

He only smiled and clapped me on the shoulder. "I'm glad you finally found her," he said. "It was about time our High Dragon Lord found his *dragaria*. I had heard stories that you were unusually close to her, now it all makes sense why." He chuckled, shaking his head. "I can only imagine what you're going through," he said, immediately sobering up. "If my *dragaria* was kidnapped, I would destroy the entire world to get her back again." He wiped his bleeding lip once more. "I'm surprised you showed such restraint with me."

Hiram came forward and bowed deeply, the other Lords following suit. "We will help you however we can to get your *dragaria* back, my Lord," he said.

I looked back up the mountain, pinpointing one of the entrances. "First, we'll have to kill everyone to get to her," I said grimly. "We start at dawn. Anyone who resists must die."

CHAPTER THIRTY-TWO

VALORA

The next morning—or what I would assume was morning—I awoke with a raw throat and gritty eyes, having cried all night long. The pain upon finding out Dracul was the reason my family died and I'd been so scarred was agonizing. I could only imagine what sick pleasure Borthen got out of revealing that information to me, at driving this new wedge between Dracul and myself. I pulled myself over to the pail of water and splashed some on my face, waking me up instantly to this cold new reality I had found myself in.

Borthen arrived shortly after I awoke, an unreadable expression on his face. He scrutinized me from afar as I hunched in the corner, glaring at him. I could sense his eyes carefully examining every part of my body: my bloodshot eyes, my sniffling nose, and my slight trembling. After several minutes of silently staring at the other, he finally spoke.

"I heard interesting news last night," he said, inspecting his fingernails, pretending to be disinterested. "Would you like to hear it?"

"Not particularly," I mumbled, continuing to glare at him.

"Well, I'm sure you'll be glad to know that your precious Dracul's army thoroughly defeated mine yesterday," he said.

I closed my eyes, angry at myself for how happy I was at this news. Dracul was alive and well. He had done it.

When I opened my eyes, Borthen stared at me more intensely. "Do you know what *dragaria* means?" he asked.

My brain took a moment to take in this sudden change of subject. "No," I said, shaking my head. This was now the second time the phrase had been brought up—Kessland being the first. Just as I had promised Dracul, I had not asked or investigated the term any further.

"*Dragaria* is a special draconic term," he said, his golden eyes glittering ominously. "It's how we refer to our mate, our other half."

"Why are you telling me this?" I asked warily.

"We don't get to choose our *dragaria*," he continued, watching me closely. "It's something that we innately know once we see them for the first time. We feel an unexplainable pull to them and they feel the same to us. It's almost… magical." He paused, checking for any reaction from me. When he received none, he continued. "In your time with our *precious* Lord, have you felt anything like this?"

"No," I lied, an uncomfortable feeling growing within me. What Borthen described was exactly how I felt with Dracul. But that was impossible—he was a dragon and I was a human. There was no way I could be his *dragaria*. It could only be a silly one-sided crush on my side. Not to mention, his actions were the reason that I had gone through so much pain. I shook my head. There was no way I was Dracul's *dragaria*.

"Interesting," Borthen said in a clipped tone. He stared at me for several moments. "That will be all for today, I think." He pulled a hunk of dried meat from his pocket and tossed it to me, and it landed about a foot away from where I huddled. "Well, I leave you to your thoughts." As he did yesterday, he dramatically leapt from the dome, and I heard the sound of his wings once again.

Ravenously, I grabbed the piece of meat and began to gobble it down, not having eaten since early yesterday. I remained huddled in the corner, wrapped in the thin blanket, my thoughts tormenting me into an uneasy sleep once more.

CHAPTER THIRTY-THREE

DRACUL

Early the next morning, before dawn stretched over the skies, we attacked. I led the charge through the entrance I had spotted the night before, Firenze and Fangburn at my sides with the others close behind. The two measly guards Borthen had keeping watch were nothing to me—my claws killed them instantly, coating me in blood. I could feel Lora's presence nearby and let that feeling guide me as I raced through the halls, unreservedly slashing anyone who crossed my path. I did not care if my warriors or Lords followed me—my mind was set on one goal: rescuing Valora.

After several minutes of running and bloodshed, I paused, trying to sense the direction of her presence. A human servant turned the corner and yelped in fear. Instantly, I pounced, pinning them to the ground.

"The woman your Lord took, where is she?" I demanded, my teeth dangerously close to their face. I smelled the odor of urine and wrinkled my nose in disgust.

"Down the hall, that way," they said, pointing to a corridor to my left.

As soon as the words left their mouth, I launched myself off them, not bothering to kill them, and heard Firenze and

Fangburn following me. We encountered no one as we entered a large cave filled with weird domes lining the walls all the way to the ceiling. From what I could tell, they seemed empty, except I could feel a presence in only one, almost all the way at the top on the right. I flapped my wings, gaining altitude to see who was there, holding my breath that it was her.

When I reached the dome, I peered in. My heart skipped a beat. Lying on her side in the corner was Lora, wrapped in a blanket. Her eyes looked red as she moved to look at me, her expression unbelieving.

"It's you," she said softly. "You came for me."

I transformed into my human self, holding out my arms for her. "I always will."

She rushed towards me, crushing me in her embrace. Tears soaked into my neck as she buried her face there, sobs wracking her frame.

"You're safe now, Lora," I said, holding her tightly. "Never again will he hurt you."

CHAPTER THIRTY-FOUR

VALORA

He was there. Dracul had come for me. I stared at him in disbelief, my traitor heart pounding at the sight of him. I did not care that he was dirty or covered in blood—all that I cared about at this moment was that he was there. I pushed all the thoughts that Borthen had left with me deep into the recesses of my mind. I just needed to focus on Dracul. Now that he was there, everything would be fine.

I rushed to him, holding him as tightly as I could, sobs breaking from me. My captivity with Borthen had been short, but torturous. Seeing Dracul there, unharmed and well, was enough to break me. I sobbed into his neck, my hands scrambling to clutch him to me. His arms encircled me, as well, holding me just as tightly as I held him, giving me much needed relief. He murmured sweet, tender words to me, but I could not hear them over the rushing sound in my ears.

Eventually, I could make out his words. "I need to get you out of here," he said over and over again. "We need to go, Lora."

Wordlessly, I nodded and I felt him pick me up, moving towards the edge of the dome's floor.

"Hold on tight," he said before transforming into a dragon, holding me securely in his claws as he navigated us downwards.

To my surprise, he had two Lords with him—Lord Firenze and Lord Fangburn. In the hallways, I could hear fighting going on, lots of screaming.

"Well done," Lord Fangburn said, beaming at me as we landed.

I turned away, tucking my head into Lord Dracul's chest as he still held me with one claw.

"What do we do now?"

"We find Borthen and end him," Dracul said stiffly, his grip on me tightening.

"No need, Dracul. I'm already here." Borthen's voice came from behind us.

I squeezed my eyes shut at his honeyed voice.

"I see you've found your Maiden."

"What was the point of this, Borthen?" Dracul asked. I could feel him shaking in anger. "Your forces were a mere distraction. You never stood a chance."

"You and I duel, one on one," Borthen hissed. "I want my revenge for what you stole from me."

"I didn't take anything that wasn't already rightfully mine," Dracul said. He set me down, pushing me towards Lord Firenze, who stood in front of me protectively. "But I will grant you this one last request. Before you die."

The two dragons circled each other in the large cavern. I figured the domes would cause problems logistically and watched with growing apprehension.

"Lord Dracul is an excellent fighter," Lord Fangburn said quietly to me, and I looked at him in surprise. He was trying to comfort me.

Borthen struck first, launching with his jaws in an attempt to bite Dracul, who took to the air to get away. The bronze dragon swiftly followed, and the two began a deadly dance of claws, jaws, and fire. Dracul singed Borthen's shoulder before getting slammed into one of the domes by Borthen's tail, collapsing it from the force.

"You'll have to do better than that," Borthen crowed before letting out a fireball of his own, Dracul just barely able to dodge it. "You can't be fully healed just yet. You're slower than you usually are."

Though I had never seen Dracul fight before, from what I had seen of his flying, Borthen was right. He moved a tad slower than the bronze dragon, and I watched as Dracul continued to take blow after blow, rivulets of blood steadily streaming down his body. But he did not give up and managed to seriously injure Borthen, taking a chunk out of his leg and chest.

After several minutes, both were winded, breathing heavily while resting briefly on different domes. Borthen decided to use this time to gloat more.

"Loyalty does not run strong within your clan, Dracul," he sneered. "I have been kept abreast of your activities. Your Dragon Maiden there has made enemies for herself." My stomach dropped at his words. "You should have chosen more wisely instead of picking an outsider like her. Her enemies have become your enemies."

Dracul let out several short bursts of fire, catching Borthen off guard, but he still managed to dodge at the last second.

"Who has been spying for you?" Dracul hissed, anger lacing his tone.

Borthen let out another laugh. "Come here and force the answer out of me," he taunted.

A look of surprise crossed his face when Dracul immediately launched himself towards the other dragon, sinking his claws deep into his flesh. Dracul threw his whole body at him, sending them off the dome. They both plummeted towards the ground, Dracul angling their bodies so Borthen would take the brunt of the fall. My mouth opened in a silent scream as they landed with a giant crash. Debris from the impact flew towards us, but both Lord Firenze and Lord Fangburn used their bodies to protect me from the blast.

When the dust cleared, we saw Dracul slumped to the side of the cave and Borthen lying on the ground coughing up blood.

With much effort, Dracul dragged himself over to Borthen, putting a claw to his throat. "Tell me who was spying for you," he said. "And I may give you an easy death."

Borthen laughed, a gurgling sound as he coughed up more blood. "You might want to check with your friend over there," he said, gesturing to the three of us.

Dracul looked up, his gaze hard before swiping his claw, ending Borthen's struggling. Once he knew Borthen was done for, he stalked towards us, scooping me up in a claw once more. "Firenze, what has your Maiden been up to?" he asked in a low voice. "Have you been keeping an eye on her?"

My gaze shifted between Dracul and Lord Firenze, my mind trying to keep up with the conclusion Dracul had drawn based on Borthen's ambiguous hints. Surely, he could not mean that Vimery had been handing secrets over to Borthen?

Lord Firenze bowed his head. "I'm afraid I have not been able to keep as close an eye on her as I usually would," he said. "I've been too busy, but when we return, I will make sure to interrogate her thoroughly. A weak link in our forces will not be tolerated."

"See that you do." Dracul nodded. He limped along before I held a hand to his chest and he looked at me.

"I can walk," I said softly. "You're injured. Because of me."

He shook his head, clutching me more tightly to him. "I'm never letting go of you again, Lora," he said.

We entered one of the main hallways where fighting was still going on. I heard the sound of screaming and could smell the blood, not to mention the bodies that littered the hallway.

"What's going on?" I asked.

"We're wiping out the entire clan," Dracul said grimly. "Anyone aligned with Borthen is being executed."

The expression on his face scared me and I felt dread deep in my stomach. Right now, he was acting just like Borthen—

punishing others for one person's mistakes. I had to struggle against the urge to vomit.

"No, Dracul," I said. "You can't do that."

He looked at me, his eyes stony. "They must pay the price of their allegiance to him," he said.

"Dracul," I snapped.

His eyes cleared suddenly, as if he finally could see me without the bloody haze he had settled into.

"You can't do this. You'd be no better than him," I said. "Show mercy to those who would bow to you, to those who would show remorse. Do better."

After a tense moment where I thought he would not listen, he nodded. "Call the others off," he directed to Lord Firenze and Lord Fangburn. "If there are those who would plead for mercy, show them mercy. Anyone who fights must be killed. Is that understood?"

The two nodded before going to relay his orders.

Dracul turned back to me. "Is that sufficient?" he asked.

Silently, I nodded, at a loss for words. Never before had I seen him act this cruelly and callously. The dragon holding me was not one that I had seen before. Thinking back on what Borthen said, I wondered if I had ever really known him at all. I knew that Dracul could be strict with others, but never had I seen a cruel side to him. Shamelessly slaughtering innocents without a care was not the dragon I had come to know.

"We should go home now," he said, carefully placing me on his back before giving further instructions to a messenger that whoever was spared was to be brought to the Shadowvale Mountains to swear their allegiance. After everyone returned, there was to be a feast to celebrate our victory.

Then, at long last, he took to the skies and we flew back home together. Never before had I felt so lonely and lost.

CHAPTER THIRTY-FIVE

VALORA

Everyone returned to the Shadowvale Mountains less than a day after we did. The caves were quickly packed with Lord Fangburn's forces, as well as the new refugees that had surrendered. As soon as they returned, Dracul held a ceremony where the refugees swore allegiance to him, but I did not attend. Instead, I heard all the details from Alonsa, who Dracul had ordered to care for me as soon as I insisted on staying in the Dragon Maiden cavern. I could not stand to be alone with him right now.

Since we'd returned, I'd been forced to deal with Borthen's revelation of Dracul's past, and it consumed my thoughts. I was unable to eat, unable to sleep. I could only lay listlessly in bed. Alonsa stayed by my side, encouraging me to eat, but any food I ate was immediately expelled. The other Maidens did not talk to me, but I could tell that they were confused and concerned about my sudden change in behavior. I could not find it in myself to care about their opinions. I could hear the vague, hushed whispers and the awkward quiet that would settle when one of them accidentally made eye contact with me.

Upon Lord Firenze's return, Vimery was swiftly removed from the Dragon Maiden chamber and no one knew what had happened to her. Her whereabouts were kept secret. The Maidens were not stupid—they knew her disappearance had something to do with me, but in my catatonic state, they knew better than to ask questions.

Dracul came to check on me multiple times a day, always in his human form so he could come to my bedside. I could hear him and Alonsa talking about my worsening condition, but I always closed my eyes, unable to focus on their words. Often, he would try to hold my hand, but his touch repulsed me and I always pulled away. Each time, he willingly let me go and did not push.

About a week after I returned, Gwen and Hyacinth dumped cold water on me. I shot up, shocked at the sudden cold and gawked at them, spitting water out of my mouth. Their eyes were stony as they stared at me.

Alonsa spluttered in anger. "How dare you two do that! She's been through enough as it is. What do you think you're doing?"

"We wanted to shock her out of whatever funk she's in," Gwen said. She looked to me. "Did it work?"

For the first time since I had returned, my mind was clear— the cold water had shocked my haze of thoughts out of me. My mouth gaped open and I nodded. "Yes," I said. Feeling suddenly rushed through my body instead of the deadened husk I had grown into. Though the thoughts still swirled around, they no longer caused the paralysis I had been feeling.

"Can you eat something?" Alonsa asked, pushing a bowl of soup towards me hesitantly.

My stomach growled angrily and I picked up the bowl, forcing myself to eat slowly. The warm broth slid down my throat, warming my stomach, and I sighed in content. No longer did I feel the urge to vomit when eating food.

There was a noise from the door and everyone turned to look, me included.

Dracul stood in shock, staring at me. "You're feeling better?" he asked hopefully, practically sprinting down the steps to my side. "You can eat?" He looked to Alonsa for confirmation, who nodded.

"Yes, my Lord. I'm sorry for having worried you," I said, formality sliding into place. I was not ready to face him yet, to confront him with what I knew. Still, I felt a yearning for him to take me in his arms, to tell me that everything would be fine, and I hated myself for it.

He looked at me, confusion in his eyes. "Valora, you are my Maiden," Dracul said, moving his hand towards my face before I flinched and he pulled away. "Of course I'm worried about you." He suddenly took in my soaked appearance. "Why are you wet?"

Alonsa spoke up. "Gwen and Hyacinth were able to shock her out of whatever was wrong with her," she said. "My Lord," she continued gently. "Valora has been through a lot. I suggest maybe you give her more time to rest before you come back. Let her take a relaxing soak in the pool and we can let you know when she's ready to see you."

Dracul looked lost, but nodded. "Yes, that sounds… like a good idea," he said at last. "Valora, I will be here when you are ready for me, be it day or night." He directed his instructions to the other Maidens. "Do not hesitate to call for me whenever she wants."

The four Maidens looked at me after he left. I could see the questions in their eyes.

"What happened?" Bethany asked, the first to speak up.

I shook my head, putting the empty bowl down. "I don't want to talk about it," I said, my voice hoarse.

Thankfully, the others let the subject drop.

"You should take a bath," Alonsa said. "If you wish, we can help you."

The thought of bathing on my own was suddenly very overwhelming, and I nodded gratefully. "Yes, please," I said weakly.

Together, the Maidens prepared my bath and undressed me before Alonsa gently led me to the warm water. Thankfully, no one mentioned my scars, and I leaned back against the wall of the pool as the warm, pulsating water massaged my aching muscles and bones. Carefully, they bathed me in silence, somehow knowing that I needed to be treated delicately. After they were done, Bethany gathered up a soft set of pajamas and they helped me get dressed before tucking me into bed.

"We are here for you, Valora," Alonsa said, and with that encouragement, I fell fast asleep.

Chapter Thirty-Six

VALORA

Over the next couple of days, I was able to resume my duties, though I still tried to keep a distance between myself and Dracul, much to his obvious chagrin. I kept busy with the other Maidens, helping prepare for the victory banquet, and that luckily kept me away from the High Dragon Lord for most of the day. All the dragons I came across bowed to me, the sudden change was so jarring that I always checked behind myself to ensure there was not someone more important that they actually bowed to. I asked Alonsa about it, but if she knew the reason, she did not tell me.

The night before the banquet, Dracul managed to corner me alone after everyone had trailed off to bed after finishing preparations for the festivities. I had insisted on staying awake to prepare the final touches on each of the tables.

"Lora, we need to talk," he said, using my nickname now that no one was around.

I said nothing as I continued to arrange the centerpieces— vases filled with navy and teal flowers to represent Dracul and Fangburn.

"Valora, please stop and look at me."

I stopped and stood still, looking at his face, which was filled with sadness. His human face showed more emotion than his dragon face did, and right now, I wished he was in his latter form so I would not feel the prickles of guilt.

"What happened?" he asked. "When I left, we were so close and now… I don't understand what's going on."

I swallowed past the sudden lump in my throat. I could hear the pain in his voice and knowing that I was the cause was not easy. Once more, turmoil filled me at the feelings I felt for Dracul. I should not be feeling these things towards someone whose actions orchestrated the death of my parents and my suffering.

I bit my lip, trying to will away the tears that threatened to fall.

"Did Borthen do something to you?" he asked, taking a step closer to me. "You can tell me whatever is bothering you. You're just so… far away these days. Like you're purposefully distancing yourself."

"And if I am?" I asked, my voice choked with tears.

"I want to know why, Lora," he said, holding his hands out towards me, pleading with me. "I want you to tell me what happened or what I did wrong so I can try and fix it. But if you leave me in the dark, there's nothing I can do."

I shook my head at his words.

"I told you before that I would wait until you're ready to tell me," he said.

Tears began to pour down my cheeks as he reminded me of how sweet he had been all those months ago. Before any of this had been brought to light.

"And I will wait for you again." His voice broke slightly as he wiped away a tear. "I just want you to look at me the way you did before."

"How do I look at you now?" I asked.

"You avoid me," he said quietly. "If I enter a room, you practically flee. And if you do happen to glance my way, your eyes are cold. Never before have I felt this distance, this coldness from you. Even when you were first brought here, your anger was red hot."

I hugged myself, trying to ignore the agony ripping through my chest. "I can't talk about it," I said. "Not now, maybe not ever."

"Just promise me that if you are ready to talk about, you won't hesitate to come to me," he begged.

I nodded before leaving the room, no longer able to hold in my emotions and unable to see him in such pain. I ran to the Dragon Maiden cavern and threw myself on my bed, sobbing into my pillow. After a couple moments, I felt someone rubbing my back, whispering words of comfort.

"This will pass," Alonsa said, rubbing circles on my back. "Everything will be fine, you'll see."

That night as I fell asleep, I recalled Kessland's prophecy to me, that the road would be difficult, but I should like the ending. I wondered now if this was what they had meant, that this discovery would be difficult to process, but that eventually, I would be able to forgive Dracul. The thought gave me a little comfort, enough for me to fall asleep without much issue.

* * *

At the banquet the next day, everyone was in good spirits. I sat a few tables away from Dracul with the other Maidens. He had Lord Fangburn and the other Lords sitting at his side instead. I was not sure if he did not want me to sit next to him or if he was giving me the space that I had obviously been wanting. Either way, I still noticed his subtle glances at me, his gaze setting me ablaze.

When the banquet was well underway, Dracul stood, lifting his goblet for a toast. Everyone quieted, waiting to hear what he had to say. "I thank you all for attending," he said. "In light of recent events, I think it is only fair that we drink in tribute to our fallen comrades. They were brave and honorable, everything a dragon should be." He took a sip from his chalice, and everyone else followed. Then he lifted it again. "And I would like to toast to our victory against the Starfire clan. They were worthy opponents. For the part that he played in helping us defeat Borthen, I would like to place the Starfire clan under Lord Fangburn's responsibility."

There was shocked silence at the announcement before cheers rang out throughout the hall.

"That is unexpected," Alonsa said quietly, loud enough for me to hear.

"Why?" I asked, turning to her.

"With both the Starfire and Twisturn clans under his control, Lord Fangburn has control over a majority of the dragon population," she said.

Lord Fangburn stood and the cheers quieted down. "I would like all of my warriors to approach," he said, coming to stand in front of the head table. When everyone was assembled, he bowed before Dracul and his fighters followed suit. "I, Lord Fangburn, of the Twisturn and Starfire clans, pledge my fealty and service to High Lord Dracul of the Shadowvale clan," he said, bowing his head in submission. The dragons behind him repeated the same oath.

"Your Lord hears your oath and accepts it," Dracul said, smiling. "Let us consecrate the pact in fire."

Lord Fangburn stood and approached Dracul. They grasped each other's arms and breathed fire at their joined fists. The flames turned a bright red, and cheers once again sounded around the room. It seemed as if their pact had been sealed. The other dragons approached Dracul and completed the same act, the red flame appearing each time.

"What does that mean?" I whispered to Alonsa as I watched what happened.

"If any of them goes against his oath, his life will be forfeit. He will die," she said. "Something in the draconic magic makes this binding."

"Now we have one more piece of business to attend to," Dracul said. He gestured to someone in the back of the room. "We have a traitor in our midst who must be punished."

Silence filled the room as Vimery was dragged to the front. The other Maidens gasped in horror. The fallen Dragon Maiden looked ghastly. She had not been treated well this past month.

Her face and hair were dirty, her clothes ripped and stained. She looked at the floor as she was brought before the Dragon Lords.

"Vimery Cottonthrall," Dracul said, his voice filling the room. "You have been found guilty of leaking Shadowvale secrets to our known enemy. You have betrayed the clan, your fellow Maidens, and most importantly, your Lord. Do you have anything to say for yourself?"

From my vantage point, I could see that Vimery trembled, tears falling down her face, leaving tracks in the dirt that had gathered there. She looked at the ground and silently shook her head.

"Since you forfeit that right, your Lord will now deal with you," Dracul said, sitting down and motioning for Lord Firenze.

Lord Firenze stood to his full height and walked to stand in front of Vimery. He leaned close and whispered a few words to her. She began to sob, her cries echoing throughout the cavern. A quick glance at the other Maidens and I could see tears in their eyes. She spoke a few quiet words to him, but not loud enough for anyone to hear.

With a nod, Lord Firenze took a step away from her. "Your punishment is death," he said.

Alonsa gasped, holding her hands to her mouth in horror.

In one quick breath, Lord Firenze let out a blast of fire, and I flinched at the heat. Vimery opened her mouth in a quiet scream before falling to the ground. It seemed that as a final act of mercy, Lord Firenze had made her death as quick and painless as possible. When she was reduced to a pile of ash, he stopped before bowing his head and walking back to the table.

A couple servants came forward and took Vimery's remains away. Gwen and Hyacinth were trying to hold back sobs, and I made eye contact with Dracul. He stared at me, a stony expression on his face. From the look in his eyes, I could tell that he had wanted her to suffer a more painful death, but accepted Lord Firenze's way of ending things.

"I thought a Maiden couldn't be harmed by her Lord's fire?" I asked Alonsa, handing her a handkerchief to wipe her eyes.

Gratefully, she took it and dabbed at her face. "Unless she has betrayed her Lord, then that is the case," she said. "But once Lord Firenze declared her a traitor, he had the power to kill her with fire. It is also better for the Lord if he's the one to kill his Maiden. The pain he feels is significantly lessened."

I sat back in my seat, nodding slowly. The stipulation made sense—if a Maiden betrayed her Lord, that was unforgivable. To my surprise, I felt a twinge of sadness for Vimery, that she had been driven by her hatred of me to betray the clan and Lord Firenze. From what Borthen had said and what Dracul had revealed after her interrogation, she had spilled Shadowvale clan secrets and helped orchestrate my capture to get me out of the way. She had not even cared if she endangered Dracul in the process.

The room slowly returned to its usual buzz of conversation. Music and laughter filled the air, but the other Maidens and I stayed in our seats, a somber air around our table. At least the dragons seemed to be enjoying themselves. Unlike the last banquet, the Lords did not approach us for dancing, knowing how devastated the other Maidens were at Vimery's loss. A few times, Dracul and I made eye contact, but every time, I was the one to break it first.

* * *

After an hour or so, I noticed five odd figures on the outskirts of the crowd, slowly making their way towards our table. They wore cloaks and covered their faces so it was impossible to see if they were dragon or human. When they were mere feet away, all drew swords, aiming them at us. Once more, immediate silence descended on the hall. In my peripheral vision, I could see Bethany clutching to Alonsa, beginning to sob softly. Gwen and Hyacinth looked pale, but remained still. I waited, too, examining what I could of the figures. One of them had a familiar air about them.

Dracul stood, his chair scraping against the ground. I glanced at him briefly, but his eyes were trained on the interloper closest to me. "Who are you? What do you want?" he growled, starting to move closer to us.

"I received an interesting message about your newest Maiden," the one closest to me said, the clear leader of the group. "And I needed to investigate." He removed his hood, and I cried out in recognition. "Hello, Valora," he said, looking at me, lowering his sword. Ronan now had a new scar across his cheek and his black hair was shorn short. The biggest change was within his brown eyes—rather than the smiling, kind Ronan I once knew, this one was calloused.

"Ronan!" I rushed towards him, enveloping him in a hug. I could hear murmurs in the background, but paid them no mind. "I haven't seen you in so long. So much has happened."

"That's what it sounds like," he said, his arms tightening around me. "I'm sorry I wasn't able to protect you from being taken by these monsters." I could hear the hatred filling his voice.

I pulled away from him. He needed to know about what happened. "Becoming a Dragon Maiden isn't all that happened," I said hesitantly. "There's so much I need to tell you."

"What is it?" His dark brows furrowed in concern, his eyes darting to glare at Dracul.

"A year after you left, men came," I explained, my voice shaking. "They ransacked the house and… and killed Mother and Father. They're gone, Ronan."

He nodded silently, seemingly unsurprised.

My blood ran cold. "Wait. Did… did you know about this?"

"I did," he confirmed.

A gasp escaped me, and I stepped away from him, my mouth open in horror.

"But there was nothing to be done. By the time I had heard what happened, it was too late."

"And you didn't think to come looking for me?" I whispered, betrayal creeping into my voice.

In my peripheral vision, I could see Dracul shifting. It seemed the visitors were quickly beginning to wear out their short stay.

"I looked everywhere for you. I was following you."

"It was too dangerous," Ronan explained. "I couldn't come back."

His eyes showed the pain he felt, but he looked very different from the brother I used to know. With a chill, I realized I did not know him at all. The past years had changed both of us drastically. Anger filled me. His actions had had consequences.

"You don't understand—"

I slapped him, the sound ringing through the cavern, interrupting his excuses.

He held his reddening cheek in shock.

"I know very well what you did," I hissed. "Borthen told me *everything*."

His mouth dropped open in shock, and I could sense Dracul moving.

"But the consequences of your actions were a price you didn't even consider. You stayed with him. You *knew* how he was! How he would punish you for your crimes! Our parents were killed because of *you*," I spat out.

He took a step back from me, away from my anger.

"I was forced to watch, and then they turned on me, Ronan! Do you understand that? They cut me and cut me and cut me until they grew tired and left me for dead. I was left in the house with our dead parents, slowly bleeding to death while they set the house on fire." I pulled up my sleeves to reveal the scars, my voice rising in both volume and pitch. "And you weren't there! You promised you would always be there to protect me, Ronan, and you weren't." A tear slipped down my cheek.

"I'm sorry, I truly am," he said, taking a step towards me.

I backed away, shaking my head. "Your apology means nothing," I said. "I thought I wanted to see you to get answers and have you rescue me. But everything you've done has turned you into a complete stranger, a monster. The Ronan I knew would never have betrayed his family like this."

Ronan let out a hollow laugh. "You don't think *they* are the monsters?" he asked, pointing at Dracul, whose eyes had grown wide. "*He's* the one who commissioned me to steal the ring in the first place! And when I found out that you would be attacked, I rushed to him asking for help, but he refused, he sent me away! So I ask you, dear sister, who is the monster now?"

Dracul stepped forward. "I think we should take this discussion somewhere private," he said, glancing around the room.

At this point, I realized that the entire banquet hall had heard everything, their eyes glued to Ronan and I. My face flushed as I brushed past my brother, leaving the hall. Footsteps sounded after me and I knew Dracul and Ronan had followed. The banquet room remained quiet for several moments before the chatter of whispers began to rise.

I led the way to Dracul's cavern and sat on the couch, crossing my arms as the men came to stand in front of me. They both stared at me, refusing to look at each other, trying to judge my current emotions.

"Well?" I asked after several moments when neither said anything. "What do you have to say for yourselves?"

Both flinched at my venom.

"You don't seem shocked to know that Lord Dracul hired me," Ronan said, tilting his head at the unspoken question.

"Borthen told me that," I said in a clipped tone.

Dracul's face paled and his eyes widened. "Is that why you've been so distant?" he asked, his gaze clearing as if everything made sense now.

"*I'm* the one asking questions here," I said, giving him a scathing look. He at least had the decency to look ashamed. "Now, I know the ring gives you the power of a Lord who has a Maiden without actually having one. Was staying alone this whole time really worth everything that has come after?"

Dracul looked at me, his eyes pleading with me to understand. "I was unable to take the title of High Dragon Lord without a Maiden," he said. "Lying and saying I had the ring was the best way to move forward. Any delay in the process and Borthen could have easily gained support for becoming High Dragon Lord himself. And then when I found out he actually *had* found the ring, I knew there was no time to waste. I needed to have it in my possession."

"Then what was the point of appointing me as your Dragon Maiden?" I asked.

He came and knelt in front of me, reminding me of that time so long ago when he consoled my worries about the Dragon Maiden ceremony. "You mean so much to me, Valora, more than words can express," he said softly.

My breath caught in my throat. The tenderness in his expression and the heat from his eyes weakened my resolve, and I could feel myself leaning towards him.

Gently, he took my hands in his. "Ever since you came here, I've felt a connection to you, something I never even hoped to experience. I hope you know me well enough by now to know that I keep my word and that when I say that I never meant to hurt you, I mean it."

"I… I…" I wanted to say I did not believe him, the words were on the tip of my tongue, but they just would not come out.

Dracul's expression turned intense, heat rolling off him. In a fluid movement, he leaned forward, capturing my lips with his. There was an urgency yet softness to his kiss as he gently pulled me towards him, his arms circling my waist. After the initial shock, I could feel my body yielding to him, wrapping my arms around his neck. The heat that I felt so often around him flared up into a blaze. Now my feelings were staring me in the face and I could no longer ignore them. I had fallen in love with the High Dragon Lord and it seemed he harbored the same feelings for me. The thought made me giddy and lightheaded.

After a few moments, he pulled away, his chest rising and falling rapidly. It seemed the kiss affected him as much as it did me. I could tell my cheeks were flushed.

"I'm sorry," he said, putting a hand to his head.

Mischievousness rose up within me. "Why?" I asked. "Because you stopped?"

His eyes darkened with lust as he tried to hold back a grin. "For getting carried away," he said. "Now was not the right moment." From his uncertain expression, I could tell he was nervous about how I interpreted his actions.

I grabbed the lapel of his robes, pulling him towards me, crushing our lips together. I could feel him stiffen in surprise before his body loosened and he dragged a hand through my hair. The feeling was exquisite.

Eventually, I pulled away, my eyes searching his face. "Well?" I asked when it did not seem like he would say anything.

Dracul rubbed the back of his neck self-consciously. "I wasn't expecting that," he admitted. "Though I am doing my best to hold back right now, I don't think your brother appreciates the display. Not to mention, we still have topics to discuss."

I looked to Ronan, having completely forgotten about him, a stricken expression on my face.

He stared at both of us in shock before shaking his head. "I suppose if you can forgive him enough to kiss him, then I guess I don't have much to say," he said at last.

"Really?" I asked, sensing that right now, this was as close to getting his blessing as I could get.

He shrugged. "I guess so."

My questions from earlier came flooding back. "I have more questions for you," I said, and Ronan's expression dropped. "Why did you leave all those years ago? I heard part of the fight that day. I know that's part of the reason. But I just don't understand why."

He visibly swallowed and I could see that it was hard for him to tell me what happened. "Father and I fought and we both said things that we shouldn't have. He basically said that it would be best if I left. It was hard for me to leave, but I knew he was right, that I should set off on my own. I was getting tired of being cooped up and never being allowed to go anywhere. After I left, I got mixed in with bad people. The only way to leave was to join a group that worked for Lord Dracul. He sent us to retrieve the ring and we infiltrated as Borthen's servants. When we disappeared right after it was stolen, it wasn't hard to figure out that it was us. In retaliation, they sent people after our families. The other guys have no one left now. By the time I found out, it was too late, there was nothing I could do." His eyes took on a tortured look and I went to him, giving him a hug. "I never meant for it all to happen," he whispered. "But it did, and I have no one to blame but myself."

"Ronan, I…" I took a deep breath, trying to wrap my mind around everything. "When you left, I could not understand why, and when the men came, I blamed you for a long time. I searched for you, trying to dredge up every ounce of information I could about where you were, to find you and ask what happened. It was difficult, having to live on my own, figure out everything by myself." I pulled away from him, unable to meet his eyes. "I could only get Father's book of stories and Mother's brooch out. I had to leave everything else behind." Tears spilled as the memories I thought I had conquered came rushing forward.

"I'm sorry."

"It was horrible," I choked out, needing to tell him. "The smoke grew so thick that I couldn't breathe, but I managed to get out through the back door. They had left right after setting the house on fire, thinking I was too injured to move. They wanted me to suffocate and burn to death—they laughed after they left."

Dracul came up behind me, wrapping me in his arms. I leaned into his embrace and closed my eyes, trying to ground myself in this moment.

"I'm sorry, Lora," Dracul murmured. "I should have sent people to protect you. But at the time, I didn't see the point in..." He trailed off, unable to finish his sentence.

"In protecting a useless human family that you didn't know?" I, on the other hand, had no such qualms. "I understand your reasoning. You had gotten what you wanted. We didn't matter."

He buried his face in the crook of my neck, breathing deeply. "I'm sorry," he said, his voice muffled. "I would do anything to go back and redo that moment."

"Even if it meant we never would have met?" I asked softly.

Dracul let out a snort. "I don't know if I would go that far," he said. He turned me to face him, his expression solemn. "Although there is one thing I need to tell you, Valora."

My heart stopped at how serious he seemed. He'd used my full name. "Another secret to share?" I asked.

"I wish there was a better way to tell you. I had a whole plan, but the timing just hasn't lined up," he said, shifting slightly from foot to foot. "But my feelings for you? You're my *dragaria*."

Ronan gasped at his words, and I nodded, having felt it deep within me. Since returning, Borthen's explanation had stuck with me and I realized that I had been most afraid of being wrong, that I was not Dracul's *dragaria* and that my feelings were one-sided. But now, knowing that he felt the same way for me, it was impossible to ignore.

"Do you know what a *dragaria* is?" Dracul asked.

"Borthen said that it means I'm your mate," I said.

"And... how do you feel about that?" Dracul was hesitant. I could tell he was nervous about my answer.

"Well, how much of our feelings has to do with that bond rather than our own true feelings?" I asked.

A smile slowly crossed over his face when he heard my question. "'Our' feelings?" he asked. "You feel the same way?"

"Even if my arrival here wasn't what I wanted at the time," I said, "you have shown me such kindness. It would have been so difficult not to fall in love with you, Dracul. I've felt this pull to you, this connection, and I've tried to fight it." My voice dropped. "I've tried to fight it for so long."

"And why is that?" Dracul asked, his brow furrowing in concern.

"Because you're the High Dragon Lord," I whispered. "And I'm a human. I didn't think something like that was allowed. I thought it was a foolish hope to have."

"Valora, listen to me." He put his hands on either side of my face, his eyes molten silver. "A *dragaria* is the most sacred bond in our society. To refuse or reject your *dragaria* is seen as a grave sin. While you being human may have… difficulties, once others find out you're my *dragaria*, they'll have no choice but to accept you. This isn't something I take lightly, I want you to know that."

"But how do I know you really care for me and not just because of this *dragaria* bond?" I asked.

Dracul came forward and kissed my head. "Lora, I think even without the bond, I would have fallen for you," he said. "You are so full of spirit and somehow always manage to surprise me."

Tears filled my eyes as I embraced him, holding him tightly to me. I could hear the rhythmic thumping of his heart, and my chest felt like it would burst. His arms wrapped around my upper body and he patted my head, smoothing my hair.

"So what happens next?" I ask.

"Next, we officially introduce you to the clans as my *dragaria*," he said. "Although those who fought alongside me against Borthen all know."

"What?" I pulled back from him, my voice rising in pitch. "What do you mean?"

Dracul rubbed the back of his neck. "Well, I might have accidentally let it slip rather loudly when Lord Fangburn said that you being captured wasn't a big deal. I pummeled him pretty good."

"And he wasn't mad?" I asked.

"I told you, a *dragaria* is one of our most sacred bonds," he said. "More than anything, everyone was happy that I found my mate."

Something finally clicked in my mind. "Is that why everyone has been bowing to me since we returned?" I asked.

He let out a chuckle. "Yes, I would imagine that would be why," he said.

"If you are Lord Dracul's *dragaria*," Ronan said, "then I guess I have no choice but to give you my blessing. That's a lifelong bond."

"But Dracul's still going to outlive me," I pointed out. "Being a Dragon Maiden elongates my life, but nowhere near the lifespan of a dragon."

"Lord Hiram has been doing research," Dracul said. "He has found in cases where a dragon has had an exceptionally long life, their *dragaria* has lived a similar lifespan as well. I don't know how it works, but I would assume it may work the same for you." He pulled me to him. "In any case," he said, resting his head on top of mine, "that is not something we need to worry about for a long, long time."

CHAPTER THIRTY-SEVEN

VALORA

Announcing that I was Dracul's *dragaria* went more smoothly than I expected. The Maidens were shocked—rightfully so—before congratulating me, and most of the dragons from the Shadowvale and Twisturn clans were already aware. What remained of the Starfire clan did not seem to care—they were too busy dealing with the aftermath of the attack and assimilating with the Twisturn clan. Notices were sent to the Lords of the Hysta and Grathal clans, who swiftly replied with their congratulations. To my continued surprise, there was no vocal opposition to me being Dracul's *dragaria*.

"Now that everyone knows, what happens next?" I asked Dracul shortly after the announcement was made. We were on the couch together, each reading different books. Dracul's head was in my lap and once in a while, I would play with his hair.

He set his book down on his chest, looking up at me. "Typically, there's a ceremony, similar to a human wedding," he said tentatively.

I made a face. There had been enough ceremonies lately and I was not sure I wanted another one. Only a couple months ago, I had become his official Dragon Maiden.

"We could always do something small," he said.

"But you're the High Dragon Lord," I said. "Isn't it expected that we invite everybody?"

"That usually is how things are done, yes," he said. "But nothing about the two of us is normal. Having a ceremony with just the Lords would be sufficient for witnesses. What would you think of that?"

"And the Dragon Maidens too?" I asked. "And Ronan?"

Ronan had taken up residence in the caves now. He helped Lord Lorka oversee the crops, glad to finally have a chance to slow down and work with his hands again. In the past few years, he had not had that chance, ever since he had left home.

"They would be more than welcome," Dracul said, nodding.

I leaned over and kissed him, savoring the taste of his lips. That was something I did not think I would ever get used to— every time gave me butterflies. I pulled back, glad to see a smile on Dracul's face. My cheeks flushed as I felt a warmth spread through me.

"What was that for?" he asked. "Not that I'm complaining."

"Just because," I said, leaning forward to give him a quick kiss. "Are there different duties I would have to take over as your *dragaria*?"

Dracul sat up, facing me. "That is something I wanted to talk to you about," he said. "Because there *will* be different duties. I was wondering what your thoughts would be on scaling back on your Dragon Maiden duties. You would still bear the title, but less of the manual labor."

"Who would do that instead?" I asked.

He shrugged. "I had the other Maidens do it before you came along," he said. "Or we could have one of the servants clean up around here if you want."

"I don't mind the cleaning," I said.

"But you'll have your *dragaria* duties on top of that," Dracul pointed out. "You'll be accompanying me on tours to the different clans, attending the council meetings with me, and you'll be given tasks to deal with the administration of the cave."

"Doesn't Lord Verhorn do that administrative piece now?" I asked.

Dracul chuckled. "He does, but he shouldn't be," he said. "It's one of the tasks that got assigned to him since I did not have a *dragaria* when I was appointed High Dragon Lord. There were a few things over the course of my reign that have been unusual."

"I see," I said. "Then why don't we see how things go with me doing both sets of tasks for a while? If it becomes too much then we can go with your plan of having someone else do the manual labor."

Dracul kissed me, making me lightheaded. He pulled back and I had to gasp for breath. "That sounds like an excellent plan," he said. "Now that we've decided on a small ceremony, when would you like to hold it?"

"How about late summer?" I asked. "It's a few months away and gives us time to get everything ready."

"That sounds perfect, Lora," he said before lunging at me.

I shrieked in surprise, which turned into giggles as we began to kiss each other, running our hands over each other's bodies. The heat within me flared up and I could not wait for us to be officially tied together.

CHAPTER THIRTY-EIGHT

VALORA

The next few months passed in a blur, excitement filling the caves. The Dragon Maidens once more worked on my dress for the ceremony—my wedding dress this time. After taking my measurements, they refused to let me see them working on it, wanting the dress to be a surprise for the day of the ceremony. They had done such a wonderful job with my dress for the Dragon Maiden ceremony that it was easy to let them take the lead with my wedding dress. Ronan had agreed to walk me down the aisle and the Dragon Maidens had volunteered to make him a custom suit as well.

Each of the Dragon Lords had a role to play in the ceremony. Lord Hiram would be officiating the ceremony since he was Dracul's closest advisor. Due to Dracul wanting to incorporate a few human wedding traditions into the ceremony, Lord Noxus created our rings, taking prized gems out of Dracul's hoard for the bands. Lord Verhorn was tasked with documenting the ceremony for historical records. For food, Lord Lorka was in charge—he had everything harvested directly from the clan's crops, as well as flowers. And lastly, Lord Firenze was tasked with music. Surprisingly, he was a gifted lutist.

230

As the day drew near, palpable excitement filled the caves. Everyone was thrilled that the High Dragon Lord had found his *dragaria* and we would officially be joined together. Every time I saw Dracul after being away from his side, no matter how short that time apart had been, I felt giddy. Officially, I had moved into his quarters and being able to fall asleep next to him every night was a dream.

The morning of the ceremony, when I awoke, Dracul was already gone. There was a note on his side of the bed wishing me a good morning and that he could not wait to see me at the ceremony. He wanted to keep to the human tradition of not seeing his bride on our wedding day so he had snuck out last night after I had fallen asleep. His sweetness made my heart melt and put a smile on my face.

Shortly after breakfast, the Dragon Maidens bustled into our quarters, dress in hand. Lord Firenze had found a new Dragon Maiden by now, a sweet blonde girl named Chutney Sweeten, and she was with the group as they dressed me.

Taking a look at myself in the mirror, I gasped. They had outdone themselves. The dress had a curved neckline with long sleeves, intricate navy embroidery, and diamonds covering the bodice. The skirt billowed out from my waist in swaths of fabric, diamonds continuing to drip down to the hem. A long, scalloped train flowed behind me. My necklace from Dracul rested in the hollow of my throat.

After fixing my hair into a smooth twist at the back of my head, Alonsa had the honors of affixing my veil. Tears entered my eyes as I saw everything together. It was absolutely breathtaking, *I* was breathtaking. Our eyes met in the mirror, and there were tears in her eyes as well.

"You look beautiful," Alonsa said, leaning to give me a warm hug.

The other Maidens gathered around to hug me, as well, echoing similar sentiments. I felt so lucky and grateful to have such a warm group of women surrounding me on this special day.

Ronan entered, stopping short when he saw me. "You look wonderful," he said. "Lord Dracul is going to be speechless."

I blushed at the compliment, looking forward to my groom's reaction.

Ronan stepped to my side, offering me his arm. "Shall we?" he asked.

I took his arm, taking a deep breath. Unlike my Dragon Maiden ceremony, I was not nervous this time. "I'm ready," I said.

The Maidens led the way to the ceremony chamber. Along the way, dragons of the Shadowvale clan lined the hallways, everyone bowing as I passed. I had to hold back my tears at the sign of respect, the sign that they approved of me. Ronan squeezed my hand in encouragement.

At last, we were at the room. The Maidens entered first, lining up by their Lords. I could see Lord Hiram and Dracul at the end of the room, waiting for me. And now it was time.

Lord Firenze played beautifully as I walked down the aisle. As soon as the music started, Dracul turned to look at me. Immediately, I could see his deep intake of breath and blushed. He was in his human form, wearing a formal, light-gray suit that matched his eyes. My breath caught as our eyes met and I could feel the butterflies in my stomach. Ronan escorted me down the aisle, placing my hand in Dracul's outstretched one. Together, we stepped onto the dais, facing Lord Hiram, who smiled broadly.

Lord Hiram looked around the room. "Thank you for joining us here today," he said. "Today, we celebrate the joining of High Dragon Lord Dracul Shadowvale and Valora Marchton as soul-bonded *dragaria*. *Dragaria* is a special bond between a dragon and their mate, a bond that no one can break. Dracul and Valora, please turn towards each other to recite the *dragaria* vow."

Dracul and I faced each other, holding hands. He squeezed mine lightly and I squeezed his back, feeling the warmth from our connection spreading throughout my body.

"Dracul, please repeat the following: 'I, Dracul, take you, Valora, to be my *dragaria*. I will remain yours now and forever, letting no others forsake us. I will be your fire in the cold, warming you during your lowest times, and the wind beneath your wings, lifting you up to your highest moments. You are mine and I am yours, today, tomorrow, and forever more.'"

Dracul repeated the words with a giant grin on his face. Next, it was my turn, and I repeated the same vows, mirroring his smile. Speaking my love and vowing to be his forever made my chest feel like it was about to burst—it was a magical moment.

Next was the exchanging of rings.

"Dracul, please take your ring and place it on Valora's finger, reciting the following."

This part of the ceremony was not standard, but Dracul had worked with Lord Hiram to add the human tradition of wedding rings into the script. Dracul repeated the words, slipping the ring on my finger. It was a beautiful silver with a deep-navy sapphire, reminiscent of his scales.

"This ring is representative of my never-ending love and commitment to you. I will love and cherish you for all of eternity."

I took his ring, made from a black meteor with light-blue sapphires lining the band. He had insisted on sapphires to match my eyes. Carefully, I slid it on his finger, reciting the vow. When I was done, he clutched my hand tightly and when I looked up, I could see tears in his eyes.

Lord Hiram gave us permission to kiss, sealing our vows to each other. Dracul wasted no time in pulling me towards him, crushing our lips together. I wove my fingers through his hair, pulling him closer to me while his hands clutched my waist as if I would fly away if he did not hold me tight enough. After several moments, we broke apart, smiles on both of our faces.

Cheers erupted now that the ceremony was complete. We were now bonded together—forever and always.

Dracul leaned towards me, whispering in my ear, "You look breathtaking," he said, his voice husky.

I blushed at the compliment. "And you look very handsome, too," I said, pulling his head back down for another kiss.

The rest of the night passed in a blur filled with feasting and dancing. My dancing skills were much improved from the last banquet. Dracul and I had practiced for hours over the past few months. I wanted to dance with my husband and not make a fool of myself.

He held me close the entire night. We always had at least one part of our bodies touching the whole time. It was as if we were magnets, drawn to each other.

When we both fell into bed afterwards, the night was filled with sweet lovemaking. It was the first time for both of us and I was extremely nervous, but Dracul was patient and caring as always. We focused on each other's bodies, how they would react to certain caresses and kisses. We remained busy until early into the morning, unable to get enough of each other.

Before falling asleep, I thought with a smile on my face that he was mine forever and I was so happy that we had chosen each other.

Kessland had been right after all—the future was bright and promising, one I was sure to enjoy.

EPILOGUE

DRACUL

5 years later

The day was here, the day was here! At long last, Lora was giving birth. Though both of us were excited, I was extremely anxious, as there was no record of a dragon-human pairing before. We were in fully uncharted territory. I hoped everything would go smoothly, and so far, the pregnancy had progressed normally. But I was still worried.

Lora had taken everything in stride. While she had her own worries, she did not ever seem as worried as I felt. For the past nine months—since we had found out we were expecting—she had been planning for our baby's arrival. Everyone was ecstatic when we shared the news and absolutely no one let Lora do anything by herself anymore. Everyone wanted to help her, much to her chagrin.

"I'm an independent woman I can do a simple task!" she had complained to me after a dragon insisted on carrying a small pile of paperwork for her to Lord Verhorn.

After the eighth month, Lora had been put on bed rest upon the midwife's insistence, and much to Lora's dismay. I brought her as many books as she requested, checking in on her every hour throughout the day. The Dragon Maidens also took up shifts so she never was alone. Someone was always there at her beck and call, although she rarely took advantage of that.

Only a few days ago, she'd complained about the baby and how she wanted to give birth already. We both were excited to meet our little one, but I also knew what human birth entailed, how dangerous it was. Just in case, I had prepared multiple potions to help with her healing process should the worst happen. While I was excited for the baby, I worried about what the cost would be. We had not even been sure if procreation was possible between us, but Lora had been beside herself with happiness when she realized she was pregnant.

Now the baby was on its way and I was at Lora's side, my hand tightly gripped in hers while she panted and screamed, pushing the baby out. The midwife encouraged her to push again and there was more screaming. My heart broke for her. I wanted to take the pain away, but it was impossible. She was the only one who could bear this pain.

A couple more pushes later and the baby was out.

"It's a healthy baby girl," the midwife said, handing the baby to Alonsa to clean off before a freshly swaddled baby was placed in my arms.

I held the baby towards Lora so she could see the newborn. "She's beautiful," I said softly.

Lora's face suddenly grimaced in pain.

"What's going on?" I asked frantically, turning to the midwife.

"It looks as though it's twins," she said. "Valora, you need to push."

This time was only three pushes total before our little girl had a sister.

Lora lay back in the bed, completely spent from giving birth. I crawled in next to her, showing her the two newest members of our family.

"You did wonderfully," I said, passing them to her to hold. Alonsa moved to wipe Lora's forehead of sweat, but I took the towel from her and started cleaning her myself.

"They look human," she said, staring at both of our babies in awe. "We did this, Dracul. We made them."

"That we did, my love," I said, kissing her forehead. Never before had she looked so beautiful. "What would you like to name them?"

Both girls had wisps of hair, dark navy like mine. When one opened her eyes, I could see that she had Lora's eyes, a brilliant, bright blue. The other one was a surprise—she had one silver eye and one blue. But I could tell both had my *dragaria*'s nose and I knew that it would crinkle when they smiled, like hers did.

"How about Valia and Calantha?" she asked, kissing each one as she named them.

"Perfect," I said. She looked to me, and I kissed her once more, capturing her lips with mine. "I love you."

"I love you too," she said, her eyes bright. She glowed— motherhood already suited her. It only made me more excited to see what was to come.

ACKNOWLEDGEMENTS

I would like to thank my amazing husband, Zachary Lesperance, for his unwavering support. Without his encouragement and steadfast support, this book would not have been where it is today.

My family's support and encouragement of my writing over the years has meant the world to me.

Valerie and John Lampinen, Mom and Dad, who encourage my imagination and voracious reading habits. Without that encouragement I would not have come this far.

Hannah Lampinen, my SEESTOR, who gives me a healthy dose of reality sprinkled with the snarkiness only a sibling can provide. I can count on her to give me honest feedback while also assuage my fears.

Richard and Marty Butler, Grandpa and Grandma, who shared their love of stories and words with me. Through their own stories and books we read together, my vocabulary and love of language grew.

I would not be able to get to where I am today without the support of my wonderful friends.

Audrey Cramer, who has encouraged this journey and offered hilarious commentary on scenes.

Kathryn Maes, who participated in many late night writing sessions in college and is always willing to read my work.

Charlotte Marlinga, my ever eternal writing companion who I bounce ideas off of and can always turn to in times of crisis.

Ashley Oldenburg, who provides excellent feedback and criticism to add additional clarity to my text.

Kate Wareham, one of my oldest friends who shares the love of a good story and whose opinion I value greatly.

Shannon Westman, who listened to my ideas and explanations over countless cups of coffee.

About the Author

Kendall Lesperance has loved fantasy from a young age. Since high school she has dreamed of publishing one of her numerous stories for people to enjoy. Kendall is a business analyst and lives in Wisconsin. Publishing her debut novel, *The Dragon Maiden*, is a dream come true in combining her love of writing and dragons.

Visit her at www.kendall-lesperance.com